THE ATLANTIS CIPHER

OTHER TITLES BY DAVID LEADBEATER

The Relic Hunters Series

The Relic Hunters (The Relic Hunters, #1)

The Matt Drake Series

The Bones of Odin (Matt Drake #1)
The Blood King Conspiracy (Matt Drake #2)
The Gates of Hell (Matt Drake #3)
The Tomb of the Gods (Matt Drake #4)
Brothers in Arms (Matt Drake #5)
The Swords of Babylon (Matt Drake #6)
Blood Vengeance (Matt Drake #7)
Last Man Standing (Matt Drake #8)
The Plagues of Pandora (Matt Drake #9)
The Lost Kingdom (Matt Drake #10)
The Ghost Ships of Arizona (Matt Drake #11)
The Last Bazaar (Matt Drake #12)
The Edge of Armageddon (Matt Drake #13)
The Treasures of Saint Germain (Matt Drake #14)
Inca Kings (Matt Drake #15)
The Four Corners of the Earth (Matt Drake #16)
The Seven Seals of Egypt (Matt Drake #17)
Weapons of the Gods (Matt Drake #18)

The Alicia Myles Series

Aztec Gold (Alicia Myles #1)

Crusader's Gold (Alicia Myles #2)
Caribbean Gold (Alicia Myles #3)

The Torsten Dahl Thriller Series

Stand Your Ground (Dahl Thriller #1)

The Disavowed Series

The Razor's Edge (Disavowed #1)
In Harm's Way (Disavowed #2)
Threat Level: Red (Disavowed #3)

The Chosen Few Series

Chosen (The Chosen Trilogy #1)
Guardians (The Chosen Trilogy #2)

Short Stories

Walking with Ghosts (A short story)
A Whispering of Ghosts (A short story)

THE ATLANTIS CIPHER

DAVID LEADBEATER

This is a work of fiction. Names, characters, organizations, places, events, and incidents are either products of the author's imagination or are used fictitiously. Any resemblance to actual persons, living or dead, or actual events is purely coincidental.

Published by Thomas & Mercer, Seattle

www.apub.com

ISBN-13: 9781503903128
ISBN-10: 1503903125

Cover design by Ghost Design

Printed in the United States of America

For Keira and Meggy,

there's a message here for you . . . in the memories.

CHAPTER ONE

Guy Bodie paced the hotel room's threadbare carpets, hands clenched into fists at his sides and a resolute frown set like concrete. His familiar team of expert thieves was seated around the room, waiting for him to say something.

"We go after Pantera now," he growled. "Before Heidi bloody Moneymaker calls upon our services again."

"Hey, man," Cassidy Coleman drawled. She lounged on the windowsill, looking as beautiful as ever. But, as her enemies would attest, beneath the beauty was a deadly killer. "It's only been a week. We helped out the CIA once already. Almost got ourselves killed searching for the Statue of Zeus, and all for Agent Moneymaker. How often can ancient relics get themselves lost anyway?"

"Oh, I dunno," Sam Gunn cracked at her. "If only we knew some relic hunters we could ask."

Cassidy shut him down with a stone-cold glance. Bodie finally stopped pacing and faced them.

"Jack Pantera was our boss, my mentor for five years. He brought me into this game, showed me the ropes. A man like that does not simply . . ." He paused to find the right words. "Decide to end you by throwing you into a Mexican prison and sending in a bunch of killers."

Eli Cross, an experienced career thief, took a sip of water and crossed his legs, comfy in the room's only armchair. "You've been apart for, what? Four years? People change, Guy."

"Maybe," Bodie conceded. "Either way, we should pay him a visit."

"And risk all that we have now?" Gunn said. "I quite like our new status. Working for the CIA, with access to their resources. Doing what we like to do but with government backing."

Jemma Blunt, their planner and organizer, sighed. "Working for the CIA is harder than working for yourself, Gunn, believe me. Instead of developing and initiating the ideas, we now have a new layer of scrutiny to pass them through. Nowhere near as easy. I guess geeks don't see that side of it, though."

Gunn was seated beside Jemma on the sofa. He ran a hand through his carefully gelled hair. "I meant that we're on the right side of the law now." He looked around. "Aren't we?"

Bodie blinked twice. The hotel room was tight, crowded. He felt just a little too close to everyone. "I'm not sure Heidi and the CIA are familiar with that concept, Sam, but I understand what you're saying. Let's see how it plays out. The fact remains that Jack Pantera screwed us once and he could do so again." He shook his head. "I never thought I'd hear myself say that, considering all we've been through."

"If I remember correctly," Cross said, scratching his head, "you mentioned that the guy who put you in prison—Pantera—wasn't responsible for the weird dudes who then came after you."

Bodie nodded. "If by 'weird dudes' you mean those eastern Europeans who really knew their business, then yeah, you're right."

Cross shrugged. "Seems to be a mess, that's all."

"Bloody right it's a mess, my redneck friend. Another reason to head south."

Over the past week the team had taken leave of Heidi Moneymaker, their new boss by default, agreeing reluctantly to stay on high alert and await her call, and had flown to Atlanta via Hartsfield-Jackson International Airport, the busiest in the world. Bodie was pretty sure Heidi's influence would have taken them off a dozen watch lists, and his team reasoned it was better to conduct their business in plain sight while knowing that they could rely on the CIA's help, rather than at a later date when relations might have soured. They wouldn't be happy being at the CIA's beck and call, but they would try to find a way out from under the heavy governmental thumb. And for now, they were content to search out the few relics that their new paymasters would send them after. They expected lots of downtime, since ancient relics didn't exactly pop up every day. For now, it worked *for* them, not in conflict with their needs. Heidi had offered immunity so long as they performed. The CIA gained deniability, a team they could disavow if caught. They also gained expert help and unparalleled experience in matters of relic hunting. The team knew they were being blackmailed by the government agency. The question was, Was there anything they could do about it?

Just the thought of blackmail made Bodie's top lip curl. There was no way they would work for the CIA forever, but first they needed time to devise the perfect plan.

They had found a nondescript place in the center of Atlanta, checked for tails and bugs, and then settled down to make arrangements. Bodie had triple-checked Pantera's whereabouts—Florida, specifically a gated community close to Kissimmee. When the subject of their supporting the CIA and its worldwide hunt for ancient relics grew monotonous and unsolvable, they turned right to the thorny matter of Jack Pantera.

"Have you thought about the approach?" Jemma asked. "I will need to see the place first but already have a few ideas."

"Damn," Cassidy moaned. "You have too much time on your hands, girl. Let's go out tonight and get you a boyfriend."

Jemma looked hopeful for a moment but then clouded over. "The way we have to move at a moment's notice? That's not gonna happen, Cass."

"All right, how about a one-night stand, then? At least it'll divert those energies."

Jemma blushed. "Not sure I could handle one of those. It's been a while."

Cassidy made a face. "Like riding a bike," she started to say, then grinned. "Literally."

"Can we get back to the job at hand?" Cross said, a pained expression on his face. "Maybe you two can discuss boyfriends later."

"Cool, ancient one. Carry on."

Cross gave her a long-suffering look. "I believe it was Jemma who mentioned a plan."

"Who else would it be?" Gunn grinned, fingers ready at his laptop.

"That's all fine," Bodie interrupted. "But we should get a look at the place first. Now . . . the tricky part. Jack's married, with a son."

"Yeah, but they're separated, right?" Cassidy said. "Last I heard, Pantera was reduced to watching his kid from afar."

Bodie lowered his head. "I believe so. His wife took out a court order. A situation that could break anyone. The op has to be handled with care, people. Clearly, Pantera isn't the guy we used to know. I don't want to bust in and damage him . . . not straight away . . . but I do want to find out why the hell he betrayed me. Now, we can't go barging in there because we don't know what may have changed. We study, and plan, and plan again. Got it?"

"As ever, boss." Cassidy saluted.

"And Heidi?" Gunn asked.

Bodie stared at him. "What about her?"

"If she calls, I mean."

"Fuck her," Bodie said impulsively.

"Okay, dial it back, Guy," Cassidy said. "But hey, I did see a bit of carnal friction between the two of you."

"No, no," Bodie said a little too quickly and without smiling. "I meant that we ignore her until this op is complete. I don't like being used as a puppet, not by anyone. They want us—we want out. But for now . . . we'll play along."

"Play hard to get, you mean?"

"Yes . . . I mean no. Look, the CIA may employ us but they don't own us. And they're not gonna employ us for long. Understood?"

Cassidy grew serious. "They'll never take their hooks out, Guy. That's not their way."

"Well, we have the best planner in the business," Bodie said, nodding at Jemma. "And the rest of us aren't bad at slipping in and out of places and going unnoticed. I think we can handle the CIA."

A hush descended across the room. Bodie stared around. "Don't you?"

"Let's wait and see," Cross said finally. "Who knows? We might get to enjoy a little relic hunting."

Bodie shrugged and shook his head. "Whatever you say, Eli, whatever you say. Personally, I can't see it being much more than creeping around in the dust and scratching at old rocks, but maybe I'll be proved wrong."

They arrived in Florida, rented an SUV, and headed south toward Kissimmee and the gated community of Shingle Creek. Bodie, a many-year resident of London, never ceased to be amazed at the size of America's highways and the ease of driving straight roads rather than the twisting warrens of Europe, and sat back to listen to a rock music channel and let Cross drive.

"Good to be driving through the homeland again?" he asked the older man.

"Yeah, really missed the place. Homecoming is always good."

"Of course," Bodie said. "Being a part of this crew means you always take your family with you."

Cross glanced over, sunlight glinting off the metallic rims of his sunglasses. "Sure, man. What is it you always say?"

"Family is a sense of belonging. It's what I believe."

The interstate appeared to roll on forever, eventually becoming a shimmering haze in the distance. Cross turned off at the next exit, following the sign for Kissimmee and a GPS directive toward Shingle Creek. Twenty minutes later and with Kissimmee still some miles distant, they slowed as a large, ornate stone set in the middle of a wide grassy area proclaimed their destination in delicate, swirling letters.

"Cruise by," Bodie said unnecessarily, since Cross would be doing just that without thinking. The man was as good as they came, and Bodie's closest confidante. Someone he could turn to when he could turn nowhere else. One day, maybe, he'd have to tell Cross that.

Cross didn't slow but took his foot off the gas. They spotted a high wall, lots of trees, and a guard house. Cassidy pointed out the enormous double gate, which appeared mostly ornamental.

Still, nothing good ever happened easily.

"Let's get to work," Bodie said, "and see what Jack Pantera has to say for himself."

CHAPTER TWO

Heidi Moneymaker flung the federal-issue Chevrolet around a tight corner, allowing the back wheels to squeal slightly. When the road straightened she stepped on the gas again, seeing a gap in traffic and exploiting it. Another quick left and right with the wheel and she was past another car and saw the next corner approach rapidly. The engine protested as she downshifted. The tachometer surged and the gas consumption readout no doubt dipped alarmingly, but time was of the essence.

Seeing her target ahead, she aimed for the single space in the on-street parking, flung the wheel, and ended up parked at an angle, the car's ass slightly askew and protruding a good meter into the road.

Screw it. The target is more important.

She jumped out, locked the vehicle, and ran into the nearest store.

The man behind the counter shook his head at her. "Made it by the skin of your teeth again."

Heidi flashed a smile that made her blue eyes light up. "I do believe you should have closed over a minute ago, Georgio."

The man smiled back. "I heard you coming."

Heidi grabbed what she called her "lifesavers"—a big cup of strong, black coffee, a bag of Skittles, and, to even it out, a bulging bag of red grapes and a healthy yogurt. This sustenance would keep her going through the long night, which she envisioned would be spent at home sorting through mounds of paperwork.

"Thanks, Georgio." She paid for her goods. "Same time tomorrow?"

"Maybe a little earlier, eh, Heidi? Just a little."

She acknowledged the tiny reprimand with a sheepish grin and left the store, climbed back into her car, and drove home. The DC night was chilly; a fine drizzle laced the air. Heidi thought it felt good on her face as she walked up to her apartment block and searched for her keys. On a night like this the loneliness always struck her where it hurt most, but a heart that yearned for two goals at opposite ends of a vast, sliding scale would never be happy, its desire never stilled. Law and order was her calling. The husband and child she left back home remained her passion, despite divorce and the total lack of communication from her daughter. One passion fed the other. Keep the world safe; keep them safe. Her family wouldn't accept it. Complex emotions made a battle arena of her heart.

Inside, it was clean and warm. Heidi switched on the lights and sipped at the coffee, moving around the main room. She flung her cell onto the low coffee table and was startled as it began to ring.

Heidi stared at it in surprise. *They can't do without me for one night?* But then the truth kicked in, that they would only call in an emergency, and she scooped it back up.

"Yeah? I just got home."

"Sorry. The call just came in."

"What call?"

"You need to get down here. I can't say much over the phone, but I wouldn't call if it wasn't urgent. Another relic may have surfaced. The sooner you get a look at this, the better."

Heidi closed her eyes for a long moment, then opened them and drank in the appealing, safe, quiet haven that was her apartment. More than anything right now, it represented what she needed—a good night's rest. "Now? Is it time sensitive? It won't wait till morning?"

"If that were the case I wouldn't be calling you."

"Watch your tone, Scottie. I'll be there in an hour."

She ended the call before he could protest, gulped more coffee, then jumped in the shower. A change of clothes later and she was ready for the second shift of her already long day. With a sigh, she threw the grapes and yogurt in the trash, not knowing if she would be gone a day or a month. She knew the existence she led was draining, debilitating, but remained addicted to its emotional rewards.

Driving back to the office in silence, Heidi kept to the speed limits. When she arrived she saw the lights in every window on her floor blazing. Security had been alerted, and she was entering her office in less than the hour she'd promised.

Scottie looked suitably sheepish, his boyish face strained, and his mop of gelled-back hair hanging limply as if in apology.

"Sorry, boss."

"Just explain why the hell you've ruined a perfectly good night of sifting through paperwork." It was a poor attempt at a joke and he knew it.

"Ah, yeah, sorry again. They called a half hour after you left. It sounds . . . interesting."

Heidi inclined her head, trying not to look too concerned.

"There's been a significant find in South America."

Now she shrugged off her coat and poured bad, stewed coffee from the machine. "Go on."

"I can't drink that stuff." Scottie stared at her steaming mug. "Makes my guts squirm."

"I'll be sure to order in a supply of half-and-half. Now, go on."

"All right. Well, I have to assume that where there's an old myth or an old dig site there's probably an archaeologist hanging around. A group of underfunded, mostly misled kids just came across something near the eastern Brazilian coast. Then they called a goddamn press conference." Scottie shook his head sadly.

Heidi couldn't stop a sharp intake of breath. "That's not good. Publicity is the last thing they want at a new discovery site."

"You said it, boss. Full disclosure isn't always the way to go. So, it appears these young archaeologists were investigating an archaic site believed cleared out years ago. To cut a long story short, they unearthed five statues."

Heidi set her mug on the table. "I'm guessing they're not bronze representations of Dwayne Johnson?"

"No, though that would be cool." Scottie paused, caught her eye, and then blushed. "Right, so the statues are obviously thousands of years old. *Many* thousands. In fact, they perfectly match four other statues found on the Azores over a decade ago."

Scottie let it hang. Heidi worked through it in her head.

"The Azores?" she repeated. "Which is . . ."

"Off the coast of Portugal, near Spain and Morocco."

"Right." She nodded. She felt a surge in her chest but held it in. "And you say they match *perfectly*? How perfectly?"

Scottie sat back. "Perfectly perfectly."

Heidi ran it through her mind. *Perfectly perfectly. From South America to Morocco? How could that be?*

"So what we have here are essentially nine statues. Crafted by the same person at the same time. Now found . . . what? Four thousand miles apart and across the width of the Atlantic Ocean."

Scottie nodded. "That's about right."

Heidi switched off for a moment, preventing the euphoria from carrying her away. While locating ancient wonders wasn't exactly within the CIA's purview, stopping global conspiracy was. Chasing down the all-powerful shadow organization that she later discovered was the Illuminati had started her on this path, and now her bosses realized there was more reward than simply arresting criminals inherent in finding anything from an old statue to a lost continent. Oddly, it wasn't simply the lure of discovering ancient relics that inspired her, it was also the chance to work with Bodie again. *And the other guys,* she qualified quickly in her mind. In addition, after working for the CIA for over a decade this was fresh, new, and exciting. But they needed a period of calm, rational reasoning right now. She focused on the details. Their office was small, well lit, and functional. She gazed at the walls and at the desk, seeing a noticeboard still bristling with photographs and sticky notes from their last mission—the quest to retrieve the Statue of Zeus and take down the Illuminati. At least half of that mission had been successful—the ancient wonder would now reside in the devastated museum at Athens, bringing much-needed tourist money into the city and the country.

I wonder if there are more ancient wonders out there. The Hanging Gardens of Babylon? Now that would be a find.

The only desk was black and scarred, its surface the place of many wars with hot liquid, sandwich knives, and broken ceramic. The computer was clean. A photo of her daughter drifted around the screen while it was in power save mode. People sometimes asked her why she used the old photo. *Because I don't have any recent ones.* But she always kept that part to herself. Her eyes moved to the water cooler in the corner, which grew enough algae for its own manicured front lawn. That corner was a no-go zone. She kicked a chair from underneath the desk and sat down heavily.

"Okay, I'll forgive you for summoning me back to the office on one condition."

"Yeah, sure."

"After we're done, you go get a shower. Now, tell me more."

Scottie looked relieved. "Well," he said softly, "everyone knows this is a big press release. Clearly, not everyone will make the connection you just did. That the statues were all made by the same person. I even ran it through a computer process. The carvings, markings, color, and detail on the new statues match the Azores statues perfectly. That's even without any form of dating. They were made by the same man. So . . . how did that man cross the Atlantic Ocean ten thousand years ago?"

"The Azores statues have already been dated to that time?"

Scottie nodded.

Heidi gulped coffee. "The answer is simple," she said. "He didn't."

"You say everyone knows about this?" Heidi asked after a few moments of reflection.

"Yeah, it's gone worldwide."

"Unfortunate. Have we identified any potential aggressors yet?" Heidi assumed other nations would immediately see the significance of the find and try to be aggressively proactive in what may well be the greatest treasure hunt of their time. It would all come down to what they might find and how they might use it. Some ancient knowledge might suddenly put any nation light-years ahead of the competition. And Heidi knew that the US would want it first.

"Well, in the last two hours, chatter has naturally increased. Langley and our NSA contacts report half a dozen potential aggressors. A local gang." Scottie shrugged. "Small fry. Other unknowns. And, unfortunately, the Chinese."

Heidi stared. "I'm assuming you don't mean the Happy Wok on New Hampshire?"

"No, no," Scottie quickly said to cover his mistake. "A hardcore government faction. Not the government per se," he said with air quotes. "Not that they would ever admit to."

"Right." That was indeed an unfortunate development. The Chinese would hold nothing back in their search for items of value. Within the politburo, she knew, were men of influence who wanted all westerners and their wares out of the country, gone forever, and used hard finance, bottomless influence, and ransom-worthy items of enormous importance to further their agendas, while there was an equal number who thought it could be achieved by doing just the opposite. *Keep your enemies close, and all that . . .*

Which made her think of Guy Bodie and his team of social misfits. If ever there was a perfect job for a certain group of rebels, tracking down such an intriguing and mysterious treasure was it.

"Where are the relic hunters?"

"Right now? They're chasing down that old boss of Bodie's somewhere in Florida."

Heidi had known that. She was thinking rapidly while Scottie spoke. "Call them. Tell them the job has changed."

"They won't like that, boss."

"Look at me." Heidi stood, her face looking more lived-in than usual and her naturally curly hair listing badly to the east. Her scarred hands and holstered gun spoke of intense fieldwork. Her tired eyes spoke of incredible responsibility. "Do I look like their travel agent to you?"

"Umm, no."

"What do I look like?"

"Their . . . boss."

"You got it, Scottie. So, what are you gonna do?"

The younger man reached for the phone. "I'll call them right away."

Heidi put out a hand to stop him. The human contact made him flinch just a little. She didn't move her hand, but held on to his wrist.

"You know the significance of all this, don't you?"

Scottie couldn't help but grin. "Sure, I do."

"The only way those two groups of statues could reasonably have made it two continents apart and four thousand miles across an ocean over ten thousand years ago is if there was no ocean."

"And no split continents," Scottie said.

"Just one body of land," Heidi said.

Scottie took a deep breath. "Atlantis."

CHAPTER THREE

Guy Bodie was in charge of the infiltration of Pantera's property. With the assistance of Cassidy and Jemma, he sneaked in under cover of darkness. Jemma in particular seemed to delight in returning to the field, possibly reliving her former career as a cat burglar.

Bodie had reminded them constantly that while the job wasn't big and it wasn't dangerous, they should treat everything as if it were life or death. The risk was that they missed noticing something they didn't know was there—especially where Jack Pantera was concerned.

This worried him the most.

But Bodie had known Cross the longest of his team, and trusted him the most. If the forty-three-year-old insisted Bodie could make it to Pantera's domain and back with absolutely no issues, then the matter was closed. Cross was the closest Bodie had ever come to an ally as capable as Pantera, and as good a friend. Following Pantera's betrayal, Cross had taken on that role.

Bodie had hooked up a series of covert cameras, gaining them a 360-degree view of Pantera's house. The cameras themselves were high-tech, enabled with seamless zoom and motion detectors. Small and thin, they were practically unnoticeable, hidden as they were among the leaves and branches of trees and bushes. Bodie had even checked the gardener's schedule and learned he wouldn't be around for another three days.

"Let's review what we know," he said. The team was lounging on the furniture in the terrace bar at a large hotel. White canvas shutters rolled across the timbered roof to keep the direct sun at bay, and a heart-shaped pool glistened to their left. The area was quiet at this time of day; most of the hotel's occupants were cruising one of the nearby theme parks or filling up at a restaurant.

"Two days of watching have given us more than a few headaches," Jemma said.

"Explain." Bodie stretched out on the rattan sofa. Cassidy had ordered mocktails all around, and now brought them on a tray with a little curtsy.

"Found your calling," Gunn said, smirking.

"You have a problem with waitresses?" Cassidy growled.

"Umm, no. Not at all. I was just—"

"Then shut your smart mouth."

Jemma took a quick drink and then continued explaining her plan. "Pantera is in the house, as you know." Bodie had identified the man for his own peace of mind during the initial hour of surveillance. "I have half a dozen signals coming out. Nothing unusual. House alarm, Wi-Fi, broadband, etcetera. Nothing suspicious, which, knowing Pantera, is suspicious in itself. Bodie knows the man best and he helped with snooping out any would-be surprises. But . . ." Jemma spread her arms. "We can't find any."

Gunn took over. "I hacked his system. Took a look at his computer. The man has solid firewalls, great protocols. As Jemma says, it all seems above board, which makes me very skeptical."

"We're thieves," Bodie said with a chuckle. "What would you expect?"

They laughed and drank. A small fountain sprayed arcs of water into the pool. A happy-looking couple walked slowly by.

"Anything good?" Cassidy asked.

"That *is* the good," Gunn said. "Weren't you listening? Of course, there is some bad news too."

"Naturally." Cassidy waved at him. "Spit it out."

"It appears that somebody else is watching Mr. Pantera."

The team went silent, eyes on Bodie. It was his decision as to how to proceed. Some jobs would be aborted, others wildly transformed, dissected. This one had roots that were beyond fragile, though.

"Methods? Routines?" Cross asked eventually.

"They're decent, but they never saw you, Eli. Barely any movement at all. If I were put on the spot I'd say it's a long-term watch. Complacent. They even have a house."

Bodie pondered this. "That makes it even more intriguing," he said. "Does Jack know? How long have they been observing him, and what for? Who else knows? To plant an extended watch in a gated community speaks of power."

"CIA?" Cassidy suggested.

Bodie stared at her. "Nah, that'd be too messed up. The CIA watching Jack after rescuing me, the man he got sent to prison. The same CIA we now work for."

"Pantera has made no effort to hide anything," Gunn said. "He's alone. Hasn't been outside the property's boundary in two days. Never looks directly at the long-term watch or at our cameras. How observant is he, Guy?"

"Jack is the best." Bodie shrugged. "Or used to be. The guy taught me how to read body language, how to properly assess a target, how to lift and return a guard's ID card without him even knowing it was gone. Every skill I have came from Jack. He treated me . . . like a son. Shit, how is his behavior? Anything suspicious or out of the ordinary?"

"Seems fine. Coordination is all there. Drinks a lot; I see evidence of wine and beer bottles on the kitchen shelves as well as in the recycling. Buys local and at supermarket prices, judging by the contents of his trash, which suggests he's not hiding any golden nuggets under the bed. There's a two-year-old Dodge in the garage, plates registered in his name. Everything else"—Gunn shrugged—"is textbook.

Mundane. Pantera is living like a model citizen right here in the heart of the Sunshine State. I'd expect to see him skipping out of that house chomping down on a juicy orange next."

Cassidy swatted him across the head. "Idiot. Stop typecasting everyone."

Gunn sighed deeply. "Is there anything you feel that I *do* do right, Cass?"

"I'm sure there is, but it's gonna take some thinking. What do you say, Jemma?"

Caught off guard, Jemma's usually quick mind couldn't construct a fitting comeback to that one *and* look at the plan. "Leave it with me," she said. "Now, Jack Pantera—the man. We need to understand how to anticipate his reactions. I'll let Guy brief you."

Bodie went instantly from repose to sitting on the edge of his seat. *If I still didn't care for the man, it would be easy.*

"A quiet, keen observer, Jack is reserved, intelligent, and shrewd. He would always steal the old way, but with state-of-the-art tools. I'd say from being the solid *numero uno* he's dropped down the charts these past three years. The man lost interest. He will undoubtedly have lost sharpness too."

"Violent?" Cross asked.

Bodie shook his head. "Never, unless threatened. But you put one foot the wrong side of Jack and he'd crush it. Literally. With a hammer. He taught me to be courteous, respectful, and as tough as a prison-yard brawler." He reflected for a moment. "Couldn't have been easy for him. Living two lives."

"Sounds like my dad, or what I remember of him," Gunn commented, looking at the ground. Like Bodie, Gunn was an orphan. Bodie's own bereavements were markedly different—his parents were killed while he attended an eighth birthday party—but he was reminded of his own life both before and after their deaths.

Two existences. The first—real fun-filled glory days where legends were made. The other—a slide into obscurity and self-loathing. He didn't have to ask how Gunn had fared; he never had—the answer was obvious. Sam Gunn had become a child of an imperfect system, placed with new parents who didn't show love or care as only real parents can. Without love, he'd grown up hard. At least Bodie had old, perfect childhood stories to hang on to. Times of friendship and belonging.

"So, Jack?" he said. "Treat the dude with the utmost caution, if not respect. He did, after all, somehow land me in a Mexican hellhole."

Jemma waited a moment, then eyed the crew. "We good to go?"

"What?" Gunn spluttered. "Now? But I haven't finished my Lava Flow."

"No, dummy." Jemma sighed. "Tonight. We go tonight. When it's dark."

"Oh yeah, that's what I thought you meant."

Bodie saw their faces set, their eyes determined. Right here, right now, he knew he was among those who cared and looked out for him. There was nowhere he'd rather be and no one he'd rather be with. Cross, in particular, held his gaze and nodded slightly, reassuringly.

Tonight would be different. Tonight they would find out why one of their own had betrayed them.

Jemma broke a profound silence. "All right. Dark will be here soon. I have a few rough edges to smooth off. Maybe Gunn could help me with that. I don't need the rest of you."

Cassidy finished her mocktail in a single gulp. "Sounds great. Who's up for cruising Kissimmee to see if they have any decent night spots?"

"And when would you *hit* them?" Cross asked. "Tonight's out."

Cassidy shook her head at his assumptions. "You kidding me, old-timer? First we hit Pantera, then we go clubbing."

"The only clubbing I'll be doing is in my dreams." Cross smiled.

Bodie felt his phone vibrate against his thigh and fished it out. One look at the incoming caller ID and his heart sank. "Oh hell," he said. "It's Heidi."

Cross plucked it out of his hand and answered, pressing the speaker button too. "Yeah?"

"That's not Bodie. Who is this?"

"Well, hello to you too, Agent Moneymaker. This here is Eli Cross."

"Is Bodie there?"

"Indisposed, I'm afraid."

"Indis . . . what the hell does that mean?" Heidi sounded taut.

"Well, I guess it means he can't come to the phone right now. What can I help you with?"

"You'd better not be covering for him, Eli." Heidi took a deep breath before continuing. "I need the team. Right here, right now. We have an urgent job."

Bodie mouthed "So do we." Cross exhaled and scratched his head. "I gotta say, we're close to moving on *this* op. Coupla hours is all we need."

"You don't have Pantera yet?" Heidi sounded appalled.

"Flawless jobs take meticulous planning. They don't just happen."

"It doesn't matter. This new job eclipses everything. Forget Pantera and get back here now. I can't tell you how important this is."

"It can't wait until morning?"

"It can't wait until you get back. Time is an issue. Listen, there's new, strong evidence that Atlantis actually existed. We have to get on top of it before anyone else does. I need you . . . right now."

The team members stared at each other and then straight at Bodie. This was his call. It occurred to him that if ever there was a time to make a stand against the CIA, to lay down the ground rules, this was it. Blackmail or not, they weren't broken enough that they would roll over at every command.

But Atlantis? That was huge. Yet he couldn't let it take his attention away from Pantera.

He took the phone from Cross. "This is Bodie. We're finishing here first, Agent, then we'll head in."

A long silence spoke of Heidi reining in the anger and calming herself down. "One more time . . . this is bigger than the last job. Do you get that? The Illuminati . . . they were a secret organization. This is a lost *continent* filled with potentially explosive knowledge. It's top priority. I need the team."

Bodie studied the middle distance. "You'll get the team. Tomorrow."

He hung up.

Cassidy whistled. "Phewee, I bet the air's a bit blue around DC right now."

Bodie didn't smile. "I feel like a jerk," he said. "We work for her. This will look bad on her. But . . . then there's Pantera."

The phone rang again. Bodie answered immediately. "I only need tonight."

"Send someone. You gotta let me have someone. Jemma or Eli. Even Gunn."

Bodie studied the team, seeing the compromise and wishing he'd thought of it before. "Actually," he said, "you can have all three. I only need Cassidy."

Cross tried not to look hurt. "Hey, I wanna see what this asshole has to say. Don't you need me too?"

Bodie nodded, feeling guilt at having to send his best friend away. "I'm trying to be diplomatic here. I don't trust Heidi. I don't trust Jack. It works better if I have my team in both places. And I value your opinion on Heidi's new job, Eli."

"You don't trust anyone," Heidi complained.

Bodie ignored it, thinking, *Duh.*

No one liked it, but the decision had been made. Bodie and Cassidy would deal with Pantera while the rest of the team headed north to hook up with the CIA. The goodbyes were short, perfunctory. Tension was rising.

Bodie saw nothing but conflict ahead.

CHAPTER FOUR

Heidi Moneymaker sat in the middle of the highest tier of shallow steps that led up to the Lincoln Memorial at the western end of the National Mall, staring without seeing along the length of the Reflecting Pool. She didn't realize she was shivering. The view, enhanced by spotlights and with the black vault above, was tremendous, the vastness awe-inspiring, but her heart was heavy.

Torn between her duty as a CIA agent and her life as a mother, she fought hard to tackle them both, but she was fighting a losing battle. First, she had been career-motivated all her life. She loved her job and the satisfaction of bringing hardened criminals to justice. Second, the harsh demands of her job had all but alienated her from the husband she was now trying to reconcile with after he left her. Thirty minutes ago, she'd managed to get through to Jessica.

"Hey, honey."

"Hey."

"How are you?"

Silence.

"What you up to?"

"Nothing."

"I miss you so much."

Silence.

Heidi felt the tears spring into her eyes, fought to keep control of her voice. "So, what's new with you?"

"You don't have to do this, Mom."

"Do what?" She wondered if Jessica believed that this was a call borne out of duty.

"Keep in touch. You're where you want to be and that's not here. With us. Look, I have to go."

Heidi tried to speak but her throat was too constricted. The call ended with nothing further said and a hole the size of a football where her heart should be. *Is it time to give it all up? Priorities, right? That's what it's about, or so they say. Damn, but what if every man and woman who upheld the law and fought for the rights of decent civilians decided to do the same? What then?*

She gripped her knees tightly, wiped the tears from her eyes, and looked up, straight into dark skies illuminated by a silver moon. *No help up there.* The conflict of career and family was very real for her. Both were incredibly important, but if either one didn't exist then she would become a more shallow person. She needed both to function.

Movement came from the left and she checked her gun before turning to see Eli Cross. Gunn and Jemma were walking along behind him.

"Been a long, bumpy trip," Cross grumbled as the newcomers all sat beside her. "It better be worth it, Agent."

Heidi swallowed the pain and nodded, showing her game face. "I'll say thanks for coming to the few who came. No doubt Bodie and Coleman will be able to catch us in the field. I'll give you a quick briefing and then we're off. Got it?"

"Why the clandestine meet?" Gunn asked.

Heidi stared at him. "We're the CIA, dude."

"Ahh, sorry."

"Briefly . . . five statues were recently unearthed in South America that match *precisely* to four others that were found on the Azores a decade ago. I hope I don't have to clarify the significance of that, considering what's between both places."

Gunn shook his head dubiously. "You mean the ocean? Nope. Bodie and Cassidy are the ones that will need the full documentary. But that's a big presumption, Agent."

"Understood. But the idiots who made this find announced it to the world several days ago. By now we'll have every crackpot and his pet alligator on the way to Brazil."

"Brazil?"

"The statues have been taken to the National History Museum in Rio de Janeiro for examination."

Gunn's mouth fell open. "Rio? Now that's pure bucket list. I do like the sound of that."

"Yeah, Rio. But don't get sidetracked. I meant it when I said it's attracted an awful lot of international attention. And an entire pigpen of unsavory characters."

Cross grunted. "Always the same. Why did they announce it so publicly?"

Heidi blew her cheeks out. "I have no sane answer to that question."

"And why are you in such a rush?" Gunn asked. "I mean—so what? Atlantis has been there a bloody long time, Agent. It'll be claimed by Morocco or some other nation. And it's not like they're gonna dredge it up very quickly."

Heidi sighed. "Are you kidding me? The stakes are huge. First, it's *international* waters. Second, Atlantis was an advanced civilization. There could be devices, engineering, ideas, and medicines that could change our planet. We want a new frontier, a big step forward. The world is ready for it now more than ever. And guess what . . . Uncle Sam wants it first."

"Naturally," Cross said, nodding.

"These original Azores statues," Gunn said. "I'm guessing they had Phoenician origins?"

"You'd be right. The Phoenicians were an ancient civilization who spread across Lebanon, Turkey, Gaza, and even to the Atlantic Ocean. It has been suggested that they were the remnants of Atlantis, all that remained after the great cataclysm."

Jemma made a noise. "They were also supposed to originate from Bahrain. Another classic history quarrel. I remember that much."

"And this is why I'm looking to enlist the services of a history expert," Heidi admitted. "For this mission, at least."

Gunn shuffled on the cold concrete. "Not a bad idea. Look, is there a reason we're sitting around like this? It's bloody freezing up here."

"I like it," Heidi said. "It helps me think about . . . things."

Cross might have seen something in her eyes, for he spoke quickly. "You want to go to this museum and get a look at the new statues?"

"Yeah, to make a definitive ID."

"How long have they been on display?" Gunn asked.

Heidi shook her head. "Stop being so naive. They're *not* on display. There are *no* good photos. Why do you think I called the relic hunters? The press conference was a few days ago, and the statues have since been transported to the museum—"

"For examination?" Jemma asked.

Heidi raised a brow. "Yeah, for investigation."

Gunn finally understood. "My bottomless computer skills are at your service."

Cross looked out toward the distant Washington Monument spearing up at the scudding darkness. "You want to use us as deniable assets," he said. "Again. But that won't happen. We should be able to form a plan by the time we arrive in Rio."

Heidi nodded gratefully at him. "Perfect. We can let Bodie run his eyes over it." She paused. "I'm assuming he meant what he said?"

Cross shrugged. "All being well, they should have no problem taking Pantera tonight."

Heidi took a moment to remain completely still and consider what she was doing right now. Twenty minutes after losing it over the conversation with her daughter, she was once again traveling farther afield. The hurt deepened, but the quandary didn't have the decency to unravel itself. She still felt drawn, driven. The search for Atlantis or any ancient myth may take a back seat to current affairs—it also had to remain under the radar—but it was no less important. It all went back to the excitement about everything that might be discovered. Imagine the concerns that may arise if an enemy state found it and the secrets contained therein.

She rose and joined Cross, staring toward the Mall. "Beautiful, isn't it?"

"It evokes a sense of internal contemplation, yeah."

"We touch so many lives, help so many people, and yet we can't do a damn thing about our own."

Cross nodded carefully, saying nothing.

Heidi knew the choice was to quit then and there or to compartmentalize her daughter for a while. The trouble was, at the moment, she could do neither. Every time she went away, she made it worse. The odds of a reconciliation diminished. She sensed right now that it was at a tipping point. Yes, she was a good agent, one who could put personal issues aside for the job. But the more she did that, the closer she came to losing one of the reasons she was so good at her job. Without one, there could not be the other.

To be good at this job, you not only had to be driven—you had to be obstinate. Headstrong. The rule book couldn't tell her what to do. The head and the heart were always at war.

Feeling a further upwelling of emotion, she turned away and faced the cold concrete steps where her team waited.

"So, what the hell are you guys still standing there for? Plane's waiting, c'mon."

CHAPTER FIVE

Bodie narrowed his eyes. The bastard was right there, looking out of the window, staring practically straight down the hidden camera's lens. Jack Pantera was bald and distinguished, and always cut a dashing figure, which some might have believed would make his trade even harder. It was quite the opposite. Jack could tape on a wig, slide a pair of sunglasses over his nose, and blend in to any scene, anywhere. He had always been a privileged son of a bitch too, Bodie reflected. Born into wealth, he had chosen his own path with the time and ease to do it. No worrying over security and bills for Jack.

So why choose to be a thief?

Bodie remembered the conversation well. Pantera had never been closed with him, never lied . . .

You're joking, right?

Bodie set the prison events aside for the moment. Pantera had never lied, never covered anything up. Every risk, every occurrence, was laid out for Bodie in black and white. Jack watched his young protégé come to his own conclusion that, in the end, usually matched Jack's.

He'd taken up thieving for the classic reason—to rebel. Jack had chosen to go against the grain, taking what he could easily afford, making a name for himself on the dark side of the law. But even that decision had good connotations. He didn't need the money, so everything he took from the rich he gave back to the poor.

"What are you thinking?" Cassidy's whispered question snapped Bodie out of his reverie.

"Just dwelling on old stuff." Bodie sifted the significant memories from the trivial, trying to find something that would explain Pantera's actions. With every job Bodie pulled, he preferred to go in with all the answers, every scrap of information. Here they were, ready to go, and he knew nothing.

"He once told me why he became a thief," Bodie said quietly. "His words were: 'Because I like the *ideal* of Robin Hood.' Jack liked to take from the rich and give to the poor. That's how it all started out. Of course, even in that game, you soon learn there are rules you can't break. By the time Jack realized, he was already in too deep." Bodie shrugged. "So, he evolved. Got better at it. Became the best."

"I never knew that about his past," Cassidy said. "We talked, sure, for hours, but never about how he got started."

"You didn't work for him long enough. He kept that stuff for his closest confidantes."

"I barely worked for him at all, but he never seemed the one to betray his best friends."

Bodie stared into the eyes behind the camera's lens. Cassidy was right. It was time to find out what drove a man to betray his friends.

Bodie led the way. Cassidy wasn't his equal in covert infiltration, the same as he wasn't hers in combat. They each had their strengths. From their vantage point to the rear of the gated community, over a high wall and into somebody's backyard they went, a silent step at a time. Every parameter had been accounted for. They chose the houses without dogs, and one particularly large yard that was empty, to regroup and assess. They chose a circuitous route and a time when the guards were at their most lethargic. They chose Pantera's habitual heavy sleeping time. They watched their path carefully through the magic of mini surveillance cameras and Bluetooth. They moved easily, slowly, and with infinite care. The night hummed around them, populated by small creatures. The skies were dotted with stars, the great vault otherwise pitch black. A barely noticeable breeze stirred trees and bushes, chilling the sweat on their faces.

Bodie halted finally at the foot of the hedge that bordered the rear of Pantera's property.

"We good?"

Cassidy nodded. "Ready when you are."

"You have the restraints ready?"

"Always."

Bodie concentrated on the hedge. It was in poor repair, being out of sight of the main internal road. He found a way through quite easily. Pantera's house lay a quick sprint across well-tended lawns, which Bodie now made, Cassidy at his back. They checked all the cameras one last time.

Nothing. No sign that they'd been compromised by security, neighbors, or Pantera himself, although several houses and many windows overlooked Jack's property. Bodie wondered if, for the sake of blending in, Jack had been forced to temper his cunning. The old Pantera would employ a warning device of some sort at the very least.

The rear double glass doors were secured by a high-end device, Bodie noticed. They would have to make a lot of noise going in that way. Most people fitted advanced security to the ground level of their houses and tended to neglect the upper floors. Pantera should be different, but here, Bodie betted that he wouldn't be. They scaled a rear porch and inched along a conservatory roof, glass to both sides of the half-meter ledge. Exposed, they took just seconds to reach the end and duck down beside a second-floor window. Bodie quickly examined the lock, and knew it could be forced inward with minimal noise. That fact in itself made him wary. The Jack Pantera that Bodie knew wouldn't use a lock like this for anything other than a setup.

"This is it," he murmured. "Looking at the state of this lock, Jack should be ready for us inside. It's an easy in, so burglars will be drawn here. Make sure you're close."

"I'll be so close to your ass you'll be issuing a restraining order."

Bodie shook his head, then broke the lock. Instantly, he forced the window open and levered his body through, dropped to the carpeted floor, and moved aside to give Cassidy room to cover his back. He expected light, he expected sound, maybe even a flare of some kind to debilitate the senses—but he didn't expect what happened next.

Pantera stumbled into the room, looking worn and tired, a bed sheet wrapped around his frame. He jabbed at a lamp, illuminating the room with a low light, face stretched with agony as he recognized who stood before him.

"No, no, *no*, Bodie. What the hell have you done?" Panic tautened the vocal cords and made Jack's face as white as the sheet that covered him.

Bodie recovered quickly. "You'd better explain yourself fast, Jack."

Pantera clutched the sheet in fear. "Did they see you?"

Bodie glanced at Cassidy, who shrugged eloquently.

"Who?" she asked sweetly.

Pantera lurched, fear sending his eyes huge. His feet tangled in the sheet, ripping it away from his body.

Cassidy made a show of covering her eyes. "Whoa, I never bargained for that. You put that bad boy away, Jack."

"You don't understand." Pantera came forward, holding a hand out to Bodie.

"Right. Well, until I do, let's get out of this room and go somewhere dark. And for God's sake put some bloody pants on."

Pantera tried visibly to get a grip on himself, picking up the sheet and tying it properly. Then he did something else Bodie would never have expected. He walked over to the darkest corner of the room and threw himself down on the floor, sitting with his back to the wall.

Then he motioned for Cassidy to turn the lamp off.

"I assume you chose this room because it was the easiest entry?"

Bodie nodded. "Identified it yesterday. I guess that was part of your plan?"

Pantera sighed raggedly. "Yeah, yeah, but a long fucking time ago. When . . . when things were better."

Bodie sat opposite the older man while Cassidy roamed the hallway outside the door, checking for traps.

"Tell her to make no noise," Pantera said. "No noise at all and no shadows against the curtains. I don't know where I'm safe anymore."

Bodie didn't try to hide his confusion. "What are you talking about? You're acting like you didn't collude to get me thrown into a Mexican prison for the rest of my life, which, by the way, was going to be measured in days."

Pantera, to his credit, only gave a pained sigh. "One of the worst moments of my life. I'm so sorry, Guy."

Bodie had never heard Pantera apologize before. Cassidy returned to the room with a shrug. "All clear up here."

"Please," Pantera hissed. "Do not go downstairs."

Cassidy appeared to take that as a challenge and turned toward the door. Bodie called her back.

"Wait. Just give him a minute. I want to hear what he has to say."

"Could be a trap. No matter how you think of him, he's not your father."

Bodie was staring at Pantera's darkened face. "I don't think so. What's got you so shook up? If I didn't know you, I'd swear I was looking at a totally different man from the Jack Pantera I used to admire."

"To be fair," Cassidy said, "I think we've seen a little bit *too much* of him tonight."

"It didn't scare you off," Pantera said, managing his first buoyant comment of the encounter.

"Things like that never do. As you know, Jack, I'm not shy."

Bodie clicked a finger. "You have sixty seconds before I set her on you. Don't waste them."

Even in the dim light thrown by the starry skies Bodie saw Pantera's shoulders slump. A ragged sigh came from his mouth, and then he glanced up toward one of the houses that overlooked his property before fixing everything on Bodie.

"You have to help me, my friend. You have to help *them*."

CHAPTER SIX

On the plane, Heidi provided what information she could about the mission, backed up by Gunn on his laptop and the few things that Jemma knew. Between them they knitted together the drifting sands of time as best they could. Several times Heidi mentioned the new historian they were trying to appoint.

"She should be with us by the time we return from Rio."

"What . . . she doesn't like the beach?" Gunn asked.

"She's somewhat difficult," Heidi admitted, "so should fit in with you guys perfectly. But do feel free to tell us when you expect to visit the beach."

Gunn sank back into his work, saying nothing. Heidi let it go, knowing he was happiest there. The gelled hair, the snappy clothes—they were all for show. Gunn was an introvert and never more content than when he could lead from behind a flickering screen.

She turned in her seat to stare at Cross. "Did you try Bodie?"

"Yeah, no reply. Must be in the thick of it." He looked anxious.

"Try not to worry. He's not your kid and he can take care of himself." Heidi wondered why her own heart was tensed with worry. The two of them had big issues to sort through when he returned. His selfish actions may have jeopardized this mission. Even then, she was looking forward to seeing the well-shaven, strongly built man with the incredibly white teeth.

Hey, Flash, she wanted to say when she first saw him but knew it would have to be a far sterner greeting.

It wasn't to be. If only this group of recalcitrant children would fall into line.

"He might not be my kid," Cross responded, "but behind actual family, he's the person I care about most in this world."

She'd guessed just that, seeing their interaction. Cross was almost as much a father figure and mentor for Bodie as Pantera had been.

She caught the team's attention by standing up, and told them everything she knew.

"The nine statues," she began, "are of Phoenician origin. They are a representation of the god Baal. You may be wondering why the Phoenicians keep coming up in reference to Atlantis . . . well, the Phoenicians were a great seafaring people who destroyed most of the major powers around the Mediterranean a few thousand years ago. Even Egypt and Ramses III fought them. Some say these sea people were the remnants of Atlantis. Others, that the Phoenicians were founded many years before that, again from what remained. The fact is that many of the kings of Atlantis were the gods of the Phoenicians and the Greeks. Through time, there have been inscriptions found on Egyptian temples that tell of these sea people, the fall of a continent, and the attack of an advanced race. And it was the Egyptians themselves that started the cowing of the Phoenicians by sending their mighty armies up the coast, demanding to be recognized as their overlords, and claiming a large tribute also. Of course, the Phoenicians later rose again, with supposed help from the so-called sea people, and created such cities as Carthage, Tangier, Cadiz, and Beirut."

"And why was this guy Baal so important?" Cross asked.

"The *god* Baal was important to a race that dominated both the Atlantic and the Mediterranean so much so that his and other names they gave ports and towns were the names of their gods and remain so even now. Gades in Spain was one such town, named after Gadeirus, the son of Poseidon, god of the sea."

Jemma scrunched her nose. "I never heard of Gades."

"That's because today they call it Cadiz."

"Sorry, I still don't get the link between the Phoenicians and Atlantis," Gunn admitted.

"Well, there's a lot more to it," Heidi said, "that I'm just not qualified to relate. For instance, a purple dye they brought to the Med that can be found in only one other place on the entire earth—Oaxaca, Mexico. Ancient Roman artifacts made from Canadian spruce. It all points to the fact that these so-called Phoenicians, at some point in their history, lived on a continent that stretched from the Med to South America at least."

"I remember a documentary that stated the Phoenicians themselves claimed their civilization went back thirty thousand years." Jemma shrugged. "Most of it lost to the mists of time."

Heidi nodded. "The fact is that they were probably the very first civilized nation on earth. But back to Baal. His real name was Baal Hammon, worshipped as both a fertility god and a supreme god. He was probably their greatest deity."

"I also remember there were an awful lot of other places where Atlantis could have been," Cross said, playing devil's advocate.

"From the Caribbean to the Sahara and even to the North Sea. But let's not forget major cities like Amsterdam and Rotterdam are even now many feet below sea level. They could be the incredible sunken cities of future generations. But Atlantis speaks of mythical worlds and millennia ancient. It is captivating."

"I understand that Atlantis would be a major find," Gunn said. "Especially today. But why are the CIA involved?"

Heidi poured water from a bottle, steadying her glass as the plane flew through a little turbulence. "Obviously, they're not."

"What? Well—"

Cross tapped his arm. "She means officially."

Heidi wished that were the case. "The CIA does not undertake these missions. They do not manage teams of . . . relic hunters. They do not believe in myths and legends. Imagine the indignity . . ." She shook her head. "But they *do* believe in undiscovered technology and new medicines that would solidify America's position as the strongest nation in the world. All they're doing is safeguarding our future."

"We just found one of the ancient wonders of the world," Jemma pointed out.

"Sure you did. Do you really think the bean counters, the wizened old men in their towers, the fly-by-the-seat-of-their-pants kids in their bespoke suits give a shit about wonders? About legends?"

"They would if it lined their pockets," Jemma said.

"Oh yeah, but they can find far easier ways to do that. A coup here and there. A coal deposit cleared of locals."

"What exactly are you saying?"

"I'm saying that the whole thing is transient at the moment. A bit like my personal life. Understood?"

"Isn't a transient homeless?" Cross asked caustically.

"You got it, Eli. For now, you're homeless. You're off the books, which is perfect for the CIA. You're expert, capable tramps. We all are. Until somebody finds a home for us."

"You seem to have adopted us pretty quickly, though," Cross pointed out. "What did you do before this?"

"None of your business. Now listen, we should talk about what to do when we land in Brazil."

CHAPTER SEVEN

Jack Pantera launched himself at Bodie and Cassidy, thrusting his bulk up from the carpeted floor. It came as a shock to Bodie. When the bald man came at him, he launched a head-butt that Bodie barely avoided. Pantera straight-armed him across the top of the chest. It was like walking into a low beam. Bodie flinched and went down to one knee.

Cassidy didn't even try to talk Pantera down. There may even have been a slight smile across her lips as she confronted the bald man.

The older thief struck her like a hammer, his attack lacking any sense of craft. He just wanted to get her out of the way and find freedom, bulldoze his way to victory. Bodie saw Cassidy skip aside and grab Pantera's right arm. He flew one full rotation on his journey to the ground, landing hard on his spine.

He didn't groan, just kicked his feet.

"Stay down," Cassidy warned.

"Bastards," Pantera fumed.

Bodie rose. "You seriously think you can fight your way out of here? You're not even better than *me*, mate, never mind Cassidy here."

Pantera made a noise and then Bodie realized, with profound shock, that the man was crying. His face was red, crumpled. Nevertheless, he rose and ran for the door. Cassidy moved fast, planting a foot in his spine and altering his trajectory.

Straight into the doorjamb.

Pantera bounced off the wooden frame with a crunch that made even Bodie wince. A streak of blood marked the impact. Pantera fell to his knees. Bodie moved to stand over him.

"What the hell are you doing?"

Bodie knelt at Pantera's side, took hold of his face, and turned it until they stared eye to eye.

"What's the deal, Jack? You sold me out. Left me to die. A Mexican prison? Betrayal? European assassins?"

Pantera struggled. "I didn't send anyone to *kill* you. They said it would be a tough year in prison. That was all."

Bodie spluttered a little. *A tough year?* That was some understatement.

"Fucksake," Cassidy echoed his thoughts. "That's harsh."

"*Who* said that, Jack?" Bodie asked.

"They did. The people watching the house. Did you see anyone else watching?" Pantera hissed. "When you came here? Did you?"

"There's nobody else out there, Jack."

"Are you positive?"

"Not entirely." Cassidy shrugged. "But if there is, we can deal with them easily enough when they arrive."

Pantera closed his eyes. "You don't understand."

"Dude, we've been saying that since we first saw your ass. Literally. So why not enlighten us?"

Pantera couldn't stop crying, it seemed. Bodie was trying very hard not to conceal his bewilderment. Through all the years of training, of comradeship, he'd never seen Jack so upset.

"You hate me, but it is them you should hate. I don't hold anything against you, Guy. I have no strife with you. But they do, and they are very, very, *seriously* bad people."

Bodie sat back, shaking his head slightly. "You're making no sense at all, pal."

"*The watchers.* They watch for you."

Bodie ignored a shiver. "Mate, I'm gonna slap you so hard if you don't start talking sense."

"These people." Pantera looked like he feared speaking their name. "They are seriously evil. No morals. No compassion. Not even the slightest sense of consideration or family unless it is for themselves, where it is absolute. They are brothers," he whispered. "They are *Bratva.*"

Bodie took a moment to process what Pantera had said. "Russians?" he asked, even more confused. "You mean the Russian Bratva? Gangsters, thugs, that kind of thing?"

Pantera nodded slowly.

"Sorry, mate, I'm not buying it. Those people would never have scared a man like you."

"You really pissed them off, Guy. You and your band of"—he glanced at Cassidy—"brothers."

She clucked her tongue. "I know what you wanted to say there. You wanted to say 'bitches.' Well, don't worry yourself. I *am* a bitch, happy to be, and a good one at that."

"You pissed them off," Pantera reiterated. "You stole something from them after we parted ways. Some bloody artifact that belonged to the old man. Apparently, he suffered a heart attack three days later and died."

Bodie frowned hard. The cause of the heart attack wouldn't matter to these people. They would only see the circumstances surrounding it. He knew of the Bratva—that they were a close-knit, ruthless organization founded in Moscow and part of the Russian Mafia. They were well organized and incredibly far-reaching.

"They're the real deal," Cassidy said.

"Yeah, I know. And you're saying we stole from them?"

"Not just that. They know you stole a priceless sentimental statue from them," Pantera said. "When the old man died they made it their business to track down the person who *employed* you. When they finished with him and his family"—Jack gulped—"they tracked me just because I was your old boss. They couldn't find you at the time, so they came straight to my door."

"But we broke up our partnership."

"You think they care that I agreed to let you follow your own path? That we parted on the best of terms? That I was actually proud to see you leading your own team? They don't care about that shit."

Bodie looked toward the bare window. "What . . . and now they watch in case I drop by for a coffee?"

"You're a fucking idiot, Bodie, you know that?"

"If I'm understanding this right, you gave me to them in order to save your own skin. You put me inside that jail and let them know I was there. It was Bratva that attacked me inside . . ." He remembered their appearance, their tattoos. It seemed a lifetime ago now. "Makes sense."

"The Bratva entered a Mexican cartel–run prison?" Cassidy wondered.

"They have ties," Bodie said. "They do business. These real-life crime syndicates are plugged in everywhere, and with each other."

"So they threatened your ass and you ran squealing to protect it?" Cassidy stared at Pantera. "Man, I thought you were better than that. *More* than that."

"No, no, no." Pantera shook his head wearily. "Is it that hard to understand? Here . . ." He crawled over to a wooden chest, opened the bottom drawer, and pulled out a plastic folder and a small flashlight.

He opened the folder, spread the contents onto the floor and flicked on the flashlight.

Bodie blanched as reality hit home. "Shit."

Over a dozen Polaroid photographs showed a woman and a young boy: eating cereal at a breakfast bar, driving to school, and, in one case, even lying asleep in their beds.

"This is your family?" Cassidy asked, knowing the answer already.

"How long?" Bodie asked.

"Six months maybe?" Pantera shrugged. "Sometime before the Mexican prison. They send me more every month."

"And are they just watching?" Bodie asked. "Or . . ."

"No. Just watching. Endlessly watching. Both my wife, Steph, and my son, Eric. And me, I guess."

Bodie read between the lines. The Bratva saw Pantera as their best route to getting close to his entire team. Their modus operandi was heavy threat and extreme coercion. Family was the weakness, and ruthless criminals would always exploit it if they could. Somehow, then, they had found a way to Pantera's family.

"You lost your edge."

Pantera shrugged. "Yeah, happily. I quit three years ago. After you left, the whole bloody vision lost its edge. Felt hollow, somehow. I took excessive precautions when I quit. I never thought someone on this scale would come hunting. But I guess we never kept our alliance a secret. People knew."

Bodie had to agree. They had always been fastidious about who they worked for and who they deprived of objects. Somehow, somebody had deceived *them*.

"What's the world coming to," he muttered. "Stealing old relics is a bloody victimless crime. Or it's supposed to be, at least." He shook his head, depressed.

"You realize how big a problem this is?" Pantera asked. "The Bratva are vast—worldwide. A million-man army. You may have escaped the watch on my house, but they will *never* stop coming. This is a matter of honor to them. Pride. It is out of respect for their boss, their father. This debt might never be repaid."

"We'll talk about that later," Bodie said. "First, what the hell do you mean—*escaped* the watch?"

Pantera blinked. "You said you'd escaped the watch."

"No. I didn't say that," Bodie said. "If they're watching—they know we're here."

"No." Now Pantera rose ramrod straight. "It's the anxiety, the constant unease, the lack of sleep. I find it hard to focus."

Bodie couldn't find the words. Cassidy found them for him.

"Get it together, Jack."

The fear that crossed his features was terrible to comprehend. "Please, God, no. Please—"

"Your family! Jack, your family. Where the fuck do they live?"

It took a moment for Pantera to say anything. "Winter Park."

Bodie dragged him up and motioned at Cassidy. "We go now. We have to get there. We have to help them."

And he knew, as she turned away from him, that the fear he saw etched on Cassidy Coleman's face was not for herself, not for them. The fear was for a woman and her child.

CHAPTER EIGHT

The National History Museum in Rio de Janeiro sat a twenty-minute drive north of the famous Copacabana Beach and nearby Sugarloaf Mountain. The entrance was fronted by palm trees, bordered by banks of grass, and framed by the golden sun. Heidi could think of worse places to be.

After landing they had been taken to the hotel and then for a ride, courtesy of the local CIA station, through the colorful streets of Rio, threading between small parked cars and marveling at the multitude of wires crossing above their heads. Delivery bikes and motorcycles were plentiful, and pedestrians walked in the roads because the sidewalks were crammed. They passed high walls decorated with excessive, beautiful street art, futuristic-looking trams, and the yellow-and-green flag of Brazil flying above boulevards chock full of market stalls. The pace was lively and the noise raucous. Heidi found herself being grateful they were cocooned inside the black, air-conditioned, noise-reducing bubble all the way to the front of the museum.

Gunn climbed out first, ignoring the others as he got his first real gulp of Brazilian air. "Ah, paradise." He sighed. "So perfect."

Jemma pushed open the door he'd let swing back into her knees. "You'd better sunscreen up, geek. I hear hair gel really attracts the rays."

Gunn turned to her anxiously. "Does it?"

"Mister Practical," Jemma said, sighing, "you should read up on the real world."

Gunn turned away. "Why should I when mine is so much better?"

"It may have helped you in the past," Jemma said. "But we're in a whole new situation now."

Heidi came up beside them, not commenting on their conversation as she waited for Cross. He took a good look at their surroundings before sidling up.

"We expecting company?"

"Not that we know of. Why?"

"Just checking. You mentioned 'other factions' involved here."

"Well, I guess it's possible." Heidi realized he made a good point and reassessed the view. "Intel suggests a Chinese faction, among others. But they won't be wearing signs around their necks."

During the flight they had probed the museum and its security measures. Cross had found the first loophole, an outdated sensor array, and Jemma the second, a hackable security system. Together they had worked up a plan. But it was Heidi's responsibility to find out exactly where the statues of Baal were being kept.

"We have the vault," she said quietly. "One floor down, and then the main workrooms next to that. Our man only managed a quick flyby, but reports he saw the statues sitting in the third workroom to the right of the vault. Three people working on them. He reported no security upgrades, but like I said, he only managed a quick look."

Cross nodded knowingly at her. "AC problem? Internet issues?"

"No. Something far simpler. Coffee-machine upgrade. They've been asking for one for months."

"And a mysterious benefactor bought and paid for plumbing it in." Cross nodded. "As you say, simple and forgettable. The perfect recon."

Heidi nodded in acknowledgment. "And now over to you, Eli. Time to implement your plan."

"Sure. Well, let's get inside the museum and take a look. Make sure there are no surprises."

They spent the time until dark investigating both inside and outside the museum and then gathered on the grounds in a deep nest of shadows, properly attired and tooled-up, again courtesy of the local CIA. Heidi had arranged everything nicely, and Cross commented that thievery was so much easier with the help of the American government.

She shrugged. "I guess we're pretty well versed in it."

The team laughed quietly and made ready to move. Gunn was using a mobile tablet, which made it possible for him to join them in the field. A fact he was not entirely comfortable with.

"First time for everything, my friend," Jemma said. "You gotta get your toes wet sometime."

"It's not my toes I'm worried about. It's the rest of my body. I'd feel better if Cass and Bodie were here."

She slapped his back. "Can't sit behind a screen forever. Some jobs need to be done up close and personal."

Gunn nodded. But he didn't seem convinced.

"Use your strengths first," Jemma said, laying it out for him, "in any situation."

With midnight almost upon them, the team tuned out the relaxed atmosphere of a warm Brazilian night and crossed a gray paved area to lose themselves in a tangle of bushes that ran all the way to the back of the museum. With care, they crept through, keeping a close eye on the windows and the grounds. Sensors were easy. Gunn had identified two by hacking the museum's antiquated system and knew their exact placement. The team merely hopped over the infrared beams. The windows, though, were another matter. Gunn could only initiate a brute-force overtake, which gave him control of the museum's systems for just a few minutes. During that time Cross took a small glass cutter and hammer out.

Heidi glared at him. "Really?"

"Don't worry. It's just for the last bit, and I won't use the steel."

Cross proceeded to cut a circle, tap out the glass, and then reach inside to lever open the window lock. Once they were inside, he made sure all the sensors were touching again and stuck a large piece of clear tape over the small hole.

"A bit rudimentary," Heidi said.

"If you think it's shit, just say so," Gunn said. "I mean, I do."

"Keep your opinions to yourself," Cross whispered. "Unless you want me to tie you to the urinals for the night."

"Whatever works," Jemma said. "We didn't have much time to make a perfect plan here."

Now Heidi looked surprised. "We had the entire plane journey, Miss Blunt."

"I don't know how it works in your world, CIA," Jemma said, "but in the world of the elite thief, a job even as basic as this takes weeks of planning. That is—if you want to do it right."

"Really?"

"Yeah, oh yeah. You don't just look at it and live with it. You move in. You move in like it's your brand-new permanent home. It's your whole life for as long as it takes."

Heidi saw a new level of dedication. Of course, that was the reason these guys were the best. And that the CIA was now using them.

"Still nothing from Bodie?" she said, changing the subject.

"Alone, I'd be worried. But the man's with Cassidy." Cross shook his head. "I doubt there's a single situation on earth that girl couldn't handle."

They were slipping quietly along a corridor, confident that the cameras were looped out to play an empty scene supplied by Gunn. The young computer expert kept a constant watch on his feed and plotted the paths and stations of all the guards.

"Wait," he said, holding a finger to his lips.

A shadow passed the end of the corridor, not stopping.

He waved them on. Heidi would have preferred a bit more warning but assumed the kid knew what he was up to. She concentrated on the job at hand, taking Jemma's advice literally in an effort to quell the distracting voices in her head. Distractions would get them caught, or killed.

The stairs were unmanned and went straight to the below-ground floor. Cross paused at the end as Gunn rechecked his systems.

"Interestingly," he said, "when I rerun the loop and check the system, which I do as a precaution, I am seeing evidence of a similar loop implant . . ." He paused. "Maybe from an hour ago?"

"What does that mean?" Heidi asked.

"Simple," Jemma said. "He's found digital footprints. Somebody has been here before us."

Heidi gritted her teeth. "You're sure?"

"Yeah, I'm sure. Somebody followed protocols similar to mine. Somebody well trained. If I weren't this good, we'd never have known."

Heidi ignored the bravado. "So, who's that good?"

"A few," Gunn admitted. "But it's not exactly a cutting-edge system. From the list you gave us . . . the short list of interested parties? I'd say the Chinese. I've seen their work before on a couple of relic-hunting missions. This mirrors their MO perfectly. The way they bypass protocols. The redundancies they leave in their work. Hackers like me . . . they leave trails like fingerprints."

Heidi thought it sounded plausible, given the Chinese's competency and dedication to any mission, the time they had already had to reach Rio, and Gunn's certainty, but there was nothing they could do about it now. "Are we still okay?"

"We're good to go."

"Surely they have more security in here," Heidi whispered. "For the vault and the labs."

"Trust me with this," Gunn said. "It's my job. Move out."

Cross pushed open the door. Heidi tried not to cringe in expectation of sudden, whirring alarms. The place remained silent, eerily so. Part of the lab ahead was illuminated while other areas lay in darkness. A smattering of shadows played games with her imagination—the broken blinds in one window with the marble head behind them might have been one of Hell's demons, waiting to pounce. The half-finished coat of armor in a far corner might have moved once . . . twice . . .

Cross craned his neck up at the camera mounted on a white-painted swivel, set into the place where the wall met the ceiling. "I see lenses twitching up there, bud."

Gunn checked his tablet once more. "We're in the clear, Eli."

"Could someone else be watching?" Jemma asked shrewdly.

Gunn caught her meaning. "An enemy piggybacking on my signal? Interesting," he mused.

While Heidi did not think it interesting in the least, she found herself enjoying how this team complemented each other. Their strengths were widespread, not singular; nobody could rely on just one person. Cross pushed ahead as Gunn mulled over the situation. Together, they approached the room where the newfound statues should be kept.

It was dark, but the light shining from other windows was enough to illuminate that which they sought. Inside the lab stood a long bench-like table, and resting on its waist-high top were five statues. Heidi almost pressed her nose to the glass, so intent was she on getting a closer look.

Then Cross picked the lock.

"Shall we?"

They moved quickly inside, Jemma taking pictures with Heidi's phone, as they'd agreed. Gunn shifted to the corner of the room, still thinking. Cross took out a flashlight and studied the statues more closely.

Standing less than a foot tall, they were bronzed figurines. Baal had been called the King of the Gods, also known as Yahweh and Beelzebub, and was one of the ancient Phoenicians' greatest gods. Heidi saw them as small, decorative objects, potentially nondescript and unappealing, influenced probably by the artist's neighboring countries or regions—Egypt, Mesopotamia, and the Aegean Islands. To the untrained eye the figurines would be hard to distinguish from other cultures—crude, wearing a conical hat, and with one arm raised.

"You see the patterns there and there." Heidi pointed them out to Cross, indicating the gold leaf around the hat and body. "You see the feet? The carving? I need pictures of that for comparison."

Jemma took the photos.

Gunn spoke from the corner of the room. "I think we need to go."

"Why?" Heidi asked. "Problem?"

"We're all good, but there's definitely another signal in the vicinity. I can't pin it down."

Jemma looked over. "Really, nerd?"

"I'm by no means the best when working in these conditions, and this tablet's not powerful enough," he said. "Really! There just isn't enough processing power to isolate a signal. It's a lightweight."

"We talking about the tablet, or you?"

"Piss off."

By now, Heidi had all she needed. To her mind, the decision was already made. The evidence was standing right there before her eyes. But care had to be taken and the chain had to be followed. "We can go," she said.

"Are they of the same provenance?" Cross sidled up close. "I only ask 'cause it's kinda important to the mission that these statues were made by the same person."

Heidi hid her exultation, trying to maintain a professional face. "You're quite right, my friend, but we will leave that to the scientists."

"I've seen the photos of the Azores statues," he said, moving out of the door before her. "And I've just seen these with my own eyes. If I'm not mistaken, they're very much the same, Heidi."

She grinned. "I know. But we don't want to get carried away."

"Yeah," Cross agreed with a sigh. "Don't wanna lose the edge, I guess. So Gunn? Same way out?"

"We're clear," Gunn replied. "I could leave the loop on all night and they'd never know anything different. It's what they expect. Just got to watch out for the random patrol."

Up the stairs and back to the window they crossed paths with only one guard. He paused briefly as if hearing something and peered down the darkened corridor in their direction. After a few minutes he moved off, and they waited another ten. With that, they left the museum the same way that they'd entered.

On the ground, in the bushes, they crouched.

"You hear that?" Cross asked, listening.

Jemma scrunched her face up. "Shit."

Gunn tore his gaze away from the dimly lit screen he held. "Do not say my first op is about to go pear-shaped."

"I believe I know that sound," Heidi said. "I've heard it too many times before. What do you think, Eli?"

"Feet," Cross said with an unhappy shrug of the shoulders. "Lots of feet. That is the sound of several people running toward us."

"Bollocks," Gunn hissed. "I bet you wish we had Cassidy here now."

Cross didn't reply, but the expression on his face was enough to show he agreed with the computer geek.

CHAPTER NINE

It became clear that the rushing feet knew exactly where to go.

Cross rose just a millisecond before Heidi. "The good news is it's doubtful they're the Chinese because they should have left a while ago. And it's not guards as they're still inside," he said. "I don't know who these guys are."

"That's good news?" Heidi said. "Let's just hope it's some local gang blundering in the dark."

"Well, they're not blundering now," Gunn said urgently. "They're heading right this way!"

The men were dressed in jeans and T-shirts, faces dark; some wore headscarves and others face masks with skeletal images. Several carried knives and at least two carried .38s. They made little sound but ran right for the team.

She reached for the gun she'd left behind in the room just in case the museum used weapons detectors. *Shit!* They were not equipped to fight these opponents.

She radioed the car before running hard to the left, veering away from them. Gunn loped at her side, hissing for an odd kind of aid.

"Keep me straight. Make sure I'm not going to trip over anything."

He was tapping at his tablet as he ran.

Now? Some people just can't put their phones down.

She'd met what she called the phone zombies—and Gunn was a prime example—on the streets of DC and London. Even bumped into a few. But never before had she seen one in danger, running for its life.

"Gunn! Put Sonic down and *run*!"

He glanced up, evaded a bush, kept sprinting.

"What the hell are you—"

Then it became apparent he had a plan. The sprinklers turned on behind them, several high jets of water suddenly shooting up in wide arcs, surprising their pursuers, and tripping a few up. Then, the brightest of floodlights glared on, shining in their faces. Alarms sounded just as Heidi made it to the road and saw the black car pulling up.

"Get in!"

They piled in and the vehicle squealed away from the curb just as their pursuers reached them. One aimed a kick at the car that connected perfectly and must have practically broken his foot. Another attempted to jump onto the trunk, missed, and face-planted in the road.

"Well done!" Heidi congratulated Gunn. "You kept them off us just long enough."

The younger man blushed. "Happy I could help."

Heidi punched him. "You fucking British. So well mannered. Take a fucking compliment and own it, brother."

Gunn just grinned, rubbing his shoulder where she'd hit him. Heidi squirmed in her seat to look out the back window.

"All hell breaking loose at the museum," she said, wincing. "But we left no trace and nothing was taken. Problem is, those lunatics have a car."

Cross twisted. "They do? That's not good at all. Let's move it, Lucas."

Heidi echoed his statement and the car lurched ahead. Lucas knew his way around, speeding up several narrow streets to attempt evasion. After two minutes, though, their pursuers were closing despite it being clear that their car was beyond full.

"We have guns in the car, right?" Heidi asked.

Lucas motioned to the glovebox. Gunn, in the front seat, opened the latch and plucked out a single black Glock and two mags.

"That's it?"

Heidi sighed. "Make 'em count."

"Oh, thanks for the advice."

The car wound down a sharp hill and bounced across a junction. At the bottom, a curve sent them to the left, toward the sea. Heidi watched as the pursuing vehicle, a dark-blue Toyota sedan, moved up to their rear bumper.

"You gonna shoot them, or what?" Cross asked.

"They haven't actually fired on us yet."

"They want the pictures."

"Possibly. But how did they blunder on us at the museum?"

"Well, they blundered across the gardens. And they blundered into our car. And now they're blundering up our ass. Maybe that guard tipped them off. Maybe they were watching for days. It'd make sense."

Heidi agreed with Cross but said nothing. She watched their pursuers closely as they whipped through more streets. Another few minutes passed. The road broadened and Lucas was able to stamp on the gas pedal.

The car behind veered wildly as it pushed hard to keep up. Men hung out of the windows, losing scarves and weapons as they bounced around. Heidi saw a ragtag organization, a reckless one, but nonetheless dangerous. At the first sign of a raised gun she would—

The car swerved left, making her lose her balance. She was flung against Cross, knocking him into Jemma. Reaching out, she managed to grab the seat back and haul herself up. "A little warning next time," she panted.

Copacabana Beach appeared ahead. The broad, white sands arced away to the left, a vast expanse leading to the foaming surf, mostly empty now apart from a few lone strollers. Thousands of lights illuminated the curve, bright and golden and reflected in the far waters so that they appeared to bleed into the sea. High-rise buildings rose to the right, their own lights blazing, and between them a wide roadway stretched, following the line of the beach. Rows and rows of cars were parked in front of the hotels.

They hit the Avenue Atlantica at speed. Heidi knew it would only be a matter of minutes before they were seen by cops.

That can't happen.

The op would be busted before it had a chance to even begin.

The car raced hard down the beachfront highway with Sugarloaf Mountain at their backs. The area before the beach and the road was packed with bars and refreshment stands, hordes of tourists, and locals lounging around on their motorcycles. Palm trees and barriers flashed by. A man was forced to dive out of the way, rolling headlong into a bush. Another man climbed a metal fence, his right foot almost brushing the top of their car.

Heidi pointed at the rows of parked cars to their right.

"Stop. Either we're gonna kill someone out here or we're gonna get arrested. Just pull in there."

Gunn squirmed uneasily. "Won't the bad guys catch us?"

"Not if you run fast enough. You all ready?"

Lucas didn't wait; he spied a row of empty parking spaces and swerved the car. Tires screeched. The vehicle skidded sideways, then straightened. Doors flew open. Heidi and Gunn were out first, closely followed by Cross, Jemma, and Lucas. The hotel area stretched for miles and was packed with people. Heidi knew she'd made the right choice, especially when she saw the two motorcycle cops a few blocks down.

"Run," she said. "Try to keep up."

They flew away from the car as the chase vehicle pulled up. Its own maneuver was ungainly and it ended up across two parking spaces. Nevertheless, seven men climbed out and gave pursuit.

Heidi mingled with the crowd, but they weren't far enough ahead to slow down. Their enemy would see them running. She flitted left and right, wishing she knew the layout of the hotels. Then she remembered.

Turned to the driver.

"Lucas? Do you know this area?"

He nodded. "Some," he said, panting.

Heidi sidestepped through a crowd. "We need one hotel or restaurant," she said. "Multiple exits. Do you know of one?"

"There's the Toledo," Lucas said. "But any of these restaurants will have a rear entrance."

Heidi knew that. But she didn't want them ending up in some dark back alley. Thinking fast, she decided to stay with the crowds. Gunn and Jemma were not fighters; neither would be able to handle a confrontation like this. They raced across a narrow intersecting road, then slowed past the motorcycle cops. She glanced back, getting the first proper look at their hunters.

Two with ponytails, others with short hair. All were well muscled and wore tight clothing. Heidi might have thought they were part-time models if it wasn't for the twist to their faces, the scars on their exposed skin, and the weapons they concealed.

They left the cops to stare at the men and turned into the next restaurant. It was worth the risk to put some ground between them. Putting on the pace, she sped between tables and chairs, alarming guests. Quickly they reached the far end and she checked that everybody was together. They were, Gunn panting and clinging to his tablet like it was an Uzi. She slipped through to the back and then found herself in a gleaming kitchen. Pots and pans hung everywhere, and the surfaces of sinks and worktops glared under bright lights. The noise was tremendous, several cooks not even noticing them as they squeezed by.

The far door was ajar. Heidi pushed through, leaping into the warm night. As expected, the team found themselves in a narrow alley stinking of old food and trash. Happily, though, both ways were unblocked. She turned back the way they had come, found the rear exit of a neighboring restaurant, and pushed inside. A man crouched close by, leaning against the wall and smoking a cigarette.

She turned to Lucas. "Pay him. Tell him to say we went the other way."

Lucas explained in rapid-fire dialect. Heidi reversed their earlier run through the restaurant, ending up back on the main street. The thugs were nowhere to be seen.

We still need to get out of here.

A good crew would have spotters on the street. Heidi doubted this particular crew had the guile to forward-think that, but every scenario had to be considered. She spied a cab arriving by the side of the road and quickly pushed her way to the front of the queue.

"Emergency," she said as she hopped inside, urging the others to come quickly. Shouts went up from angered civilians, but the driver never blinked.

"Where to?"

"Just drive." Gunn's voice cracked a little.

They were all breathing heavily, sheened with sweat. Heidi watched the windows, looking for the thugs, but saw nothing until the very last minute. A ponytailed individual appeared, looking both ways, shouting at the sky, and looking very distressed.

She grinned.

"Well," she said. "Wasn't that fun?"

"Oh yeah, let's do it every day." Gunn could barely speak.

"You should. It'd help you reach your ten thousand steps."

Gunn paused for a second. "What? You're talking about my Fitbit, right? That's not because I'm putting on weight. It's to help regulate my body's routines."

Heidi grinned wider. "I said nothing, dude. Nothing. That's all on you."

Jemma nudged him. "I'd sit straighter too. When you slouch like that it looks like you have a paunch."

"I *do not* have a paunch."

"Those guys didn't look happy." Cross had been staring through the back window. "Mean, yeah; happy, no."

"Local motley crew," Heidi said. "We come across gangs like that all the time. Some are a joke, but all are incredibly dangerous. When they fail, the first thing they do is resort to violence."

"Let's hope we don't cross them again," Jemma said, shivering.

"That depends on the significance of these statues." Heidi tapped her phone, where the pictures were stored. "And if we can decipher their real provenance."

"We?" Jemma looked surprised. "We're not history buffs, and even Gunn here won't find an answer to ancient statue markings on the internet."

"Don't worry," Heidi said. "I have that covered, remember? We just have to get back to DC first."

"And contact Bodie," Cross said. "What the hell is going on with him?"

"I just tried Cassidy too," Jemma said. "No reply."

"Bodie will be fine," Heidi said. "I haven't known him long, but I get the feeling he could handle anything."

Cross shrugged. "Anything but Jack Pantera. They go back a long way. Jack, I believe, once wanted Bodie to take over when he retired."

"Take over?"

"You know, look after Jack's clients."

Heidi stared at him.

Cross adjusted his seatbelt as he changed position. "Jack's a rogue. A deceiver. A man who could confront the Devil and talk his way right out of Hell, and then back in again whenever he wanted a visit. He's Bodie's one weakness."

"Shit, well, I'm sure nothing's wrong. And he has Cassidy too."

The team went quiet and Heidi sensed their worry. That was easy, of course, because she felt it too.

CHAPTER TEN

Bodie led the way out of the window and down to Pantera's rear lawn.

Pantera fretted all the way. Bodie had never seen him like this, but then Bodie had never seen a man whose family was being threatened before. Pantera checked and rechecked the visuals despite knowing they were out of line of sight. Even as they flitted back toward the hedge he stopped and again rechecked.

"Jack," Cassidy growled. "You're acting crazy. The more you dick around, the worse our chances are."

Pantera knew it, and shook his head. Bodie led the way over the hedge and back to the car and then buckled himself in. Winter Park was a good drive away.

"Hit 192 and then the turnpike."

"I don't know what the hell that means."

"Just drive."

Cassidy twisted in the passenger seat from which she'd had to kick Pantera to the back. "I'm guessing you got about forty-five minutes to tell us the background on this. Then, we'll decide whether to help you or not."

It was a hard ultimatum, a gravel road of a choice. Bodie knew without any doubt that he couldn't refuse to help a mother and child in danger, but Jack Pantera wouldn't be too sure about that. Pantera hadn't seen Bodie for many years and had then betrayed him.

"Oh hell, it was the worst choice of my life. In the end, though, obviously, it was no choice. If you had kids you would both know that. Doesn't matter who you are. The president of the United States. The worst gangster in New York. The newest dictator in Africa. If you're human, you'd do anything to keep your children safe. Anything."

"Why don't you explain it from the beginning, Jack?" Bodie said, keeping the road both ahead and behind in his sights.

"You just keep checking we're not being followed," Pantera said. "And I'll explain. Maybe a year ago, this big fellow came to see me. I was practically retired, living off our ill-gotten gains, as you know. I was passing you—what?—maybe two jobs a year by then?"

"You were severing ties," Bodie recalled.

"Yeah, but the right way. Over time. Allowing my name to fade. I didn't need anything more. But this fellow—he cornered me in the Walmart parking lot, of all places. You know, the one off Turkey Lake Road? Anyway, it was early one Saturday. It was quiet. He pulled up alongside, handed me an envelope, and stared like he was studying something dead under a microscope. Those eyes." Pantera shuddered. "They'd seen death. They'd seen murder. And they would again. Sometimes you just know. Sometimes you can see a man's face and you know he has not one moral bone in his body and that killing you or your family wouldn't even register on his radar."

Cassidy nodded, tight-lipped. "I've fought a few. Even in the ring. Had to put them down real quick."

Pantera nodded. "This life-or-death situation registered with me immediately. The fellow just sat there, waiting. I opened the envelope and my heart fell through the floor . . ."

Bodie saw tears glistening on Pantera's face through the rearview.

"It was a photo of Eric. And one of Steph. They were taken inside our old home." He paused. "*This* home. Winter Park. They were both asleep on the sofa, the TV playing in the background. Someone had broken in and taken the photo so shamelessly. So blatantly. They just didn't care. These people, I knew, would kill with no inhibition."

Bodie kept his eye on the time. They were fifteen minutes from Winter Park and the more he heard Pantera talk, the faster he drove.

"Then the man spoke. Russian accent. Told me without being asked he was a member of the Bratva. He said there was something like a suffer-and-kill order out on you, Guy. He mentioned the job you took—which I remembered—and then explained what had happened to the old man. He said they wanted you and would watch me closely until you were dead. They said if I delivered you then my family would survive, but if I didn't—" Pantera swallowed drily. "Well, then he showed me pictures of what they did to another family that upset them. It was . . . horrific. I folded, Guy, I folded and I gave you to them."

Bodie saw the truth of it all in Pantera's eyes, in his choked voice. He saw the terrible gravity in it too. The guillotine hung over them, just waiting for the favorable time. There was no way out. He felt the anger at Jack simmering below the surface, but he also saw with perfect clarity the man's reasoning.

Cassidy looked over at him. "I'd say our chances against the Bratva are even less than against the CIA."

"The CIA?" Pantera looked confused for a moment but then let it go. "I'm so sorry I betrayed you, Bodie. I ran it all through my head time and time again, a thousand times. I keep remembering when we first met—you were so green. Easy pickings, really. I taught you the body-language thing all over the West End, remember? How to tail a mark. We even practiced on a mews house in Knightsbridge that night. I haven't forgotten any of it, Bodie. I just can't believe I fucked up so badly."

Bodie agreed with the man but shrugged it off for now. "Get ready. We're five minutes out."

"The satnav will get you close," Pantera affirmed. "But not to the door." He didn't need to elaborate. Bodie knew Jack would never program his own or a family member's real address into the GPS and create an open invitation to a thief.

"Quickly," Cassidy said. "Which job was it, Jack?"

"You're asking in case I lose my memory in the next five minutes?"

"Don't be silly. It's in case you get shot to death."

"Oh, that's all right, then. I'm guessing you only did the one job in Miami recently?"

Bodie remembered it well. "The word 'Bratva' was certainly never mentioned."

Pantera sighed. "I know, mate, I know. It was never mentioned to me either when I offered you the job. Nothing came up in the checks."

Bodie knew that if the Russian Bratva were living lavishly in Miami then they certainly wouldn't shout about it. Sometimes a criminal organization was a victim of its own cunning. *And sometimes,* he thought, *they make others pay for it.*

"We always tried to be better," he muttered. "Thieves yes, but *better.* We changed our ways to victimless crimes. We stop being so solitary, so antisocial. We try to be real members of the real world. And look where it gets us."

"Right here." Cassidy looked out the window. "Racing to save a little kid on a dark night. With an asshole in the back seat."

Pantera said nothing. The GPS announced their arrival.

"Where?" Bodie asked.

Pantera pointed. "Seventh house down there. White window frames. Oak tree in the front. Double garage with a horseshoe motif."

"All right. I suggest we move fast but stay hidden. We don't know the situation and we have no time. Ready?"

They exited the car and found cover near a dense row of trees and bushes. The greenery ran the length of the road, so Bodie found the place where it pushed up against a strong fence and made his way along, avoiding tree roots and climbing the odd branch. As he walked he whispered to Cassidy.

"I don't fancy running from the Bratva my whole life, Cass."

"Ditto."

"We may have to resteal that statue and make amends. I know they have a code of honor."

"Easier said than done. You know who bought it?"

"Pantera said they killed him."

"I know. But his family still has the statue, yes? They're worse. Violent. Crazy."

"Nevertheless, the Bratva do have this odd code of honor. We'll discuss later, but I feel they will appreciate the gesture."

Cassidy pursed her lips, never trusting, always questioning. By now they were opposite Pantera's old home and stopped to take a look.

The place stood in darkness save for a single light in the downstairs living room. The property was large, with all rooms facing the road, four across the top floor and three across the bottom. Bodie noted that the garage was attached to the house. All along the road in both directions cars were parked.

He didn't like it. "No telling who's watching. The place is highly exposed."

"I know," Pantera moaned.

"You chose it?" Cassidy asked.

"No! Steph chose it. I couldn't exactly state my reasons for dismissing it at the time."

No shadows crossed the burning light. Bodie calculated the risk of a quick dash to the front door against the time they'd lose sneaking around the back. "I'm thinking we bring the car up, storm the house, and get the hell out of here."

"Unfortunately," Cassidy said, "so am I."

"If they're watching the front they will be watching the back. We don't have a few days or hours to recon, to plan. We could go in tomorrow dressed as workmen, but Jack . . . they may know we're coming by then and be ready."

Pantera would have to make the final call on his family. "They'll hate me for it either way. Hate me forever. Eric, my son—he's such a good lad. Small for his age and works hard at school. He's a little hero, taking on the big boys at soccer and"—Pantera allowed a grin that completely transformed his face—"winning, more often than not. Scoring. Running circles around them. I can't let them take him. I say go. Do it now."

Bodie nodded. "I agree."

And then their outlook, and their world, changed. A pair of dark-gray SUVs came screaming around the corner, engines roaring and tires squealing. They powered down the road before slewing to a sideways halt in front of the house.

Doors flew open, slamming back against their hinges, and four men jumped out of each vehicle, leaving the drivers behind the wheel. The men carried automatic machine guns, fully exposed, and raised as if ready to fire. They wore no head gear. Bodie could see their faces clearly, their tattoos, and it reminded him of the Mexican prison.

"Bratva," Pantera whispered in dismay. "Oh hell, no."

"Shit." Bodie struggled with it.

"We can't let them take my family, Guy!" Pantera was highly emotional. *"We can't!"*

Bodie stared Cassidy in the eye. "We won't. You ready, Cass?"

"Hell yeah."

CHAPTER ELEVEN

Bodie broke cover, racing toward the back of the rearmost SUV, Cassidy and Pantera alongside. They were all dressed darkly and were able to pass without the driver's notice at first. Bodie saw the front door of the house kicked wide open and hanging from its hinges, another declaration that the Bratva cared little about exposure. No alarm bells were ringing. He didn't mention it aloud—it wasn't the time or the place to berate Pantera—but wondered where his old friend's head was at, not instructing his family on basic security measures. Then again, maybe Steph had just refused all Pantera's advice on principle.

Four men were already in the house. A scream sounded, a woman's high-pitched cry of fear. By the time Bodie reached the next SUV the other four men were inside and the two drivers had spotted them.

He ran straight at the first driver, wrenching the man's arm. Turning, he pulled until the man fell away headfirst into the street. Bodie was on him again in less than a second as Cassidy raced by, going for the second driver. Bodie struck hard, twice, rabbit punches to the back of the man's neck. Pantera ran by and caught Bodie's eye.

"Jack. No!"

But there was no stopping him. Pantera ran straight for the battered front door.

"Shit."

Bodie rammed his opponent's skull into the ground until he moved no more, then scrambled up, took the keys from the ignition, and checked on Cassidy. Her opponent was big with arms like brick pillars crisscrossed with veins. He was big, but he was slow. Cassidy could duck under his punches to deliver her own swift, stinging jabs. She was wearing him down, but he was still standing. It would take time for her to neutralize him.

Time neither Jack nor his family could afford to lose.

Bodie signaled to Cassidy that he was going after Pantera. Cassidy nodded and increased her efforts. She took a heavy blow from the big man's clenched fist, shrugged it off, and managed to repay the strike with two well-placed punches of her own, one to her opponent's sternum and the other to his exposed throat. He fell, retching.

Bodie approached the front door recklessly, feeling less the careful, renowned thief and closer to a CIA special agent. What the hell was he supposed to be these days, anyway? Partially he felt guilty for creating this horrific situation, and partially he wanted to hurt Pantera for letting it all go this far. He was sure he'd heard somewhere that you were supposed to challenge yourself with new and difficult situations, place yourself outside your comfort zone.

But this?

As he reached the front door he realized that some of these men might know his face. Surely, they would have been briefed. Would *he* then also be a target?

Inside, a dark vestibule led to a large kitchen with a central breakfast bar. The light switches were right next to him but Bodie preferred the dark. He stole quickly across the room, entering a hallway. All the noise was coming from upstairs. The banister rails began to appear one by one to his left and he saw the boots, then the legs of someone rushing up.

Cassidy appeared at his back, tapping his shoulder to signal all was well.

Bodie kept caution to a maximum, checking the rooms on the lower level. It was Jack Pantera who'd taught him to ensure there was never an enemy at his back. Now the man was up there and struggling to save his family judging from what Bodie could hear. By the time Bodie and Cassidy had swept the lower level there was movement on the stairs.

"Wait! Wait! What the hell are you doing? I kept up my end of the bargain."

"Bargain?" Pantera's wife, Steph, could be heard crying. "What bargain? What have you done to us, Jack?"

"Nothing! It's these Russian assholes. They . . ."

Jack grunted as though someone had punched him. Knees hit the wooden floor directly above Bodie's head.

Sneaking a glance out of the front room, Bodie saw two men descending the stairs.

"Be ready for these two, Cass. They have semiautos."

"We did all right in Olympia and all those other places. We can't just let this happen."

Bodie had no intention of doing so. "We do it the best way we know how."

Cassidy grabbed his arm. "There's a kid involved."

"Don't you think I know that?"

Bodie waited for an opportunity. He was at ground level, way below their eyeline. When the first man set foot on the ground floor he could see Pantera struggling at the top of the stairs, his family behind him. Burly men stood all around, guns pointed menacingly.

"Get down the goddamn stairs," one snarled with a heavy accent.

Bodie scanned the usual assortment of faces. Hard and cold and vicious, void of anything that might be called sentiment. These were men who had killed their whole lives and forgotten how to be essentially human.

"Change of plan," he admitted to Cassidy. "Finesse isn't gonna work."

"Duh."

Cassidy fell down alongside him, scanning the hallway. The space to the right led to another door—a utility room and a side exit that she knew led to the garage. A peek through the window revealed a car sat inside—a family Chevy which again, she knew, had no chance of outrunning the Russians. The options weren't promising. They sure as hell couldn't outgun their enemy in a closed environment.

But across the street . . . ?

She knew it was a hell of a risk, but saw no alternative. There was no easy or quiet way out of this. "Bodie," she said. "Create fucking mayhem, 'cause otherwise—we're all dead."

She knew instinctively they had to let the entire group come downstairs. To force them back up would create an impossible bottleneck and then a desperate battle, because there was no real escape, and Pantera, or his family, would be in even more danger. She used the time they had spare to whisper into Bodie's ear.

Not sweet nothings.

More like ruthless affronts.

When the last man came down, pushing Pantera's wife from behind, Cassidy waited a moment and then slid out of the darkness. She was a creeping, toxic shadow, bringing mortality to those who sought to force it upon others. The last man never saw her coming, so intent was he on pushing Pantera's wife in the small of her back, so intent was he on causing her discomfort.

When his boot raised for an unnecessary kick, Cassidy slipped her arm around his throat and choked him out. As he fell she caught his gun. When he hit the floor she let his skull bounce off the heavy oak planking.

Pantera's wife whirled around, gasped.

Up ahead, another man turned to check on the progress of his comrades and saw her.

Bodie made as much noise as he could, breaking windows in the living room, smashing the TV, the mirrors, and the French windows. He also shouted, "Police!" for good measure, then ran across the hall and caused more havoc.

Cassidy fired above everyone's head. The Russians turned and sprinted toward the door. Cassidy pulled Pantera's wife out of the jostling bunch and hurled her toward Bodie.

The Englishman grabbed her before she hit the side wall and pushed a finger upon her lips. "We're trying to help. Stay here, away from the Bratva."

She nodded but looked like a rabbit caught in the headlights. Bodie knew there was no way of telling what she would do next.

Cassidy couldn't bring herself to shoot a man in the back. Instead she grabbed hold of the next Russian and, when he whirled to strike, smashed his head against the plaster wall to the right, creating a huge dent and sending out a plume of dust. Of course, he was Bratva. She didn't expect him to go down. He was raising his gun once more, shoulders tensed, even as his face ran with blood and his eyes flickered in agony.

She gave no quarter, saw the barrel of his gun, finger tensed on the trigger. She broke the arm at the wrist and tried to wrestle the gun away as he held on and fought and tried not to scream. He pushed her back against the wall as the others escaped. He punched her in the gut as she fought for the gun.

Bodie came up, fired a shot into her opponent's ribcage. Cassidy grabbed the gun. "Didn't want to shoot the bastard; just wanted to incapacitate him. Stupid."

"Today, Cass, it's kill or be killed. Don't hesitate."

She nodded, then ran ahead. Already, she saw Pantera's wife following them. Of course, she couldn't blame the woman—the Bratva had her son. Cassidy saw the rearmost Russian turn now and level his weapon. She fired first, spraying him across the shoulders with bullets. He fell back in the hallway, unleashing lead into the ceiling and through the empty floors and roof above.

Guess I'm over my inhibitions, then.

Survival was everything, and these goons still had hold of Pantera and Eric. She saw the next in line, disappearing up ahead—a large Russian pulling Pantera along by the scruff of his jacket. The older man was bleeding profusely and limping, looking like he'd been beaten. Cassidy sprinted, catching up rapidly. The big Russian heard her and let go of Pantera, who sank to his knees. Cassidy hit the Russian with the butt of her rifle, once, then twice across the temple. His head barely moved. The skin split and blood leaked into his eyes, making him blink. Cassidy saw his gun coming up and punched it down, centering on nerve clusters now, because she realized that these meat machines appeared to feel no pain.

The gun kept rising. Cassidy struck as hard as she could, dropping her own weapon in the process. The man's eyes registered nothing at all, no pain, no fear, no acknowledgment that he fought for his life. A gun went off, the bullet passing Cassidy's midriff with barely an inch to spare and continuing down the hallway. Bodie flung Steph aside in case there were more. Cassidy resorted to a knee in the groin and a punch to the throat.

Nothing. This wasn't a man she was fighting—just a slab of unfeeling, unwitting muscle and bone. And all the time, the four other Russians with Eric were getting away.

She found herself forced back against the wall, the mountain pushing her with the bulk of his body, his knee pressing into her stomach, his chest against hers. His gun was wedged between them and she couldn't move anything but her hands, which she used to pummel and break bone.

The breath was being forced out of her.

Fuck, I've never felt anything like this before.

They had been foolish to think they could take the Bratva head-on, that was clear now, but what other choice did they have? She was weakening, and even several point-blank eye punches had barely moved her opponent. He couldn't see, he could barely breathe, but still he crushed.

Bodie was coming up fast behind, but it was Pantera in his desperation who saved her. Staying on his knees, shuffling across the hall, he located and withdrew the big Russian's small but wickedly sharp, curved blade and sliced him across the kidneys.

Cassidy saw the strength leave him. She kicked and pushed him away then ran headlong down the now empty corridor, Bodie at her back. She could hear Pantera struggling to climb to his feet and Steph screaming at him as she ran by.

She halted before the ruined front door, instincts kicking in. A bullet grazed the frame as she pulled up, showing at least one man was out there waiting for her. Sirens wailed in the distance.

Now what?

Pantera grabbed her gun and ran out into the open. He didn't care about the gunfire. He was focused on one goal: *Eric.*

A bullet passed Pantera, barely a hairsbreadth from his neck, but Pantera just stood there and fired back. Surprisingly, the dense bush his opponent sheltered behind did nothing to stop the deadly lead from entering and rifling his body. Pantera turned the gun toward the rest of the Russians.

"No." Cassidy pulled it away from him. "Too risky."

The main group was already at the cars, helping the beaten-up drivers and throwing them behind the wheel. They were six strong now, but they carried Eric between them, the crying child the main focus of everyone involved in the battle.

"Don't let them take him!" Steph screamed, her voice breaking.

Pantera stumbled down the path, fully exposed.

Cassidy shook her head, then grabbed and flung him to the ground for his own safety, feeling more than a moment's satisfaction when he grunted painfully. The asshole had brought this on everyone—from the moment he accepted the statue job and didn't check its provenance properly, to letting the Bratva control him without asking for help.

Now Eric was bundled into the car. Cassidy saw guns being shoved out of the windows.

"No!" Steph saw what was happening.

Cassidy only had one option: a beautiful Dodge Challenger in a driveway to their left. Even in the darkness its bodywork gleamed an incandescent orange. She glanced around at Bodie. "You up for a car chase, bud?"

"Anything," Bodie panted. "What did you have in mind?"

"That." She was already running as the Russians fired up their engines.

"You can hot-wire something like that?"

Cassidy didn't even respond. The leader of her group knew her background as a young adult on the street, as a hustler, as a struggling actress and a cage fighter. He knew where she came from.

"I guess it's older than it looks," Bodie then said to cover his mistake.

She broke the window, then climbed in, brushing the glass to the carpeted floor. The Russians were squealing away. Cassidy looped the wires and started the car, hearing the deep-voiced and beautiful V8 engine explode to life.

"Get in, Bodie," she said as she swung out of the driveway. "And buckle up."

CHAPTER TWELVE

The night skies over central Florida glittered with stars as Bodie fastened his seatbelt and tried to hang on. Cassidy squealed the tires and set off in pursuit of the Bratva. Pantera and his wife were wedged into the back, entirely too close to each other at that moment and possibly for the rest of their lives. Pantera was glum and Steph was fraught, neither of them risking a glance at the other for fear of anger or tears, and both sat with lips so tight they appeared to be thin white lines.

Bodie had never been entirely happy with someone else at the wheel. Most times he explained it away as motion sickness but the truth was somewhat different—he preferred to be in control.

"Steady," he whispered as Cassidy almost clipped the curb. "Steady . . . big wheels and rims on this thing."

She took a moment to tear her eyes from the road while accelerating. "Are you questioning my driving skills?"

"I can't remember ever seeing you drive before, Cass."

"You kidding me? On the film sets I was a legend. Even replaced a racing stunt double after he broke an ankle."

"Shit, that was almost a decade ago."

"Excuse me?" She negotiated a bend, keeping the SUVs in sight as they sped along a tree-lined boulevard.

"I'm not questioning your age, Cass. Lighten up."

"But you are questioning my driving skills, right?"

"I question everyone's driving skills except mine."

She shook her head. "Asshole."

Bodie closed his mouth, hanging on. Cassidy gave him a sly look. "Don't shut your mouth. It's still dark out there and we're gonna need the light from those teeth."

"Bollocks."

Cassidy revved the engine, the deep, sonorous growl of the Challenger's supercharged Hemi V8 filling their heads and pounding their chests. Bodie stayed practical and sneaked a look at the fuel gauge. *Half full. Shit, that's not as good as it sounds.*

Cassidy smashed her foot to the floor, turning more fuel into fire. The car lurched and howled and negotiated another corner, gaining on the SUVs. Bodie could see one man in the back and carefully prepared the semiauto he'd taken back at the house.

"We ready?"

"Navigation shows a half mile straight up ahead," Cassidy said. "I'm going for it."

He lowered the window. Pantera did the same on his side. "Eric's in the front vehicle, but still . . ."

"Not taking any chances," Pantera muttered.

They leaned out either side of the car. Cassidy used the Challenger's power to pull up behind the SUV and then whip out until she raced alongside it. Windows were already down in the other car, guns pointing.

Everyone opened fire. The Russians were at a disadvantage, being on higher ground. Shots flew over the Challenger and grazed the roof. Bodie fired up through the door skin of the other car, riddling the closest man with bullets. Pantera fired two shots at the rear windshield, taking care of the remaining passenger.

All that was left was the driver.

Cassidy swung the Challenger into the side of the SUV, counting on the driver's shock and distractedness. Sure enough, he didn't correct quickly and ran headlong into a tree. The front end crumpled, metal folding and shredding. The engine shot back into the car, pinning the driver just as Cassidy sped past.

Steph choked in the back seat, tears falling freely, unable to comprehend their plight. Pantera stared ahead with grim resolve. "They got my boy in there, Cass. Get your damn foot down."

Without reply, she goosed the gas, drawing everything from the Hemi engine. Bodie held on to the seatbelt, almost losing his grip on the gun as the car leapt ahead. Among gaps in the houses and trees they could see a slow-rising dawn, a faint orange blush just visible. A ninety-degree bend approached, which both vehicles swept around with difficulty, neither sufficiently balanced to take it with a true racing line. The gap between vehicles stayed the same. Cassidy was aware of other road users. The Russians were not. They eased ahead.

A junction came up as the road sloped downward. The SUV barreled across at high speed. Cassidy saw both ways were clear and did the same. She held it better than the Russians, though, their SUV fishtailing under braking. Cassidy barged right up the car's rear end.

"What now?" Pantera asked.

Bodie knew only one course of action. "We have to disable that car. Get them on foot."

"The only way we can control the situation?"

"Partially," Bodie said. "Some risk remains."

"Some?"

Bodie wasn't about to say they were outgunned, outnumbered, and outmatched. For the first time he wished Heidi Moneymaker was among them; the skills and opinions that she could bring to the situation would be welcome, not to mention her own experience as an agent. *And Cross,* he thought. *I'd value his calm and clear judgment even more.*

"Squeeze their back end," he said.

Cassidy sent him a smirk. "Really?"

"You know what I mean."

"Sure do, boss."

Steph cried louder in the back seat, unable to comprehend what was happening. She was a civilian who had never seen combat, which made her a liability as much as anything. Cassidy nudged the SUV at the three-quarter rear end and accelerated, effectively making the nose turn. Tires squealed. Smoke billowed from underneath both cars. The sound was horrendous, like ancient leviathans clashing. Bodie leaned out and lined the tires up in his sights, but a wild shot from the Russians sent him tumbling back inside. Pantera followed suit, managing to keep his aim steady.

"Jack," Cassidy warned.

He fired just as the SUV swung wildly around and ended up facing them. The bullet went recklessly wide. Without pause the SUV accelerated, front-ending them. Bodie saw emotionless faces staring at him from the front seat as he rebounded, the belt grazing his shoulder. Cassidy's hands came off the wheel. The SUV reversed fast and two men leaned out of the windows.

"Down!" Cassidy cried.

Bullets penetrated the car but not the engine, which was, Bodie knew, the place they should have been aiming at. The closest thudded into the center of the back seat, parting Jack and Steph more clearly than any harsh sentence.

Cassidy hit the gas, their car lurching forward and following the reversing SUV, right up against its front grille. Bodie held his enemy's stare and gave a malicious grin. Down the slope they raced, nose to nose, approaching another even steeper road junction. Cassidy piled on the pressure, seeing rows of parked cars and a tree-lined central reservation.

"Push 'em," Bodie murmured.

"Eric!" Steph cried.

The Russian driver tried to slow and turn, but Cassidy drove even harder. The SUV hit the junction and took off, all four wheels leaving the ground for whole seconds as it still traveled backward. When it landed, Cassidy was right there, grinding her matte-black custom fender into its dark-gray one. The driver cursed and fought the wheel. The front-seat passenger tried to fold himself through the window, gun in hand, but ended up smashing his head against the frame. Bodie caught a glimpse of Eric compressed into the back seat, an enormous man at his side. Truth be told, his size offered the best protection the lad was likely to get.

"Do not let them squirm away from this, Cass," Pantera said.

She put the hammer down. The SUV twisted wildly, nose flinging around almost full circle and then ending up buried into the side of a Jeep. Bodie acted as fast as he was able. While the Russians were still being propelled forward from the impact, he was pushing the Challenger's door open. Cassidy jammed on the brakes and Bodie jumped out. The Russian driver fought for control of his vehicle as Bodie approached, gun raised.

Pantera was still trying to join him.

Bodie flung open the SUV's rear door and saw what he needed wedged into a sheaf inside the Russian's waistband. A knife was the quickest way to get the huge oaf's seatbelt open. It sawed through the material instantly and then Bodie grabbed hold of an arm around the pronounced bicep. With a heave he dragged the man into the street before stomping on his forehead.

"Stay down, Boris."

Looking back inside he now saw Eric; the boy looked befuddled and slow from the accident. No other injuries were evident. Bodie reached inside, cut the belt, and pulled the young lad across the seat toward him.

A huge arm reached for the boy from the front seat, encircling his throat. It was bare and tattooed and as hairy as a gorilla's. Eric screamed. Bodie saw no reason not to use the knife again, this time parting flesh and drawing blood. The arm withdrew and Eric scrambled free.

Bodie pulled him out of the car just as the Russian with the bleeding arm clambered out. The sheer bulk of the man hampered his journey, but Bodie knew he had to deal with the threat.

"Stop." He pulled up the gun. "Stop right there. I don't want to have to kill you—"

The Russian pulled up his own gun and fired without hesitation.

CHAPTER THIRTEEN

Bodie felt his heart stop as the bullet flashed past his face.

Still fighting his better judgment, not wanting to kill anyone, he fired back, hitting the man in the left shoulder. The gun fell and he twisted away, groaning. Bodie hefted Eric in one arm and turned to flee.

Straight into the bulk of the Russian he'd dragged clear of the SUV.

"Where you going, assboy?"

The man shoved him back into the car's frame, jarring his spine.

Assboy?

Bodie easily blocked another punch but didn't expect the man to then start pressing right up against him. The strain built and he lost his grip on Eric. The boy hit the ground on his knees, crying. The gun was trapped between them, pointed down. Already, the driver was opening his door.

This rescue attempt was disintegrating by the second.

Bodie head-butted, and felt the other's blood spray across his eyesight. The pressure only increased. Where was the bastard's gun? The Russian driver then climbed out alongside his assailant, weapon ready and a grim smile on his face.

"I wish I had time to let him crush you"—his accent made the words hard to decipher—"and watch. But sadly it is not to be."

He raised a handgun, pointed it at Bodie's head. The blur of motion that occurred next confused Bodie, but no shot came, which was promising. Then he saw Pantera grappling with the driver. Relief flooded his body. Pain and energy galvanized him and he fought back against his opponent. To his credit, Eric read Bodie's situation and aimed constant kicks at the Russian's shins. Still, the man bore down.

And now the passenger, despite being shot, was coming around the back.

Bodie let his body hang, hoping for space, but his opponent only pushed harder. Cassidy passed him by, focused completely on the passenger. Bodie didn't blame her. The passenger was three feet away from Eric.

The knife clattered to the asphalt at Bodie's feet. The Russian saw it and his eyes went wide. Bodie saw it, too, but was starting to get double vision as the breath was crushed out of him, the edges slowly blurring to black. Eric stopped kicking for half a second, mesmerized by the blade and knowing what had to be done.

"Don't you do it, kid," the Russian grumbled. "This assboy deserves what we do to him. We take you to better place."

Young as he was, Eric knew bullshit when he heard it. He raised the knife, which made the Russian move, pulling away from Bodie. The thief welcomed the easing of the pressure but still gulped for air, unable to take advantage. Eric raised the knife but then saw his wrist grabbed by an enormous hand.

"Let go, or I break bone."

Suddenly, Eric's mother flew in, an avenging angel. She wrenched the knife free with the brute strength of parental desperation, reversed it, and plunged it so quickly into her enemy's ribs that he didn't have the time to react. Still screaming, she scooped up her child and backed away.

Bodie now saw the man reaching for the knife as full vision returned. Though weak, Bodie concentrated on lifting the gun.

By the time the Russian had plucked the knife from his ribs, grunted at the pain, grinned, then turned back to face Bodie with the blade in an underhand grip, the thief had leveled his own gun.

"Assboy?" he repeated, and pulled the trigger.

Now completely free, he breathed huge gulps of air. Energy flooded his body. Cassidy was dealing effectively with the passenger at the back of the SUV while Pantera grappled with the driver—all fighters evenly matched. Bodie breathed deeply and went to help Pantera.

The driver was strong, young, and wiry; proving to be a handful. Pantera was going at him like the man that Bodie used to know—fitter, faster, and with the ability to land debilitating punches. The kid waited until Pantera overcompensated, then hit hard, wearing him down. Bodie saw a gap and entered the fray, charging in with a heavy front kick that was blocked, turned aside. But Bodie was ready for that. As the kid angled him away, Bodie swung fully around, left elbow out, landing a heavy blow on the cheek. Staggering, the driver grunted and raised a hand toward the point of pain. Bodie waded into the exposed area, pummeling flesh and making sure the spine connected solidly again and again with the car's framework.

Pretty soon, the driver was sliding to the ground in agony, all clear thought receding.

Pantera knelt down and finished him off. Bodie's first thought was for Cassidy. He looked over to see her grab her opponent by the shirt and slam him into the back window of the SUV. Glass shattered. The Russian's head lolled. Cassidy wiped blood from her cheeks and her hair.

"You took your time," Bodie murmured, breathing hard.

"Hey, what can I say? He was cute."

Bodie walked over to Steph and Eric. "Any injuries?"

Pantera's wife shook her head, tears flying like raindrops, but the steely glint in her eyes telling him she was ready to do exactly as she was told.

"Get back in the car," he said. "We should get out of here and make a call."

Cassidy and Pantera came up to him. "A call?" Cassidy asked.

"Bratva keep coming," Bodie said. "They will never stop. There's only one person in the world who can help us now."

"Don't tell me." Cassidy exhaled. "Your goddamn girlfriend?"

"She's *not* my girlfriend. But if you mean Heidi—then yes."

"Right." Cassidy controlled her breathing as she headed back to the battered Challenger. "Right."

CHAPTER FOURTEEN

Rio sat brooding, a sweatbox of mystery, immorality, integrity, and dreams. The city was never still, always vibrant, the monolithic granite giant that watched over it rising straight from the water's edge.

The team was secure, ensconced for the past few hours in a Santo Cristo–area safe house, surrounded by restaurants and cafés and burger bars. Heidi could see the incredibly blue bay from just one small area of the room. She took Bodie's call, tried to hide her relief, and then explained the situation to the rest of the team. Cross took it with no response, his deep, experienced gaze weighing all options. Jemma narrowed her eyes, assessing the likelihood of Pantera's story. Gunn listened silently, then started tapping away on his tablet, no doubt investigating the words "Bratva" and "Russian brothers."

Heidi paced the room. "I've arranged a safe house for Pantera and his family. They won't be comfortable, but they won't be dead either."

"The Bratva will not stop coming," Cross said.

"I know that."

Cross winced, also knowing something of the Pantera family history and why the man's wife had taken out a court order on him. The truth was—Heidi knew also. It had formed an important part of her research when the man and his protégé came into the picture. Steph, his wife, discovered the length and breadth of his nefarious dealings.

Fearing her son might follow a similar path, she had sought to save him by cutting all ties with Pantera.

But Heidi couldn't concern herself with that now. Their Rio contacts had put the feelers out among the local informers and identified the gang who had attacked them. As expected, they were small fry but deadly, able to react with significant force. Heidi thought it best to simply melt away and hope they did the same.

"Time to wrap this up," she said. "Plane's ready."

They called a car and met it on the street, ready for anything. Heidi found her mood buoyant, practically bouncing as she jumped into the passenger seat. At first, she couldn't figure out why, and then she pushed the obvious answer to the side.

Don't be an idiot.

In more ways than one. The situation at home was perilous already without adding another man to the story. It had only been a few days, but Heidi found herself picturing her daughter. The mood became mixed, the situation pulling her in many ways.

If I don't do this, who will? Why should anyone? Then . . . then where would we be?

The words that passed unendingly through her mind. The words that broke her relationship. She was a woman who wanted to protect far more than she was physically or mentally capable of doing.

I am a CIA agent, torn between my family and a career.

The reminder didn't help. By the time they arrived at the airport, her mood had deteriorated beyond sour to dire. She focused her mind on the job, on the components of their hunt for Atlantis. And, to her mind at least, that included a refresher course on the members of her diverse team.

Of the three members of Bodie's crew with her, she found Sam Gunn the most interesting. This man possessed all the potential, all the capabilities, and a fascinating mix of fire and innocence. She knew about his youth growing up in foster homes and how hard it might have been, but that wasn't the thing that made Gunn hard to judge and even harder to get close to. It was the combination of introvert and wannabe showman; the brains that came with no brawn, but had a hidden cache of courage. She felt herself wanting to mentor the nerd, train him, but knew she'd never be able to find the time.

As she watched him, he glanced over at her, offering up a shy smile. Then he smoothed back his gelled hair. Heidi grinned in return. Right there, just that, was the epitome of what Gunn was all about.

Cross, on the other hand, was set in his ways. And make no mistake—they were polished to perfection. But therein lay the biggest flaw for her. A man, and especially an experienced career thief, should be prepared to roll with everything and anything that presented itself during an operation. She understood that her requirements went against the grain of the team's desires and that they were always looking for a way out, but she could see Cross being a casualty of his own accomplishments; she just hoped he wouldn't become a casualty of war.

Jemma Blunt was the hardest to read of the entire misfit bunch. Heidi hadn't found the time to scrutinize her past, but knew her strengths. Before now, she'd shown relatively few weaknesses, but there was always something. Always a button well hidden. Heidi thought Jemma's was a lack of human social experience, something Cassidy was constantly trying to change with offers of days and nights out, but she never quite seemed to connect with the quieter woman.

Heidi found herself becoming more and more interested in the story of how this varied group had come together. That had to be some tale.

For now, though, she settled back to relax as the jet blasted through the skies toward DC. Within minutes her rest was interrupted by the ringing of her cell phone.

"Now what? I was trying to sleep."

"Agent Moneymaker?"

She came more awake. "Who's this?"

"Lucie Boom. History expert."

The English tones were clipped, almost military style. Heidi could imagine the girl standing at attention.

"Oh, hi. I didn't expect to hear from you for a few more hours." She thought about the time difference to DC, but the strain and weariness of the last few days was taking its toll. "What time is it there?"

"Eleven hundred hours."

Heidi raised an eyebrow in amusement. The CIA primarily used military timing terms, but she couldn't get used to a civilian using it. Already she could imagine how uncomfortably Lucie Boom would fit in with the relic hunter crew. "You mean eleven a.m.?" It was a gentle dig.

"That's what I said, Agent Moneymaker."

"Ah, right. Must have missed that. I'm guessing we're an hour away from touchdown, Miss Boom. Can this wait until we reach the office?"

"Of course. I was merely checking in. I'll be here when you arrive."

The line went dead. Heidi stared at her screen for a moment before tapping her fingers against the phone's surface.

Cross was watching her. "Trouble?"

Heidi grunted. "Could be. Too early to tell."

"Was that the new history buff?" Gunn asked.

"Yes, Gunn. Were you listening to my conversation?"

"Umm, no. Just a wild guess."

"Wild guess, huh? Well, let's not judge until we get a face-to-face. How you doing with that internet crap?"

"If you mean the research I'm conducting into the Baal statues," Gunn said with a sniff, "then relatively well, considering I'm not a *historian.* As you know, the nine statues are from the same era, the same place, the same . . . stable. What you don't know is that there are quite a lot of inscriptions on them; some on the base and others around the head and one even up the left arm. Let's hope it fits in somewhere, because all we have at the moment is some old guy called Plato placing Atlantis beyond the Pillars of Hercules in his works *Timaeus* and *Critias* describing events that happened nine thousand years before his time. It has been said that Atlantis was a purposeful invention, a fictional embodiment of immense power that Athens then overcame, thus proving its all-encompassing superiority. Atlantis was actually inconsequential in Plato's works, but many have picked up on Atlantis and personified it with legend and life. Others wonder where he might have gotten such a notion. His inspiration sometimes arose from old Egyptian records, accounts of the sea people and even the Trojan War, but there is no doubt he portrayed Atlantis as a grand land, full of kings and majesty and unfathomable power, rich not only in gold but in rolling green pastures and mighty mountains." Gunn shrugged. "That's how legends are born."

"It's what we want to believe," Cross said.

"Definitely," Gunn said. "But that doesn't mean it isn't true. Or certain parts of it, at least."

"You think they'll look back on the twentieth and twenty-first centuries as golden ages?" Jemma said wistfully. "Disco? The airplane? *Game of Thrones*?"

Heidi laughed and faced the front. "Whatever we do now," she said, "we do for our own reasons. Often, we put advancement in front of family time, work before play. Who wins?" She whispered, "At the end of the day . . . with all that we do . . . do we really make a difference?"

"You have to believe that we do," Bodie said. "Being the law enforcement officer."

"Well, here's a chance for all of us to help," Heidi said. "Find Atlantis first. Discover all the good and bad it has to offer. Stop our enemies from using any of it against us. History might not thank a team of relic hunters and the CIA for finding it first, but it *will* make a difference to the public that we serve. The stakes are higher than any of us can imagine, because the riches we seek are unfathomable."

CHAPTER FIFTEEN

In the end they had convened at a pleasant, quiet, out-of-the-way restaurant where a real fire crackled in the hearth and the tabletops were wooden and pitted with use. The whole team found Washington, DC, a little dire and dismal after the buoyant climes of Rio and Florida. Civilians, in general, just didn't seem as happy here. Bodie speculated that it might simply be because most of them were either at or on their way to work, but wondered if it might also have something to do with the imposing government buildings that appeared to oversee everything.

"I'm never going to Langley," was the first thing Cassidy Coleman said to Heidi now that they had reunited.

"Crap, girl, that's *never* gonna be in the cards. You think I want you in there?"

"What the hell is that supposed to mean?"

"I have a reputation to uphold." Heidi had turned away, leaving Cassidy gawping and Bodie trying to hide a grin.

Bodie ordered steak, medium to well done, with fries and peppercorn sauce. It was a strange place for an operational meeting, but with the catering available, he wasn't complaining.

"Feels like I'm being fattened up for something," Gunn said, waving the menu and peering at the walls as if he might pick out a hidden lens.

Bodie understood the reservations of a thief all right. "Enjoy it while you can," he said. "We're as safe as we can be tonight. Tomorrow . . . who knows?"

Heidi ran through the latest events involving Jack Pantera and his family, explaining how the first safe house had now been vacated for one that promised to be more long term—located just outside Miami. Pantera, Steph, and Eric were trying to stay comfortable.

And civil, considering the hardships between them that had affected their marriage, Pantera's covert business dealings, and the impact of the Bratva attack.

Bodie didn't envy any of them. The mixed feelings he harbored over the entire situation continued to curdle within him. So far, he still hadn't been able to come to terms with Jack's betrayal and preceding silence.

But you don't have a child.

A war raged within Bodie. The inner voice imploring him to see the whole picture was entirely correct, but the events and the way they had played out still niggled.

And the Bratva? Well, there was a long conversation with Heidi over several bottles of rum. Asking for help had never been his forte. The situation with Heidi was about as complex as it was likely to get. Feelings were running high.

Still, his best friend, Cross, was back now, and maybe they could come up with a plan between them.

"It's like we're in limbo," Cassidy had said on the way here. "Hanging. But also tasked with the job of a lifetime by people we don't like." She had shivered. "It's conflicting."

And Bodie felt the same. Here they were, hunting down and stealing more high-profile relics than they ever would have dreamed—and they were doing it legally with the force and resources of the American government at their back.

Legally?

Near enough, he thought, mentally shrugging off the question. So long as criminal organizations and warlords stayed in the mix, Bodie was comfortable with all the gray areas.

He dived in to the meal, enjoying the steak. The worries melted away for just a short while. Cassidy latched on to Gunn's earlier "fattening up" comment and ribbed him about his widening girth, which Bodie couldn't see but Gunn took incredibly seriously. Jemma wondered aloud if there were any decent nightclubs in the area, which diverted Cassidy's attention faster than a striking viper.

"I have an app," she told Jemma. "It's called Party Girl."

The team, even Heidi, grinned.

Cross ate and drank steadily, picking at his food with a care that had earned him the title of The Perfectionist in a different lifetime, long ago. He'd once thought those days great, but had learned since they were replete with darkness, risk, and a self-loathing that threatened his existence. Some people just didn't see when they were caught in a spiral. Cross saw it now and considered himself lucky that he'd emerged intact out the other side.

No danger to his family either. *You're a damn lucky son of a bitch.*

He knew it and he kept all of that intensely quiet. The only person who knew he had a family, Bodie, had been sworn to silence. Cross was a private man, and a careful one. Only Bodie had ever been allowed in.

Heidi looked up every time the front doors opened. Bodie saw it as a feature of her trade, but she was also waiting for someone.

That someone entered a moment later, saw them, and walked with a clipped step over to their table.

"Good evening. Reporting as requested."

Heidi got her first real-life look at Lucie Boom. In her late twenties, the blonde was tall and leggy but stood somewhat awkwardly, like a young chick unused to being upright. Her hair was scraped back into a ponytail, her expression professional and clear of emotion. In fact, the only personal element about her was a simple item of clothing.

"That's a hell of a sweater," Cassidy said, rubbing her eyes. "You wearing it to keep warm?"

Lucie flicked a glance at her. "It is made of wool, Miss Coleman. It should keep me warm."

Bodie saw no sarcasm in Lucie, just straitlaced honesty. It might be fun trying to help her fit in with a band of thieves.

"You know my name?" Cassidy drawled, mouth full of food.

"I know everyone's names, yes. I have also scanned your background checks. It pays to know who you work with. Where do you want me, Miss Moneymaker?"

Heidi was pleased Lucie knew enough not to address her as "agent" in the restaurant. "Sit here."

"Not too close to Gunn," Cassidy said. "He even gets a sniff of wool and he'll be all over you."

Heidi stepped in. "Can we move on? Listen, Lucie, I'm sorry we started without you but, hey, you are late. Can I order you anything?"

"Sorry, I'm late," Lucie said stiffly, not acknowledging the question. "The research . . . absorbed me. I did get carried away. It won't happen again."

"Umm, no, that's fine." Heidi preferred her people honest and dedicated. *Honest? Shit, where did I go wrong?* "I'm sorry. Where are we with the statues?"

Lucie sat herself down primly on the edge of the long seat. After rearranging her white sweater and tapping on the tabletop for several beats, she looked at the new faces.

"Atlantis is a myth. It has always been a myth. Most who aren't crackpots know that. But, for the sake of clarity and open-minded thought, can we suspend that disbelief temporarily? Just for a few weeks. Can we do that?"

She looked around earnestly, seeking an answer rather than shooting out a rhetorical question. Bodie respected her openness.

"I believe we can. After all, we recently located one of the ancient wonders thought lost to the world. There were times during that op when my faith was tested, but the results speak for themselves."

There were nods all around. Lucie looked satisfied. "The major problem with investigating a myth is the obvious lack of information. I mean, when you guys investigated the Statue of Zeus you had a credible history to examine. *Real*, reliable accounts from the past. But with Atlantis we have . . ." She pursed her lips. "Nothing."

"Nothing?" Bodie repeated. "I thought—"

"Please don't interrupt. My thought processes are precise and, once broken, are impossible to replicate."

Bodie blinked, then saluted. But Lucie was too focused on relaying her research to notice the sarcastic gesture.

"A real man named Solon, who was judge, lawmaker, and warrior of ancient Athens, was credited as the first man to write about Atlantis. He lived six hundred years before Christianity and was Plato's ancestor. *He* learned of it from the 'wise men of Sais,' which was an Egyptian town in the Nile Delta. We're talking 730 BC here now. You may not have heard of Sais, but it is famous for being the place where Osiris was buried. Sais, although Egyptian, was identified with Athens by such men as Herodotus, Diodorus, and Plato. Sais was built before the deluge that destroyed both Athens and Atlantis but, being in Egypt, it survived where the Greek cities did not."

"When you say 'deluge,'" Gunn interrupted, "do you mean the Great Flood?"

Lucie nodded. "Definitely, but I will come to that later. So, Solon is told the story of Atlantis when he comes to Sais. He is told how Atlantis, in its arrogance, attacked both Greece and Egypt and was later punished by the gods themselves. And in turn, today, no surviving traces of Sais exist either."

As Lucie paused, Bodie wondered whether he should ask a question. Was she simply breathing? Was she gathering her thoughts? Was she giving them a chance to raise—

"The story of Atlantis passed from the elders of Sais to Solon and then to Plato. Yes, it was a family story. A tale to be told around the hearth, and if it wasn't for Plato's importance and great aptitude, it may well have been lost forever. Who else could have related it to us? Even then, it is Plato's works, *Critias* and *Timaeus*, that immortalized Atlantis. Was it his way of preserving the legend for all time, or some sentiment, lines of prose to honor a family yarn? Any manner of reasoning can be read into Plato's intent, as it can with all ancient texts."

Lucie paused now and drank from the glass of water the waitress had left for Jemma. Bodie didn't see it as intentional or malicious; the woman was just incredibly focused.

Heidi drank from her own glass. "Can I ask a question now?"

"I'll open it up to a question-and-answer session when I'm done," Lucie said, clearly more used to lecturing students than briefing a panel of thieves and CIA spooks. "I believe the ancient priests and scholars understood the importance of preserving history. Of giving future generations an account of past lives and civilizations. Plato begins his recount by saying it is an old-world tale from an aged man. Passed down from grandfather to father and so on. The description of Atlantis begins when Plato described the greatest action the Athenians ever did. The ancient priest in the story is actually describing the greatness of Athens itself, its incomparable eminence, when there comes a threat from across the sea. It states that the Atlantic was navigable over nine thousand years ago—remember that fact—and that Atlantis was situated in front of the strait called the Columns of Hercules. It was incredibly vast, and its people sought to conquer the eastern lands with one devastating blow. Athens eventually overpowered these armies, and then the deluge came and broke the land. Nothing remained. As for the Atlanteans—well, it was told that the gods received whole segments of the earth as their own and Atlantis was the allotment given to Poseidon. Atlantis was divided into ten portions, and the eldest man, the king of kings, for Atlantis had many, was named Atlas. The kings are described as flawed rulers, with absolute control over the life and death of their subjects, reveling in debauchery and riches, and when Zeus saw that base human nature had climbed to ascendancy over majesty, he stepped in and wiped them from the face of the earth. Now, the entire country was mountainous, with towering pinnacles rising toward the skies. Perhaps they might now peek above the surface? Of course, we have a rather thin veneer of research here, and I have already more than scratched it."

Bodie drank deeply and waited. Lucie stared around the table, surprise descending onto her face. "I am used to more questions after I've finished speaking."

"We're allowed to talk now?" Cassidy asked. "Sorry, girl, I missed that memo."

"Well, what is your question, Miss Coleman?"

Bodie saw not even the merest hint of humor in Lucie Boom's expression. The girl was all work, all of the time. He wondered briefly if she possessed an extremely thick skin or if sarcasm, anger, and humor just washed right off her slim shoulders like a gallon of water.

He was pretty sure it was the latter. "The statues," he said quickly. "Where do they fit in?"

"Yes, well, the statues are . . ." She paused and then sighed. "The missing link? It sounds corny, I know, but there you are. How else could nine statues made by the same man at the same time appear on two far-apart and wholly different continents?"

"Luck?" Gunn ventured.

"Unlikely. So, let's skip past the Phoenicians, who *were* real, and yet nobody questions the fact that their mythology was derived from the same source as Atlantis. Their gods went by the same names as the old kings of Atlantis, and they had quite an affinity with Poseidon. A man called Sanchuniathon was a Phoenician author and wrote three works in the ancient language, which, unfortunately, are now lost. This man supposedly wrote before the Trojan War and around the time of Moses."

"Supposedly?" Heidi ventured.

"Like everything surrounding Atlantis," Lucie said with a smile, "the man's words, his accounts, and even his very existence are disputed. One could almost imagine a conspiracy theory designed to place a muzzle on the truth that Atlantis once existed."

Bodie finished the steak. "What an outrageous idea."

"Truly. Sanchuniathon used sacred lore, writing discovered in shrines and inscriptions on pillars in Phoenician temples, to expose both a new and ancient truth—that the gods were once real men, human beings who were worthy of worship."

"I've heard that recently," Jemma put in.

Lucie ignored her. "So the Phoenicians can't be the Atlanteans, as some scholars once thought. But the Phoenicians could be the ancestors of the Atlanteans, as well as the race who brought knowledge, wisdom, and education to Egypt, Greece, and Judaea."

"I thought we were skipping the Phoenicians," Gunn said blithely.

"I just did," Lucie said. "And again, the interruption is not welcome. According to my research, the statues are nine in number, which, along with ten, is an important Atlantean number. They represent the god Baal, another cross-related deity. Now to the best part . . . the symbols and ancient script that appear around the statues and along the base. When the first four were found in the high Azores, this lettering meant nothing—mere figurative rubbish, surprising in itself. Nobody ever thought it might be coded, with the key to the code placed on the *other* statues."

She paused. "Which it was."

She looked around expectantly. "And I have decoded it."

CHAPTER SIXTEEN

"What does it say?" Bodie asked immediately.

"That, I can't answer," Lucie told them. "At least not here. I would have to show you the statues and explain the script. In essence, though, the nine statues are one single message, made by a Phoenician and written in that language—a Phoenician who derived from the very shores of Atlantis itself."

"I see now," Gunn said, "why you regaled us with the Phoenician story. It's a long-held belief that the Phoenicians were the founders of all our modern knowledge as well as the last remnants of destroyed Atlantis."

"Any more questions?" Lucie had the habit of either ignoring or accepting statements without recognition. Bodie wondered if it was an intelligence thing . . . or maybe just the result of a lifetime of being cooped up with dusty old books.

"I have one," Cross said. "Can we get another man on the team? With four women against just the two of us I'm feeling a little outnumbered."

"You mean outmatched," Cassidy said. "Outsmarted."

Bodie was watching Gunn, the third man on the team, but the nerd never even heard the comment so intent was he on the screen before him. Bodie left him lost in the world he preferred, and shared a private smile with Cross.

"If you can't tell us what the statues say, Lucie," he said, "can you tell us what we're supposed to do next?"

Lucie nodded quickly, her blonde ponytail bouncing up and down, up and down. "Leave for Europe," she said. "That's a good start since we're definitely headed in that direction."

"Europe?" Heidi motioned at the waitress and mouthed "check." "The hunt for the statues' provenance leads there?"

"Yup. I'll explain later. I need more time to narrow it down because, as you pointed out, I was already late."

Heidi made a face. "I guess I did. And I guess you're coming along for the ride." She gave Bodie a sidelong glance. "Won't that be fun."

Lucie answered seriously, "I really hope so. I haven't been on holiday—what you guys call vacation—for two years now."

Cassidy let out a raucous guffaw. "Oh yeah, girl, don't you worry. We can all see that."

Lucie eyed Heidi. "I'm not sure exactly what I need, but I'll figure it out and let you know on the way."

Cassidy answered so that only the relic hunters heard. "I know just what you need, hon, but I'll let you discover that for yourself."

Bodie laughed and then scraped his chair back. "Shall we?"

"Can't wait," Gunn said, looking up. "Let the hunt begin."

CHAPTER SEVENTEEN

Bodie found himself on another plane, taking another journey far too soon. This fast pace was not the life he had become used to. It was like rushing head over heels to investigate shark-infested waters. Where was the careful planning, the long reconnaissance? Where were the blueprints to the bloody building?

Bodie remembered a long time ago, before his parents died, being eight years old and having a great group of friends. It was why now he ached with every fiber in his being to share that again. Back then, the five of them could live a lifetime in one day. Brian, Scott, Jim, and little Darcey. Darcey had been small for her age, but the boys had been big and promised to guard her with their lives. Once, that promise had been tested. Their time together had been relatively short, but, for Bodie at least, it left an impression that lasted for the rest of his life. The Forever Gang, they called themselves, because they imagined their period of fun, and their friendships, lasting forever.

They had been a gang of four until Darcey Jacobs blasted into their life, knocking their socks off. New to the neighborhood, she saw them walking by one night and made herself a part of their lives, so engaging and lively that they couldn't then envisage a walk or an excursion or an adventure without her.

"Darcey," she greeted them that night.

She shook their hands with a small, floppy appendage that was warmer than Bodie might have imagined and soft to the touch. She asked where they were going and they responded as proud young boys on a mission so often do.

"The old Killer Slide. They roped it off today," Jim had piped up.

"Yeah, we're down that mother like bread and butter," Scott had said with a whistle.

"Have you been down it before?" Darcey asked.

"Umm, well . . . no."

"Why now?"

"'Cause it's fuckin' there!" Brian growled, eyes laughing. Brian was always the ringleader, a trait that would years later remind Bodie of Cassidy Coleman.

They all chortled at the curse word, and at the shiver of fear that coursed through them with its use. Darcey pushed between them, shoving even the adventurous Brian aside and maneuvering Scott backward until she came face-to-face with Bodie.

"And you?"

"I know first aid." It was the only thing that came to him, but it set them off laughing so hard they fell to the ground. Darcey was all in, and she was first to push herself down the Killer Slide, then egg Scott and Brian, Jim and Bodie on after. She was the sunrise in their days of pure light, and as sweet as a honey bear.

Bodie rarely revisited this part of his past. It had been locked away in a dusty compartment of his mind simply because it evoked such a sense of loss to his emotional state that it often brought him to tears.

The Forever Gang spent a lot of time in Hyde Park, taking hold of the bright, sunny days, making them their own. They held picnics on the wide lawns under sprawling trees, played football and hockey and cricket, but always finished with hide-and-seek, which saw the shadows grow long and end yet another glorious, full day. Bodie found himself mostly sharing the experiences with Scott, who had been just as steadfast, careful, and reserved as Cross was now. His similarity to Scott was probably the main reason Bodie preferred Cross's company to any of the others.

It lasted forever. It felt like it lasted forever. They talked of nothing, they did dares, and walked until they ached. Sublime days and an endless summer stretched ahead. *These are our moments of immortality, when everything we hold in our heart and in our head is good and beautiful and infinitely perfect.* Bodie imagined parents might get a similar feeling witnessing their children experience the innocence of youth, but that wasn't knowledge he could draw upon. The long-dead past was all he had, and the long-gone friends he used to share it with.

Bodie had dwelled long enough on memories and returned now to thoughts of his current family, intrigued by the parallels he found between them and the Forever Gang. It was no coincidence, but it wasn't something he wanted to get into right now. He gave himself five minutes before daring to open his eyes and look around the plane.

The first person he laid eyes on was Cassidy Coleman. Perhaps because of his nostalgic mood and the memories of lost hopes, and perhaps because she reminded him of Brian, he mulled over the emotions that ate her up. All her life, Cassidy had been trying to organize disparate feelings and finding it was akin to scything her way through a jungle with a penknife. She gave up constantly . . . but never gave in, and those times when she couldn't detangle at least a few of those feelings, she ended up in a nightclub, or a fight.

Cassidy was as lost as he was, but in an entirely different way. She felt his eyes upon her then and looked over, smiling.

"What are you thinking?"

"How alike we are now," he admitted. "And how I always chose friends with the same qualities. We arrived here with totally different backgrounds . . . and yet it feels like we've known each other forever."

Cassidy grew serious. "The shit I've gone through would fill a book. I never lost my parents; I lived with them till I was seventeen. It didn't drop to the level of abuse, but I never knew love until years later."

"Still find it hard to accept?"

"You know it. It's like right now—I'm having to physically sit on my hands to keep from opening that hatch and running the hell away."

Bodie glanced at her hands pinned beneath her legs and the airplane's exit. "You mean falling away."

"Whatever. You started this, Bodie. As usual I'm just telling it straight."

"I had something really good," he said, "before my parents died. Good friends, not unlike you guys. It was . . . the best time. If life hadn't taken a tragic curve, I would have become a totally different person."

"Fate," Cassidy said with a shrug. "They say it always finds a way. I had someone too, at seventeen, but I was already conditioned, hardened to the world. It took my man every moment he had left to start helping me."

"I remember the story," Bodie said. "Brad, wasn't it?"

"Yeah, and I remember yours. The kids, right? I don't remember their names."

"Brian, Scott, Jim, and little Darcey," Bodie said, and try as he might, he couldn't keep the rasp from his voice. "Scott was a ringer for Cross; you remind me of Brian."

"Ever look them up?"

"Why would I? Everything ended the day my parents died. Strangers turned up and took me away." He swallowed drily. "Planted me in an orphanage. From that day on, my energies were consumed by survival."

"Maybe your friends would remember you."

Bodie shrugged. "Not in the same way. People move on, Cass. They change. My life with them, I remember it like yesterday because it was the only time in my life that I was happy, content, and befriended. To most normal people, it is a rite of childhood. To them,

I'm a misty memory of youth and they'd think it weird if I showed up at their door."

"Still, they could recall something."

"I remember *everything*," he said. "The individual sounds of their laughter. The touch of the night and day on my skin. The way they reacted to each situation. The games we played on given days. Cass," he sighed. "I remember everything."

"Brad saved me," she said. "And, at nineteen, I had to hold his hand and watch him die. That was after a year of trying. Where the hell the time has gone since then, I don't know, but I do know that I'm still trying."

Bodie clammed up as Heidi came to sit on the end of the opposite aisle. Her face was open and honest as she leaned toward them.

"Since we're sharing," she said, "and since this is a long-ass flight, I'm just about to put a call in to the husband who left me and the daughter who wants nothing to do with me. Any suggestions?"

"What did you do to them?" Cassidy asked bluntly.

"Oh, I went to work for the CIA, I guess."

"Then no, Frizzbomb, sorry. You're on your own there."

Bodie leaned across Cassidy toward Heidi. "Never give up," he said. "If you think it's worth it—never, ever give up."

"Amen to that truth." Heidi scooted toward the window for privacy and started tapping at her cell phone.

Bodie settled with Cassidy, happy in a shared silence. In ten minutes he had almost fallen asleep, but then Lucie Boom announced that she would be sharing her findings.

"Sounds like an invitation you're not allowed to turn down." Cassidy yawned and turned in her seat. "You'd best hurry on up to the front of the plane, hon. I'm not planning to get a crick in my neck from looking at you."

"That's where I was going, actually." Lucie's precise tones pierced Bodie's cloud of introspection. Maybe now they would learn where they were going.

Lucie stood at the front of the plane, hands behind her back, a teacher addressing a new class. "Straight to it, then. The first formal writing system that we know of is roughly five thousand years old, discovered in Iraq. Hieroglyphs and symbols such as this can be complex too, and when man started leaving triangles, circles, and other squiggles on cave walls forty thousand years ago it could be said that this was the first form of code. We're talking hand stencils, penniforms, other signs and symbols. There is even enticing evidence that *Homo erectus* carved a zigzag into a shell some five hundred thousand years ago . . ."

Lucie took a sip of water and continued. "There are etched teeth. Strangely consistent doodles all around the world. I posit this to give weight to my belief that writing and coding, in some form or other, existed nine thousand years ago."

She paused. The team stared. Heidi jumped in. "You don't have to prove your theory to us," she said. "We believe you."

"You believe me without a significant offering of evidence?" Lucie looked shocked. "Are you all mad? Or stupid?"

"I think what Heidi's trying to say is—time is short. Get on with the bloody story." Bodie used Lucie's own bluntness against her.

"Right. Well, this symbolic script can be deciphered. The key to deciphering it lies on the arms of all nine statues; the actual message lies around their heads and bases. The Phoenician alphabet is the oldest known alphabet, consisting of twenty-two letters, all of which are consonants. Of course, it derives from Egyptian hieroglyphics, but it's like the chicken and the egg here. Which came first? But it also harks back to the Rosetta Stone, remember that? It was carved with the same text in two languages and three writing systems: hieroglyphic, demotic, and Greek alphabet. Scholars were able to unlock the code, and without the stone we would know nothing of the Egyptians and their three thousand years of history. So, the five are the key, and the four are the message. Of course, it is obscure, as you would expect."

As Lucie paused for breath, Bodie wondered if she imagined everyone knew the things she knew and everyone had been educated the way she had. He also wondered if she was one of those critics that assume her point of view was both perfectly correct and at the peak of importance.

Lucie then took a breath. "The message goes like this:

Parted, my nine were assigned

Different soils, earth, different climate,

By me, for mine purpose which is remembering and rediscovering,

But now upon the Syrian sea the people do live,

The first noble forefathers of the world,

Who forged a new life for the next sons of men

Who found the path through vast seas unknown,

Using mine own ore, lodestone, and brass plate.

Whose true purpose remains remembering and rediscovering."

Heidi coughed. "I hope you're all writing that down."

Jemma tapped her armrests, thinking. "Don't have to."

"It *is* a dry, old portion of text," Lucie admitted. "But also, it is telling. This person, the man who made the statues, freely admits he not only fashioned them but left the message for future generations in the hope that they would 'remember and *rediscover*.' I don't like to jump in feet first, but I think it could be a way to find Atlantis. The start of a cipher. The first clue is right there. The poor man could never have imagined the destruction wrought on Atlantis a few years later or that his statues might survive, but look at the human race of today. We bury time capsules. We plant flags and build furiously. We leave our wills and hide sentimental items in safes or bank vaults. We want to remember. We want to *be* remembered. Maybe this man used the only tools at his disposal to do the same."

"That's all good," Cross said from the back, "the deciphering and all. But what the holy hell does it all mean?"

"It's a telling of his time," Lucie said, folding her fingers together and looking every inch the high school teacher. "A short telling, yes, but he didn't exactly have much room."

Bodie narrowed his eyes just slightly. Was that . . . was that an attempt at a joke? Somehow, he doubted it. He wondered if any words that weren't neat, well pruned, and precise had ever escaped her mouth, but then criticized himself. Being precise didn't preclude making jokes.

"You're wondering how it helps us." She was staring right at him. "I can see. If we're hunting for the fabled Atlantis, the stakes will be incredibly high. Men and governments kill for far, far less. Think of the wealth, the power it would bring, not to mention the enormity of wisdom, history, and technology within. A country may become a superpower overnight. Or a superpower may cement its international standing even further. But first we have to discover the true identity of this man. And then we have to find his compass."

"You got all that from that dry, old verse?" Cassidy asked.

"That verse is ancient history, incredibly valuable. Potentially, it holds the power to reshape our thinking."

"Wow." Cassidy sat back. "I didn't catch that. Maybe it's the way you tell it?"

"I'm not sure what you mean. What I do know is that ore, lodestone, and a brass plate mean a compass and that this man made that too."

"Nine thousand years ago?" Jemma asked. "I thought compasses didn't exist until around the fifteenth century."

"That was the first compass known to navigate the sea," Lucie said. "And that's where our story gets *really* interesting."

CHAPTER EIGHTEEN

Lucie began to pace, but the slight roll of the plane made it too difficult and she grabbed hold of a seat back.

"Remember I stressed that the Atlanteans were an advanced seafaring people? Well, through history it has often been believed that the mariner's compass existed long before we thought. It seems as far back as you can study ancient races of the world there is some knowledge of the magnetic stone. Europeans routinely claimed new inventions that were in fact just plagiarized from older populations. First, the compass was believed to be invented by Amalfi in 1302, but an Italian poem from 1190 refers to its use by sailors. And, of course, it is now known to have been used by the Vikings back in AD 868—*five hundred years* earlier than we first thought. Sanskrit has been a dead language for twenty-two hundred years but refers to 'the precious stone beloved of iron,' and 'the stone of attraction.' And even the Phoenicians placed a representation of the compass at the prow of their ships. Again, I mention this to back up my findings."

The team drew a collective breath, but said nothing.

"There is a clear line of progression here that passes the compass from the Atlanteans to the Hindus to the Chinese. But this is the one thing everyone is clear on—all civilizations where the compass has been found associate it with territories where Atlantean myths prevail. The compass is older than we have been led to believe, people, much older."

Bodie shifted in his seat as winds gently rocked the plane. "You're saying that the man who forged the statues nine thousand years ago also made a compass? And you're saying that's the next clue?"

"If I am reading the verse correctly, yes. Don't you see it?"

"Well, I guess so, but you're the historian."

"Of course. So true. In fact, I already found out the man's name. It is Danel, and was carved on the base of every statue. A signature."

"So we're searching for Danel's Compass, a little known historical relic, in the whole of *Europe*?" Jemma asked, looking confused. "Surely you have more to go on than that?"

"I seriously doubt you would need more."

Jemma bit her tongue. "If you're about to say 'We're the relic hunters,' I'm gonna—"

"Not at all." Lucie looked confused. "I was merely offering the floor to Agent Moneymaker here, and the CIA."

Jemma inclined her head. "All right, I admit the reasoning's sound."

Heidi moved over to stand next to the history expert. "Of course, Lucie is right. She suggested in private that we should search for an object by the name of Danel's Compass. We've been scouring the databases for the last few hours."

"You couldn't just tell us before all the . . . rhetoric?" Cassidy asked.

"Again," Lucie said with confusion in her eyes, "don't you want to know *why* you're going where you're going? Don't you want to question the evidence? I present it as best I can, but even my reasoning can occasionally be flawed."

Bodie turned to address the others. "She's right, you know. Who here would embark on a heist without questioning every blueprint, every camera position, every laser sight?"

Lucie cleared her throat. "Umm . . . laser sight? I hope this won't be too dangerous."

"Don't worry about it, love," Bodie said. "That's the least of your worries now that you're working for thieves who work for the CIA who may or may not have the full backing of the US government. Depending on who you speak to. Is that about right, Heidi?"

The agent ignored his question. "I, for one, wouldn't join an op that hadn't been scrutinized down to the last possible element. Thank you, Lucie."

"You're welcome, I think."

"Listen," Cross spoke up. "We're about halfway into this journey. Do we know where we're even going?"

Now Heidi smiled. "Oh yeah," she said. "Have you ever visited the Swiss Alps?"

CHAPTER NINETEEN

As the flight wore on, the team readied themselves for a fast assault, preparing weapons, gear, and communications devices as Heidi and Lucie continued to talk.

"Danel's Compass," Heidi told them. "One of those obscure, unknown artifacts that wealthy men and women buy at auction houses around the world. Probably desired and sold at great price on account of its age. Probably—"

"Wait," Lucie said, thinking of her history. "Surely the sale of a nine-thousand-year-old compass would have been widely reported?"

"Ah, you're sweet." Heidi smiled. "I'm talking about underground auctions. Those attended by collectors burdened with untold wealth, desperate to possess that which cannot be possessed and store their new assets where only they can see. Of all the incredible, important, relevant historical objects we know are in the world today, our inventory would double if we could include all those stolen items that we don't. From art to sculpture to crafted eggs, to golden objects and even papyrus. The list is endless. Danel's Compass was bought by a man named Carl Kirke some decades ago. A quick check into Kirke's history and we find that he is a successful entrepreneur, a man of many fortunes. The good news is that none of his ventures appear to be illegal. The bad news is that he's still a criminal, keeping an artifact once stolen from a museum without informing the authorities."

Cross shrugged. "Aren't we all?"

"Unless the CIA needs to borrow your skill set," Bodie said. "Then you're an agent." He laughed to confirm the joke before Heidi got any bright ideas.

"Well, we can always drop you off where we found you," Heidi said sweetly before continuing. "We're aiming for a hard landing in the Swiss Alps, a few miles from Kirke's house. The rest will be up to you."

"We're stealing the compass?" Cross said. "Shit."

Gunn was mouthing words like a goldfish. "When you say 'hard landing'—"

"Carl Kirke is a well-heeled hoarder," Heidi said. "Probably forgotten he even has the compass."

"Maybe. But that's not the problem," Bodie said.

"Listen," Gunn said. "Just how hard is this landing going to be?"

Heidi skimmed the faces before her. "Not too hard. What *is* the problem, Bodie?"

"You keep dumping this shit on us. We're thieves, bloody good ones. The kind of job we do—it takes months of planning. It takes discussions, sketching, more discussion, the review of several plans, options. It takes scheduling, organization, the perfect gear for the perfect job. Now, like I said, we're decent thieves but we're not magicians."

Heidi found a seat to slump in. "Well, shit. I guess we'd better turn around and forget all about Atlantis."

"If it means that we get what we want and walk free . . ." Bodie said quickly.

Lucie took it at face value. "No, no! Surely you can give them some time to plan. I must say—I don't remember the part where you mentioned they were thieves, but Guy is right. A professional in any field needs space to plan and execute a good job."

"Ahh," Cassidy sighed. "Then there's something else Heidi Hotpants didn't tell you. Atlantis, the compass, and the statues have already attracted the attention of several undesirables. Gangs. Mafias. Mercs. Thugs. You know, the usual circus show."

Lucie looked stunned. Bodie felt a moment's sorrow for her before shaking his head slightly under Heidi's gaze.

"Are you people ever up front with anyone?"

"You can leave at any time," Heidi grated.

"That's easy to say when you're flying at thirty thousand feet," Cassidy pointed out.

"I know, and I don't expect Lucie to accompany you on the mission," Heidi said. "But I do expect the best heist team in the world to have worked out a plan in the next four hours. Get on with it." And she turned away, staring hard at the bulkhead and cockpit door in front of her.

Cassidy made a face at Bodie. "See how her curls get tighter when she's mad?"

Bodie kept it professional, but with difficulty. "We're here," he said, "so we'll make the best of it to get what we want. Lucie's done her job. Heidi's done hers. It's time for us to do ours."

Cross leaned forward, a sign of excitement. "Do we have a photo of the place?"

Jemma turned her laptop around so that everyone could see it. "Already loaded up." The house was ultramodern, a three-story structure that clung to a hillside. It wasn't terribly imposing, raising no ominous warning signals, but its progressive appearance gave the impression that it would have state-of-the-art security measures.

Bodie looked around at the team. "Then let's get to work."

The airplane touched down, wheels skipping along the well-lit runway. The wings distended, dipped. Runway lights skimmed by at almost two hundred miles per hour. By the time the plane came to a halt, the team finally realized they were no longer in the air.

"What time is it here?" Bodie asked.

"Two a.m.," Heidi said with a yawn. "The night is already passing."

"Not in this club, baby," Cassidy said. "We party hardcore, right until dawn."

The team established a Bluetooth link with Lucie and Heidi, and drove away in a midnight-black Toyota off-roader, leaving them behind. Within minutes they had found a road and were climbing through the Swiss Alps. Darkness lay over the mountains like a thick fleece, wrapping the uneven land. Bodie cranked the heater up high as the team discussed the finer points of their plan.

Soon, they parked and climbed out of the car. The night air hit them like an icy dart.

"Right," Bodie said. "To recap. We gain entry via the solar panels, hack the system . . . or as much of it as we can . . . and make straight for the safe room on the second floor. Eyes and ears open for any extra security on the inside. Got it?"

Up here, the sense of vastness was absolute. Though the snow-covered mountains were dark, their shapes registered a colossal magnificence and radiated an utter silence. Bodie stood immobile for a minute, taking in the feeling. Time registered, he was sure, but the landscape did not entertain it.

A rough, lightly grassed slope, speckled with snow, ran up the sides of the mountain to their right. At this height, the slope was gentle. Ahead, where Carl Kirke's house sat, the gradient became much sharper. Initially it looked like three separate dwellings set on three huge mountain steps, one behind the other, but Bodie knew each building was joined to the one above by way of two parallel roofed bridges and also a twisting path at ground level. It was entirely built of stone but with wooden cladding, decks and balconies all the way around, and huge timber roofs that overhung everything. Yellow lights shone from several windows. An imposing, towering chimney built of stone and slate reared up out of the topmost dwelling, but no smoke emerged.

Bodie turned to Jemma, who knew their plan right down to the finest detail. "Keep going?"

Jemma pulled her thin thermal gloves even tighter. "Just up a ways, and the lighter snow there is where his property begins. We circumvent through that." She pointed at a stand of trees adjacent to Kirke's impressive home.

They moved carefully onward through the dark. The cold bit hard, but Bodie ignored it. Movement would raise their core temperature and then, he knew from experience, the job and the thrill it wrought would take over.

"It's not so cold"—Cassidy blew on her fingers—"if you're a seal."

"We're not all used to the West Coast," Cross mumbled. "It appears that *can* have its disadvantages."

"Piss off, redneck."

"That's *Mr.* Redneck to you." Cross forged ahead, the older man now playing on his age to give the redhead a feisty look.

Cassidy grinned and fell in alongside him, happy to be part of something. Bodie checked their link back to Heidi for the third time and followed close behind. They wound through the high trees, taking advantage of the thick, verdant branches. They stayed low and moved a step at a time. Kirke didn't appear to have any outside security, but Bodie's team remained ever cautious.

Eventually, they came to the end of the tree cover.

"Ready to hug the house?" Jemma whispered.

"Security measures start now," Bodie reminded them.

The care they took was infinite. Where Kirke's safety measures consisted of a swivel camera, they waited for the lens to move, watching it through a high-powered, super-compact scope. They were crawling so close to the earth they tasted snow, felt it sprinkle across their faces when they moved. The area before Kirke's home was nothing but a flat, meandering path of square paving amid rolling hills. It was entirely unassuming. Where cameras were fixed and positioned in pairs to observe everything, maybe even with infrared sensors attached, Gunn came forward and hacked their systems. He didn't try to gain entry to Carl Kirke's entire network yet—the team had discovered it had an internal server that approached military spec and was almost unhackable, and, without further investigation, thought it better to leave it alone. Kirke could keep his secrets—all but one.

Half an hour passed quickly. Bodie breathed a sigh of relief when they approached the apex of the uppermost step, and the roof of Kirke's highest building. When they reached it, they expected a new level of exposure, with no walls to hide them and the seemingly endless mountain rising toward blackness above.

They would be required to move fast.

Cross led the way, stepping lightly off the slope and onto Kirke's roof. The angle was about thirty degrees and the timbers were lipped, making it easy to navigate. Cross moved over to the first of the solar panels, which were "in-roof," the rectangles having replaced the tiles that used to live there. Where the design was secure enough, Bodie had yet to come across one that was correctly security-shielded.

Cross used a laser to break the seal, then removed four of the narrow panels with help from Bodie and Cassidy. This gave them a three-foot gap. Bodie was the first to lower himself inside, grabbing hold of a cross timber and balancing on another to pause and study the scene below.

"All good."

They descended into the loft space and made their way to a standard doorway, rather than the traditional hatch both Bodie and Cross were used to seeing. Gunn scanned it for every kind of machine-based apparatus, sensors, or spy technology that he could imagine but came up blank.

"Clear."

Bodie clicked the door open and the team eased into a darkened hallway. They waited, listening for movement, taking as much time as they needed. Nothing happened. Three thirty a.m. passed by uneventfully. For some unknown reason, Kirke's safe room was located inside the house's second "step," according to the blueprints Gunn had found in the federal state's secure registry. Switzerland comprised twenty-six cantons and so consisted of twenty-six different building laws. All were governed by the local building authority, which kept precise records.

Bodie found the staircase and studied the layout. They hadn't had time to locate every security measure, so were having to wing it more than he was comfortable with. Still, experience counted for much.

They descended to the bottom floor of the highest building, which stood entirely in darkness. Now they would have to traverse the bridge that joined it to the lower building. There was no other way down, thus the team saw this as the greatest risk.

Gunn scanned the way ahead with an infrared detector. Jemma snooped for an alarm system by checking for control panels or monitors, searching for any sign of technology. In seconds, they had found what they were looking for: interior cameras and beams linked to an internal system. Gunn set about hacking it, working fastidiously at first but then starting to frown.

Bodie tapped him on the shoulder. "Problem?"

"Yeah, they've wired in extra redundancies that I can't hack. Not enough time. I can force my way in, but it could set off an alarm."

"Shit, what are the odds?"

Gunn waved a hand. "Fifty-fifty."

"Says the best hacker in the business," Cassidy said with disappointment.

"I never said that, Cass," Gunn snapped back.

Bodie felt the sweat beading on his brow. "If the alarm goes off, how long until someone gets here?"

"Apart from the owner? Well, we're in the middle of bloody nowhere."

"That's what I thought you'd say." Bodie stared at the others for a second, all but Cross appearing just a little anxious. "Do it. Everyone else get ready to run just in case."

"We're not leaving now," Jemma said.

"He means to grab the owner of the house," Cassidy said with some relish. "Not a problem, boss."

Gunn tapped his keyboard some more, tongue between his teeth. After a moment he wiped sweat away and made an anguished face. "Damn, it's gonna be touch and go here."

"Get on with it, geek," Cassidy urged.

With a final flourish he hit the last key, attempting to loop the camera feed until they were across the bridge. Nobody breathed. Gunn clenched his fists.

"Oh shit . . ."

Bodie started forward, cursing their bad luck.

"No, no, wait . . ." Gunn suddenly held his laptop up in triumph. "It worked. Took a while but . . . it's safe to go."

Now the second building could be accessed. The safe room should be to their right, at the top of the stairs, and promised to be gigantic, spanning two floors. When Lucie asked how they would find a compass in a treasure trove, Bodie responded honestly.

"Not a clue, love. But we've done it before."

"I don't find that the most suitable reply."

"It's pretty good for Bodie," Cassidy said. "Usually it's littered with lots of curse words too."

A door protected with a Kindle-size digital keypad stood before them, but this wasn't the only worry. Soft light shone from the floor below and they could faintly hear music. Although no voices were evident, Bodie called a halt. They listened for a while, hearing nothing. The team peered through the balcony but saw no signs of life, not even shadows.

Cross shrugged. "Embrace the night," he said. "We're on the clock here."

"You can say that again," Gunn said softly. "The problem with forcing one's way into a system is that you could then be purged. You can also be noticed at any moment. Get on with it, for God's sake."

Bodie signaled for Cross to go ahead. While Gunn fretted, the thief connected a device to the keypad that crunched numbers and learned any passcode by matching processors, and waited. Soon, his minidisplay flashed red.

"Five minutes," Bodie said.

Gunn hung his head. "Not good," he whispered. "Not good at all. I recommend scanning the area and fast."

Bodie and Cassidy were already descending the staircase, but again saw no signs of life. Maybe Kirke was asleep on the sofa. From the background check they knew he was a loner, intent wholly upon himself.

They returned to find Gunn rechecking his override, gripping his laptop between white fingers, and Jemma standing over him, biting her lip in concern. Cross was ignoring them both.

"How's it going?" Bodie asked.

"It's slipping," Gunn moaned. "I've already lost control of the top-floor cameras."

Cross sighed with relief. "We're in."

Cross jabbed the code into the keypad and opened the door. Inside there were no more corridors, no partitions, just a wide room with four walls and a ceiling, a simple staircase in the middle.

The area was open plan, several large statues taking up the main space and paintings festooning the walls with color. A quick check revealed no hidden nooks and crannies. It also revealed, as expected, that the inner room held no cameras.

Immediately, Bodie discounted the top floor.

They descended to the bottom level. Disappointment set in when they were faced with a mirror image of the top floor. It took a moment for Bodie to notice the single, significant detail.

"Ah, bollocks," he said. "Now that's gonna be a major problem."

CHAPTER TWENTY

The safe measured eight feet in height and three feet in width. It was an old Gardamm, a manufacturer that prided itself on making burglary-proof products and supplying to the American government not only valuables vaults, but means of weapons storage as well.

"I cracked one before," Cross said dubiously. "Remember Milan?"

"Of course, but Eli . . . we were fully equipped."

"Dammit, Bodie, get out of the way. Can't hurt to try, am I right?"

"In the meantime," Gunn said, "we need a plan B in case he fails."

Bodie knew both men had valid points. He'd known Cross for many years now, and every time he came across something different, a new challenge, he approached it with puppy-dog eagerness. Cross was a jaded man in a burned-out world, but if there was one big reason Bodie admired him, it was that he never gave up.

Bodie turned to Gunn. "Failure doesn't exist," he said. "We don't leave this house without that compass. Get it sorted."

It was then he saw Cassidy, who stood on the other side of the room, gesticulating wildly. Instantly, he saw what troubled her.

The lower-floor security door stood wide open. Through it he could see straight to the downstairs living quarters. *Crap, is that a pair of legs?*

It was. When Bodie moved closer he saw the sprawled-out sleeping figure of what could only be Carl Kirke. The proportions were right. The hairline was right. The man lay on the carpeted floor, with what appeared to be a large poster of a woman's face clutched in his arms. Bodie could hear heavy snoring quite clearly.

"Awkward," said Heidi as he related the scene to her through the earpiece.

"Weird," Cassidy whispered. "Think I should knock him out to prevent us disturbing him?"

"Why not leave him for the moment," Bodie said. "Let's not forget at least that a Chinese government faction and one other brutal gang are hunting these statues and, possibly, the compass by now. As we know, the international artifact- and relic-hunting grapevine runs faster than a fiber-optic cable."

Cassidy took a closer look at the poster in Kirke's arms while Cross played with the big Gardamm. The man from Alabama had employed his field kit already, using a portable listening device for the tumblers and a blindfold for the concentration. He wouldn't break off to jot anything down; he wouldn't even move unless someone physically lifted him out of the way. Cross was way down the rabbit hole already, the job the focus of all existence.

Not even Gunn's anxiety could move him.

Cassidy returned. "It's a signed poster of Heather Locklear," she said. "I don't get it."

"I do," Bodie said. "Is he butt naked?"

"Eww, no. Whoa dude, are you saying he fell asleep . . ." She made a gesture.

"Maybe. Maybe millionaires like to sleep with their old memories. Let's try not to disturb him."

Cross remained as stiff as the statues that surrounded him. Bodie left Jemma on watch and cataloged all the valuables he could see. He didn't have to do that—Heidi hadn't requested it—but the careful relic hunter inside him knew that a thorough scrutiny of the safe room could pay dividends in the future.

Thirty minutes later the silence in his head was broken.

Heidi came out with something odd. "Chatter heading your way."

Bodie frowned at a reflection of himself in a highly polished Faberge egg. "What?"

"The agency set up a listening station around our perimeter. We have eight unknowns inbound."

Bodie looked over to Cross, still huddled in front of the safe as if at daily worship. "They hostile?"

"If you mean *hostile* hostile, then I don't know, but in your situation any new development is hostile. Wait, it appears they *flew* in."

Bodie knelt down beside Cross. "Like we did?"

"No, no, they flew in over the mountains and landed right beside the house. Smooth as silk. I have no idea what they used. We only caught the 'all-safe' communication that passed afterward."

Bodie looked up toward the ceiling as if his eyes could penetrate all the way to the third building and the land that lay beside it. "They're about to find out somebody beat them to it."

"Finally," Heidi groaned. "You caught up. I figure you have minutes."

"I don't agree," Bodie said. "If they're good they'll take their time, and their method of entry so far suggests they're good. They won't want to alert Kirke in case he has some kind of self-destruct system inside the safe room. Several wealthy benefactors of ours have used that method to destroy evidence and avoid jail. I believe a lost da Vinci was ruined that way."

Heidi's tone suggested she didn't like it. "All right, Bodie. Your call. But watch your damn back."

Immediately he rose and dispatched Cassidy to check for signs of the new interlopers. Interrupting Cross now would be like making the man start all over again, so Bodie chose to let him work until the very last moment. Seconds ticked away into minutes, each filled with a heavy silence broken only by Kirke's snoring and Bodie's pounding heart.

Then Cross sat back so fast Bodie jumped.

"What?"

"Do you have it?"

"Maybe."

"Crap! Maybe?" Bodie struggled to keep his voice low.

"Is there a problem, Guy?"

"Oh, there's a few. But chiefly, how do we get into this safe?"

Cross whirled the spindle. Tumblers clicked and a lock disengaged. The thick silver door inched open. Some might then have pulled it wider, but Bodie remembered Cross teaching him to always double and triple check a newly cracked safe door.

Cross took his time. Gunn practically squeaked with impatience, but Bodie saw the thin wire at the same time Cross did.

"Bollocks."

"Indeed," the older thief noted. "Connected to a secondary alarm, no doubt. There must be . . ." He leaned forward, flashlight in hand, trying to get a better look at the new obstacle.

Gunn sighed heavily. "We're fucked. My hack just failed."

Bodie swallowed the surge of worry, knowing it wouldn't help them now. Cross moved a millimeter at a time, not daring to breathe, leaning in.

"I need pliers."

Bodie found a pair and placed them in Cross's hand.

"Kirke must cut this every time," Cross murmured, "and then attach a fresh wire. Just shows the importance he places on whatever's in this safe." Gently, he snipped, the sight of his rigid frame making Bodie tense up.

The door opened. Cross grinned. Bodie clapped him on the back. Jemma pushed through and pulled hard.

"Gunn," Bodie said. "Watch for Cassidy. The moment you see her, tell me."

"We're on comms, dumbass," the redhead's voice came back.

"Not in the safe we aren't."

"Shit, the old redneck did it?"

"You can call me a redneck," Cross said, "just don't call me late for dinner."

Bodie ignored the banter and took a swift gander around the safe. The shelves were crammed with items, but at least there was room for two inside. "Jemma," he said. "Have at it."

Quickly they sifted through the items, starting low and working higher. They even started at the back, suspecting the older items would be lying forgotten behind the newer. Ten minutes later and Jemma found a compass. She took it out of the safe and sent a picture to Lucie, but the historian discounted it.

"Chinese," she said. "Ming dynasty. Probably fifteenth century."

Bodie kept hunting. No more compasses turned up. He was beginning to despair. Jemma worked hard too, the pair of them sweating alongside each other. When Gunn reported that Cassidy was seeing movement up in the loft, Bodie was ready to call it a day.

"Not here," he said. "Pass it on."

Gunn held a finger to his ear as he related the message over the comms. Cross groaned loudly, having wasted so much effort. Carl Kirke stirred in the living room, rattling and creasing Heather Locklear as he turned in his sleep.

Cross clicked a finger. "You check the other safe?"

Bodie kicked himself. There was always a safe within the safe. Wealthy clients loved it. And because it was always small and hard to get at, they usually never stored the valuables they wanted to access regularly there. *Cross does it again.* Bodie didn't know what he and the team would do if they couldn't lean on the man's vast experience.

Lying on the floor, feet sticking out of the safe, he found the portable metal box and studied the lock. Jemma kept searching. From his pocket Bodie withdrew a set of truly bespoke Allen keys, fitting one above the other into the lock and twisting. At first it protested, but then he attempted brute-force realignment and snapped off the keys.

"Bollocks, that's not good."

Jemma hovered over him, holding an object wrapped in a white cloth. "How about this?" Quickly, she uncovered it and snapped a photo.

The squeal from Lucie suggested one of two things. Either Jemma had hit gold or Heidi was turning frisky. Bodie bet heavily on the first option and rose fast.

"Out, out, out," he growled into the comms. "We have the package. Time to go home."

"Thank God for that," Cassidy whispered back. "These guys look the shit up here."

Gunn's face twisted as he waited for her. "Is that supposed to be good or bad? I can never understand you lot."

"It's *real* good," Cassidy affirmed. "And you can hardly talk, with your 'bollocks' and 'dog's bollocks.' Get a move on; I can see you."

"Which way?" Gunn asked, never too sure.

"The quickest, I'm afraid," Bodie said. "We go right past Kirke and out the front door. We don't all have combat experience and can't risk a battle. Hightail it to the car and back to the plane. Shit, is that the sunrise?"

The others glanced out of the room's only window, opaque from the outside. Sure enough, the pitch black at the edge of the horizon was turning orange.

"Bad timing," Jemma said.

Bodie radioed Heidi. "Break out all the guns," he said. "These guys are gonna be chasing us, and Cassidy says by the look of them and the way they move, they're good."

"She knows that?"

"She's that good. I trust her."

"Shit."

"Glad you see it our way."

He signed off. If Cassidy Coleman said these people were good, then the best place to be was a world away from them.

CHAPTER TWENTY-ONE

Heading downstairs, they ran through the house, staying quiet but making no extra effort to mask their movements. The car was minutes away, then the twisting road back to the airfield.

Cassidy urged the others ahead, disturbed by what she had seen coming down from the loft—a force of men, eight strong, lithe as Olympic athletes, and bristling with lethal armaments. Their faces were covered, their bodies clad in black. She heard not a single murmur between them but noticed a perfect communication through hand signals. She studied the way they moved and carried themselves. The discipline. The competence.

And she backed away quickly. These were not men she wished to cross. The sensation was an odd one for her, but something she recognized from a distant past and respected. Beating a hasty retreat, she rejoined the team, casting a worried glance at Carl Kirke as she passed him.

"I don't think much of his chances."

Bodie, ahead, answered, "Did they see you?"

"No."

"You leave them a surprise?"

"There wasn't time."

"Kirke will be fine. We're thieves, not bloody government agents sworn to serve and protect."

Cassidy kept her own counsel. The slim chance Kirke had was that his soon-to-be questioners were masked, concealing their identities, and would find him asleep. She watched out for her team as they fled headlong toward the front door. Bodie wasted no time unlocking three separate bolts and then slipping it open. Cassidy saw him slide a handgun from a holster at his back and then step outside. It was no small risk, but the coast looked clear.

"Go."

The path was dusted with snow, a mild breeze stirring the soft flakes. Cassidy ran for ten meters and then stopped and turned to appraise the bulk of the house behind them.

The first faceless man stared down at her from the top floor, hands gripping the rail of the balcony he had just walked onto; a second dark figure studied her from an adjacent window. And judging by several shadows crossing other windows, Carl Kirke had been awakened to the fright of his life. Cassidy saw a shadow fall, then shook her head as it was dragged back up again. Through the open door she heard a faint scream.

"Wait," she said. "These men are hurting Kirke."

Bodie slowed. "Can you see a way back to him?"

Cassidy eyed the faceless, motionless watchers and remembered their firepower. "Sure, I can do anything."

"That's a negative," Heidi broke in. "The op will maintain its priority. Get that compass here now."

"I could meet you at the airfield." Cassidy rated her chances pretty low but hated to see an innocent man left behind. She also hated being told what to do by the CIA.

"Kirke is a criminal." Heidi appeared to read her mind. "Didn't you wonder why we were able to locate him so easily? Shit, the man's been sticking our noses in it for years. Boasting about acquisitions in certain circles where he knew word would eventually reach us but always a step removed, always out of reach. Don't waste this hard work on him."

Cassidy tore herself away, vowing to find out if Heidi was telling the truth about Kirke, and to take it out of her hide if she wasn't. She ran decisively, turning one more time to look back at the house.

Nothing. No men standing on the balcony. No sounds. The visage was as empty as a ghost's face and now just as haunted.

Bodie started the car. The team piled inside. The engine roared as he swung it around in the direction they'd originally come. A beam of sunlight pierced the distant horizon, illuminating the side of a mountain and slowly burnishing the length and breadth of the skies.

"I remember cursing the sunrise a few times before," Cassidy said as she buckled up. "But not as intensely as this."

"I've never seen you with your knickers in such a twist, Cass," Bodie said.

"My *what*? Forget it, just step on the gas."

He drove urgently. Cassidy stared back through the rear window, her edgy mood soon infecting the rest of the team. Gunn was at her side, searching the roads with frightened eyes, and a worried Jemma sat next to him. But when Cassidy saw what terrifying wickedness chased them she quickly reached for her gun.

"Load up, people," she said. "We're about to become roadkill."

The midnight-black Toyota 4Runner tore up the road, barely slowing for the twisting bends that climbed higher and higher. Alpine passes and towering peaks stood all around, snow-capped, emerging faster as the sun rose higher. Sweeping through the skies in pursuit came three motorized paragliders, large chutes filled with air, each one carrying two men in the buggy-like frame that hung beneath. Cassidy saw front and side wheels and a tubular framework, but most of all, she saw the occupants leaning out, leaning down, semiautomatics aimed.

Gunfire rang out. Cassidy saw Bodie turn the wheel involuntarily, sending the tires bouncing from the tarmac onto the hard-packed soil at the side of the road. He corrected immediately and everyone saw a line of bullets make a suture across an upcoming bend in the road.

Cassidy used the grab handle to steady herself. Bodie gunned the car's engine, now seeing a straightaway leading to an apex. The paragliders came lower, three abreast and weighed down with firepower.

Bodie hit the crest of the hill just as the paragliders opened fire again. Deadly lead slammed into the road behind their rear tires, bombarding the paintwork with fragments. Bodie kept it straight even as all four tires caught air. The body bounced down an instant later, jostling Gunn right out of his seat and into the footwell.

"Stay there," Cassidy growled.

Gunn struggled. Cassidy pressed the button to lower the back windows, then leaned out, sighted up toward the eastern skies and the rising sun. The glare was blinding and she fired off a couple of shots. Bodie swung the car hard right, and she found her cheek mashed against the window frame.

"Call it out!" she cried.

Cross took the command to heart. "Straight, sixty feet," he cried. "Then easy right."

Cassidy steadied herself. At that moment the lead paraglider swooped and crossed over to the other side of the car. The second descended, firing relentlessly. A bullet clanged off the nearby framework and another penetrated the lower skin. Cassidy loosed a shot that broke one of the paraglider's upright struts, rendering it unstable but nothing worse. The masked occupants didn't flinch, drifting lower and lower.

Bullets raked the other side of the car. Gunn cried out. Jemma leapt away. The window next to her head imploded, showering everyone with glass. Bodie swung the wheel and the paraglider shot overhead, looping and spinning around to come back at them. Cassidy saw only one behind them now, and watched it carefully line them up in its sights.

"Hard right, thirty feet," Cross called.

She fired two shots. The paraglider shifted unhappily as the pilot flinched, losing line of sight. Her third shot winged the passenger, sent his weapon hurtling away and spinning to the ground.

The man hung on with grim determination.

Now Bodie turned the wheel again, and the other two paragliders shot right over them, bullets flying from their weapons and passing harmlessly to the right. Cross swore and then shouted, "Switchbacks coming up! A dozen of them!"

Cassidy turned in disbelief, thinking Cross might finally be losing his mind. From their vantage point, at an elevation above the road below, she saw a twisting ribbon, a crazed snake of hairpin bends and switchbacks, flowing sharply down to the valley floor below.

To her right ran a chaotic row of small concrete posts, the only barrier preventing them from flipping end over end down a thousand feet.

"We came up here in the dark?" Jemma asked, voice unsteady.

"Yeah, aren't you glad we did, though?"

Cassidy waited for the car to slow, then used the first hairpin to sight on one of the paragliders. Bullets sprayed from both parties, but none came close. The second bend replayed in much the same way, tires squealing as Bodie struggled to keep control around the tight curve. Cassidy reloaded on the straightaway, giving Jemma a long look as she slammed in the spare mag.

"Would work better with backup."

Jemma breathed deeply and then nodded. The rest of the team, except her and Gunn, was proficient with firearms. This was way outside her comfort zone.

"Don't worry, girl," Cassidy emboldened her. "Just point and squeeze. Whatever you hit in the sky, it's good."

Jemma inched her way out of the open window, as ungainly as a newborn gazelle on a treadmill. Cassidy tried something new as they hit their fifth hairpin, now about a third down the mountain. Cold wind blew between open windows, scouring the inside of the car. Cassidy leaned out, farther this time, using one hand to take firm hold of the grab strap and the other to steady the gun.

Hanging out of the car that way, she waited until Bodie straightened and let the lead paraglider drift into her sights. *There!* She squeezed the trigger three times. The first bullet flew high, but the second took the pilot right between the eyes. The man's head jerked back, blood spraying the passenger, and then the machine took a nose dive. Cassidy saw he had become entangled in the guiding rope, placing pressure in multiple places. The glider became unruly, shifting this way and that. The dead man hung over the front, dragging it down. The passenger tried to climb over him and cut him away, lost his balance, and plummeted to the ground. Cassidy watched and held on, keeping her aim steady in case either of the remaining two paragliders came into view.

Jemma fired from her side of the car. Bodie jumped on the brakes and twisted the wheel, hearing return fire from the paragliders. Bullets strafed in front of the car, blew pieces from one of the concrete posts. Bodie evaded them, scraped the front left side on the next post and saw the yawning drop beyond.

"That is *not* smooth and fucking sweet," Cassidy heard him mutter. "That is *not.*"

She angled her body even farther out. The car fishtailed one way around a corner and the paragliders shot across the other, the three machines level for one second and then roaring apart. As they switched back, Cassidy saw their fallen enemy's body on the road below, limbs bent at terrible angles. She took a moment to gauge how far there was to go.

Four more hairpins to the valley floor. Then . . .

Well, then they'd be sitting ducks. The paragliders would know that. Having lost one comrade, they would surely wait for an easier kill.

But one swooped down, coming in behind the SUV. Bullets streaked from its sides, fired by both the pilot and the passenger. Cassidy heard Bodie shouting into the comms, ordering Heidi to get the plane running and prepare some cover for them. She then blocked it all out, concentrated on the paraglider that pursued them as it started to pull up toward the clouds. She fired at the same time as Jemma, and the results were spectacular.

Bodies jerked sideways and backward, lolling lifelessly. The glider's engine stopped, and the machine lurched in midair. It then took a nose dive, which developed into a roll, end over end until it made contact with the road in a loud and shocking crunch of metal. Cassidy levered herself back into the car, right hip on fire from resting on the narrow ledge for so long. Quickly, she slipped in another mag and looked at Jemma.

"Ready?"

The dark-haired girl nodded, the tight bun at the back of her head barely moving. Cassidy knew Jemma, careful and with scrupulous morals, would be reeling inside—this would disrupt her normally faultless thought process—and tried to divert her attention.

"They're shooting at you too, Jem. You see it now. Remember it. No excuses."

"No argument here."

Gunn again tried to pull himself out of the footwell, but Cassidy planted a boot on his head and pushed him back down. "Stay there. It's safer."

"Under your boot?"

"Best place for you."

An unexpected hairpin sent Cassidy sprawling. She regained her composure and got back to the window. The remaining paraglider hovered to their right, and its occupants seemed to be taking their time as they aimed weapons. Both vehicles were running at the same level and the difficulty factor was far less.

"Shit, that's not good."

They opened fire. Bodie's window smashed, the influx of glass blinding him for a moment. Another bullet wedged into the car's central pillar, right behind Bodie's head and in front of Cassidy's nose. A third plowed through the thin door metal, grazing Jemma's knee and drawing the thinnest line of blood. The cat burglar screamed in a startled reaction, dropping her gun and staring at her leg as if it might fall off.

The paraglider passengers didn't let up, emptying their mags at the SUV. Buffeting winds and speed spoiled their aim, but still bullets grazed and punctured the car. Cassidy knew it was another desperate moment for the team, turned and fired through the open window, fired constantly and at anything—everything—in an effort to upset their attackers' aim.

Then Cassidy had no more time. Bodie had lost control of the car. It swerved violently to the other side of the road. He caught the wheel and twisted it back. Too far. The SUV tipped, went up on two wheels, then smashed back down and gained instant traction. Bodie jammed his foot on the brakes, but too late. Cassidy saw what was coming and grabbed the seat back with both hands.

Shit, poor Gunn. He's gonna feel like a pinball in that footwell.

The car crashed brutally through the nearest barrier, bouncing through the gap and heading straight down the side of the mountain.

CHAPTER TWENTY-TWO

Cassidy braced herself. Any instant she expected the big front end of the SUV to dig in, and the whole heavy lump to start tumbling.

And there was no chance of surviving that.

Bodie wrestled the steering wheel, trying to keep the tires dead straight and at least give them a chance. Cassidy saw Cross with his hands braced against the dashboard and his mouth open in a rictus of fear. Adrenaline shot through her. Gunn was being buffeted uncontrollably in his small space, but at least the area around him was leather bound. Jemma was on her side, holding her leg and trying to stay in a fixed position.

The SUV bounced, took off, then came down hard. Bounced again. The suspension screamed, the front splitter smashed. Fragmented glass washed over the front and back floors and seats of the car. Cassidy couldn't understand why they hadn't started rolling yet.

Then the ground suddenly leveled out. Bodie yelled in relief, straightening the steering wheel, and Cassidy realized they had already traversed the majority of the switchbacks before they crashed through the barrier. They were speeding across flat grassland now, hopefully back toward the road.

She pushed away from the seat, reached down to Gunn, and steadied Jemma. "Relax now," she said. "We're alive. We're fine. Sit up."

She checked Jemma's wound, but the cut was superficial at most. Then she took stock of their position. The bumpy field was full of rocks, Bodie swerving to miss the worst of them. Half a minute later and he crashed through a wooden fence back onto the smooth blacktopped road. The car shuddered, tires squealing, but Bodie wrestled it back under control.

Cassidy cast around for the paraglider.

It was right behind them, hovering twenty feet up like a prehistoric bird of prey, its tenacious riders training their weapons in the SUV's direction. There would be no respite.

Bodie made a noise then, and jammed the brakes on. Cassidy shot forward, smashing her nose against the seat back, and felt the blood flow. Pain lanced upward through her temples. The paraglider flew ahead and then a deep cacophony of gunfire erupted. Even in her position Cassidy knew it was deeper, heavier than that which the paraglider could bring to bear. Bodie was still braking. Cassidy heaved herself away from the seat back, wiped her face, and shifted to find out what the hell was going on.

The road ahead was blocked by four SUVs. Men and a few women stood in front and to the side of the big vehicles, all with weapons aimed. Others stood in the field to the side, firing up at the paraglider.

Cassidy watched as the flying machine veered away. Bullets broke several struts and perforated the chute, but failed to bring it down. With one threat neutralized, Cassidy switched her attention to the next.

"Who are those guys? Did Heidi send them?"

"I don't think so."

Bodie steadied the car, eased up on the brakes, and managed to stop about twenty feet from the gathering. He took a moment to catch his breath, as did the entire team, and their world suddenly became very still.

And silent.

Cassidy soon changed that. "Load up, people. Even you, Gunn. The more threatening we look, the better."

Bodie was already arming himself; Cross too. Jemma, to her credit, didn't say a word, just located her .45 and changed the mag. Gunn clawed his way up from the footwell and peered between the front seats.

"I could run the plates quickly."

"Great idea," Bodie said. "Do it."

Cassidy was impressed to see Gunn thinking so clearly under pressure. Perhaps he had a future on the team after all. Some people could just surprise you, she guessed.

She peered through the windshield. "I see five men to the left, four more in front of the cars along with two women. I see two silhouettes inside the middle car—probably the bosses. Rear view is blind. You guys see anything?"

"Not since I opened my eyes again," Cross grumbled. "But then my brain is still spinning."

"Smaller objects do rotate for longer," Gunn said as he clicked at his laptop. "I think."

Cross peered ahead. "Any ideas?"

"Well, they're not traffic cops," Jemma said. "Someone is going to have to get out and talk to them and show we can match their firepower."

"I have a bad feeling," Bodie said. "I've seen tattoos like that before. Stand strong and aggressive. Show absolutely no weakness."

"Not a problem." Cassidy clicked her door open before he could say more, and watched the reactions of the gathering. "They're staying cool," she said. "Not the best sign and not the worst."

She saw the middle SUV shift as the rear doors opened. A large, middle-aged bald man stepped out, followed by an older figure, also large, dressed in a beige suit. The latter wore a black fedora with a silk band. She watched as he walked patiently to the front end of his car.

Still reflecting on Bodie's words, she found herself studying the wealth of black tattoos on show.

Gunn rattled off all he could see in the short span of time. "Could be worse, I guess, but not by much. Obviously, the vehicles are registered through a shell corporation that belongs to an international bank. A quick exploration of its lineage leads us to Viktor Davydov, the current deputy head of the Moroccan branch of the . . ." His frightened gasp swallowed the next word, so he repeated it. *"Bratva."*

Bodie nodded grimly. "I thought as much. Talk about out of the frying pan and into the fire."

"I need more time to figure the rest out," Gunn told them. "But the details are correct."

Bodie clicked open his door. "Well, we can't just sit here forever." Quickly, he relayed their new predicament to Heidi, who reminded them of other factions' interest in the statues.

"But the Bratva?" Bodie said. "Doesn't make sense. They're not here for Atlantis. They're here for me."

"How could they track you down?" Heidi asked.

"Two ways I can think of. These people have connections everywhere, including the CIA. And we haven't exactly been quiet so far during this mission."

"Just make it out of there in one piece."

"Easier said than done."

Cassidy flung her door wide and jumped out, stretching as much for show as to scout the terrain in every direction. As Bodie appeared in front of her, she whispered in his ear.

"I see a way past if the chance arises. Ditch to the right leads toward that mountain, but the road also turns up ahead. Runway is what? Five miles away?"

"Six. But I like the idea."

The person they believed to be Viktor made a hand gesture. Immediately, his troops came forward, formed a line, and lowered their weapons, but only slightly. Bodie made a point of copying their lead and took a step toward them.

The bald man held out a hand. "That's far enough."

Bodie nodded. "Morning," he said. "How can we help you?"

"I think we helped you." The bald man let loose a laugh that inspired a similar mocking sound among several younger men.

"And thank you for that." Bodie remained polite.

Viktor spoke English in a low voice. "We want Bodie first. Hand him over right now and the rest of you won't be harmed. It's not personal," he added. "Our boss, Lucien, merely wishes to speak to him."

"Sorry, dude," Cassidy said. "The Wright Brothers got here first. You know"—she pointed at the skies—"came outta nowhere. We barely escaped alive."

Viktor flicked open his suit jacket and casually slipped out an Uzi.

Cassidy stared. "Fuck. That's some party trick."

"Send him over."

Cassidy knew it would never happen, and that they needed a clever distraction to attempt an effective escape. It was right then that Cross went completely off the rails and started to stride forward.

Bodie held out a warning hand. "Eli?"

But Cross appeared to have entered an alternate universe. Staring at a woman beside Viktor, he said, "Yasmine?"

Cassidy flinched incredulously. "That might not be the best idea, bud."

Cross allowed his gun to drop until it pointed at the ground and walked closer. "Yasmine, is that you?"

Bodie sent a shocked glance at Cassidy. "What's he up to?"

"I have no clue."

Viktor regarded Cross with distaste. "You know Yasmine?"

"Hell yeah, from a lifetime ago when I was freelance. Still learning the trade. It was a chance encounter," he said wistfully. "But a memorable one."

The woman, in her late thirties, peeled away from Viktor's side. She kept her face carefully neutral, her body language dispassionate. The handgun by her thigh was half raised, the hammer pulled back. But when she looked at Cross it seemed that she had seen a ghost.

"Eli? Is that really you?" Her voice sounded husky with intense emotion.

Cross continued to approach her. Viktor raised his Uzi, leveled it at Cross, and the rest of his men followed suit.

"Stop!" Viktor ordered.

Yasmine stared at Cross. "Where did you go, Eli?"

The older thief went mute, unable to string another sentence together.

Cassidy whispered, "Sheeyit, man, I gotta survive this just so I can squeeze Cross for all the gory details."

Bodie stayed professional. "You working on that distraction, Cass?"

"Me? I thought you were dealing with that."

"Me?"

"Or your girlfriend?"

"Heidi?"

"Ah, so now you admit it."

"No! Bloody hell, Cass, stay focused. I don't see a way out of this."

"Don't worry," Cassidy said. "I'll figure something out."

But being totally honest, she didn't see a way out of this either. She studied Viktor and his crew as Cross and Yasmine gawped at each other like long-lost lovers, searching for an opening. The Bratva were one of the deadliest enemies they could ever face, and they had incalculable support from all over the world. Any attempt to escape was going to be dangerous as hell.

"You know what happened," Cross said finally. "I . . . I . . . didn't change. I never left. I loved you—"

Yasmine broke her group's protocol and rushed forward to embrace Cross, still with the gun held tight and cocked. Cross held on as if he'd found the most precious thing on earth and never wanted to let go. Viktor waved his hands in angry resignation, then turned an almost apologetic look upon Bodie.

"Let us finish this business and then we can all go home. Yes?"

Bodie nodded. "I guess so."

"You can't just give yourself over to him," Cassidy whispered.

"We're outnumbered. Outgunned. We're not SAS. I'm not Keanu Reeves and you're not Maggie Q. Live now, Cass, fight later. Oh, and don't be late with the distraction."

It made sense. She didn't like it, but Bodie's words were unadulterated, true. It wasn't just *her* life. Jemma and Gunn could never hope to come out of this alive. Thus, she didn't make a move when the Englishman took a single step forward.

"Are you ready?"

Viktor nodded, satisfied. Bodie studied the man. "How are you involved in all this?"

"You step into my playground, I beat you down."

Bodie remained silent, gauging everything. Yasmine broke off her embrace with Cross, the two now standing close and staring at each other as if trying to rekindle the best of memories. Jemma climbed out of the car with Gunn. Bodie started forward.

Viktor stopped him with a raised, open hand. "I will take your compass too."

Bodie closed his eyes briefly. The Bratva were nothing if not thorough. A CIA leak could have fed them the information. It also occurred to him that a Chinese informant might be their source. And if that was possible, any of the street gangs who'd heard the initial broadcast about the statues and taken an interest could have passed on information. Once you considered it, the possibilities were thick.

Still, passing along the compass would give them more time, and they had the photograph to study.

Bodie took his time retrieving the compass and then started walking again, passing right by a bald man with the spindly arms. He handed the tissue-wrapped relic to Viktor.

"It better be the right one, Bodie. I know Carl Kirke collected more than one of these."

"It is. How did you find out?"

"I can search the records, just like you. For decades now, modern technology has built incredible transparency into everything that anyone does. We can be seen and we can be tracked. Ironically, it is only the old-timers who have refused to move on, and who are safest from the modern world and its surveillance."

Viktor opened the tissue and regarded the compass. Bodie got his first real look at it. Considering its age, it held up well, the wooden base still gleaming, the bronze runes still etched perfectly around the side. Viktor held it up so that the man behind could photograph it.

"Precaution." He grinned a white-toothed beam at Bodie.

Bodie gave it straight back, with interest. He was pleased to see Viktor blinking away his surprise at the gleaming display.

Viktor rewrapped the compass. "Our business is done. I am a man of my word." He held a hand out, indicating the battered SUV. "The rest of you may go."

Cassidy didn't move a muscle. Instead she studied Viktor's men. Nobody moved. A chill wind speared down the mountain passes and between them. Snow drifted off the top of nearby peaks and rocky formations, reminding Cassidy of spindrift thrown by a restless sea. Finally, it was Cross who broke the spell.

"So now I know where to find you."

"I would not recommend that you come knocking." Yasmine smiled. "But I wish that you would."

"They'd never see me. And you'll never know until I'm right beside you."

"Ah, yes, I remember how good you were, now."

"You never thought about me?" Cross sounded dejected.

"Don't be silly. Of course I did. Every damn day. You, Eli Cross, are the one that got away. Everyone has one, am I right? You were mine."

"And you . . ." Cross held out a hand. "Were mine. Often remembered, never retold."

She took the tips of his fingers in her hands. "Yes, Eli. Because the memories are too precious, and too fragile."

"And too devastating."

Sadness fell across both their faces. Viktor, observing the conversation, became increasingly impatient before he finally issued an irrefutable order. "We are leaving. Come, now."

They walked apart, backing away. Cross looked like he couldn't tear his gaze from her. Still, he hadn't noticed Bodie's plight. It was the first time in Bodie's recollection that Cross's mind hadn't been completely in the game.

Viktor raised his Uzi. "But be warned," he said to the others. "If I see any of you again, the result will not be so friendly."

Cassidy saluted. "Count on it."

Viktor regarded her for a moment, as if debating whether to escalate the situation. Then he shivered, pulled his suit jacket tightly around him, and spun. "Let's get out of this terrible place. I can stand it no more."

Bodie waited until the last possible moment. The distant thump of an approaching chopper finally registered with some of the Bratva before it came into view, shooting across the top of the nearby highest peak, blasting through drifting snow, its rotors hurling icy particles in all directions. In moments, a large black Predator was hovering over them, bristling with weapons aimed at the Bratva.

"You can go!" a familiar female voice cried over the chopper's loudspeaker. "And leave Bodie right there."

Guns were aimed upward by the Bratva soldiers. Viktor and the spindle-armed man shielded their eyes. Bodie carefully backed away from his captors.

"We got you covered!" Heidi shouted. "We could shoot you all. Don't be stupid. Just leave."

It was a gamble, Bodie knew. If the gunfire started, the Bratva would probably lose, but casualties would be taken on both sides. Hopefully a Bratva soldier like Viktor would see he was covered from an elevated angle as well as having threats to the side.

Bodie continued to back up.

It took a while but Viktor finally waved his arms to send his minions back to their cars. Four minutes passed before the road was clear. Bodie used the time to converse with Heidi.

"Just drive back to the runway," she said with grit in her voice. "We're on the wrong friggin' side of all this now."

CHAPTER TWENTY-THREE

The plane journey that followed was not as comfortable as the last.

It transpired that the paragliders had been piloted by a Chinese Special Forces team who also tortured and killed Carl Kirke. This news came from the surveillance net that Heidi had set up around Kirke's house when the team infiltrated it. The same surveillance that had originally warned them of the approaching force. It was safe to say that, by now, this Chinese faction knew as much as the Moroccan Bratva and Bodie's team about Atlantis, even though only one group held the real compass in their hands.

DC was furious. The Chinese government denied all knowledge of the incursion and consequent attack. *But they would, wouldn't they?* Heidi spent precious hours fielding time-wasting questions from DC stuffed shirts wanting to vent their gratuitous wrath. By the time she finished, their plane was among the clouds with nowhere to go.

"So we took a hit," she said when she'd finally found time for them. "Mr. Kirke got himself killed and you met the Moroccan Bratva, an offshoot of the friendly bunch who tried to abduct Jack Pantera's family. You lost the compass"—she sucked at her teeth in disappointment—"but you redeemed yourselves by taking a photo of it. Clearly, the best course of action here is to let Lucie examine the photos. Jemma?"

Bodie bristled at the rebuke. It wasn't simply that Heidi was correct; it wasn't that she deliberately ignored the circumstances; it was mostly that none of them wanted to be under her thumb anyway. They were here through blackmail, and they were doing their goddamn best.

"If you think we're below par," he said quietly, "call in a fucking special forces team to help you."

"Ah, but then you guys will be superfluous and headed to prison. Is that acceptable?"

Bodie gritted his teeth. "So much for the bond I thought we'd made."

Heidi inclined her head. "Look, I realize you're not soldiers and don't have military training. I understand you're doing your best. You just . . . have to do it better."

A minute later and the pictures on Jemma's cell phone had been uploaded to the plane's computer. Lucie approached the screen and started to take notes.

"And as for you"—Heidi stared down the aisle straight at Cross—"is there anything we need to know?"

Cross hadn't spoken a word since they vacated the scene. Now, he latched on to the inquisitive faces as if seeing them for the first time in a week.

"How do you mean? Sorry, no. Yasmine is a long-lost friend. Very long lost. I couldn't imagine meeting her now in the Swiss Alps. I had . . . forgotten about her."

Bodie wanted to respect Cross's privacy, but saw right away that Cassidy would not. The redhead was itching to get down to the raw, penetrating questions.

"Is that it?" he asked.

Cross nodded, more distracted than Bodie had ever seen him. In the end, though, the career thief closed his eyes and let out a long sigh. "Damn, I realize you need to know this. We work primarily from information. We need information. It's wrong of me to hold it back, but . . ." He trailed off, lost again in another world, another time.

Cassidy stepped in, handling the situation in her own inimitable way. "Dude." She walked down the aisle until she stood right before Cross. When he didn't look up immediately, she reached out, caught hold of his shirt, and shook him.

"Who's the old flame, Eli?"

Cross snapped out of it. "Stop fishing. I'm thinking it through. Just . . . just give me a minute. I'm not zoning out; I'm putting the story together."

"Yeah, you appeared to zone out for a while, mate," Bodie said, worried for his closest friend. He'd never seen Cross so upset, so obviously off-kilter.

Cassidy laughed. "I've seen men zone out during battle, in the ring, on the streets when their courage gets tested, but I've never seen a man zone out after meeting a woman. And what was all that stammering, spluttering claptrap? She got you tongue-tied?"

Cross took the barrage and then sat back. Eventually, he eased around Cassidy and poured himself a stiff drink. With the whisky glass half full, he faced them with an awkward, strained expression.

"Right, I guess you guys deserve some kind of explanation. I love my family, you know I do, but before them, before everything, there was Yasmine. She was eighteen, fiery, hot as hell, and wise as the world. I was in my early twenties and completely bowled over. First time I'd ever been in love." Cross drained the glass and poured another, three fingers high. "We shared a year, I guess. One of those times that passed me by when, later in life, you look back and see all the big opportunities you missed. But that's just part of living. We all have those. And it wasn't just for fun."

Cassidy sat herself down in an aisle seat. Bodie wasn't sure whether to feel pleased that Cross was sharing or uncomfortable because he felt he had to.

"This wasn't just Morocco—Marrakesh, Casablanca. It was Seville and Lisbon. Gibraltar, mostly. Memories everywhere."

"And what were you doing there?" Cassidy asked. "I mean apart from the obvious?"

"I'm a career thief, Cass." Cross took a sip. "You figure it out."

Jemma spoke softly. "At that age I'm guessing you learned the trade with her. You figured out the ropes."

"I lived and died with her. Took it to the next level. Failed and failed some more and barely escaped prison, twice . . . It became . . . incredibly complex. We did everything together."

"You never speak about your family," Jemma said. "Ever. For a year I thought you'd never married, let alone had a son. I understand this must be very personal, Eli."

"Damn right." Cross stared into his glass. "Damn right. But everything passes, doesn't it? The good and the bad. Change is always just around the corner."

"What happened?" Cassidy, when she spoke this time, was as gentle as Bodie had ever heard.

"Maybe it was the age gap, I don't know. She was eighteen, flighty, still in love with the world and all it could offer. But later, I noticed she wasn't quite the same. I noticed it for almost two months. Something was on her mind. In itself, that was odd, because we shared everything. I pressed her, but she never told me. I came home one day to find her gone. I waited, and she never came back."

"You didn't try searching for her?" Cassidy's question was laced with steel.

"Of course I tried . . ." Cross paused, then finished his second drink and turned toward the small window. "But I never found her. Since then, many times I've been forced to wonder what happened to Yasmine. But now"—he held out his free hand—"I can find out."

Bodie regarded his old friend compassionately. "If I can, I will help you," he said.

"Right!" Lucie Boom's voice cut across the profound, sad silence. "Now that's out of the way, can we get to work?"

Bodie winced. "So, Lucie, in addition to your other striking traits, you also have little access to emotions?"

"Emotions are for children, Mr. Bodie, not historians. And what other traits do you mean?"

"Nothing. I'd rather help the CIA one more time and then get back to my life. It sounds like you have an idea?"

"Our big question—was the compass made by the same man? Very probably, but the runes upon it are completely indecipherable."

Bodie hadn't expected that. "What? You're kidding me! The same man wrote in a different language?"

"I didn't say that. It's not an entirely different language. You have to remember the earliest known alphabet is Phoenician, known as the Proto-Canaanite alphabet. It was derived from Egyptian hieroglyphics, Greek, Aramaic, Hebrew letters, and more. Latin stemmed from Phoenician. But"—she checked to make sure the students were all watching—"if your theories about Atlantis are true, we have to assume *they* developed what we call the Phoenician alphabet many thousands of years before that."

"It makes sense," Gunn said, relaxed and back to his normal self now that they were safe.

"Good to hear we're on the same page. Well, Danel was clearly an educated man. I believe he carved these runes with vagaries to purposely test those who chased his secret. He changed the script. Deliberately. To make the cipher harder to crack."

"Vagaries?" Heidi questioned.

"Yes, vagaries. It means there are slight modifications to the Phoenician alphabet, but those differences are crucial to help us figure out the text."

"So that's it?" Gunn looked like he wanted to open his laptop and start a new search for "vagaries."

"Luckily, historians never give up." Lucie tugged at today's woolly sweater, all black and sporting the head of a moose. "I know an ancient-language expert who lives in Milan."

Heidi looked dubious. "I'd prefer to do this in-house."

"That does surprise me."

"Civilians add risk, not only to the mission but especially for themselves. The Chinese Special Forces team, working in Europe, remember, had no qualms over committing murder. Their government gives them deniability and, even if they were caught, would never admit sanctioning their actions. So . . . they're a splinter group. That's how it has to be. And a damn deadly one at that."

"Then tell me . . . who in the CIA can decipher a ten-thousand-year-old language created by a culture that never existed?" Lucie crossed her arms expectantly.

Heidi kept her mouth shut, knowing the answer and exactly why Lucie had asked the question.

"Wait," Bodie butted in. "You're not making sense. *How* could your Milan guy know the language?"

"A good question," Lucie acknowledged. "Alessandro is widely regarded as the leading expert in Egyptian hieroglyphics, Phoenician, and Hebrew. It's his calling, his lifelong career. If anyone can help us, he can. Even better, I know him and can arrange a meeting."

Bodie stared at the computer screen and the mix of runes. Would this potential dead end fool both the Bratva and the Chinese, put them out of the chase? Were the Bratva even bothered about Atlantis, or was it just Bodie they were hunting? He wasn't surprised when Heidi acquiesced to Lucie's demands and asked her to arrange a meet.

"Change of plan," Heidi told the pilot. "We're going to Italy."

Cross nodded his agreement. Cassidy leaned forward expectantly. Bodie sighed and tried not to think of all the things that could go wrong, as the pilot acknowledged the change of course.

CHAPTER TWENTY-FOUR

Milan's Galleria and Duomo cathedral sat at the heart of the city, surrounded by bustling crowds all day and through the better part of the night. A vast open square helped draw the eye to the details and immensity of the buildings that proudly rose up around and within it—the cathedral in all its Gothic glory, which took six centuries to complete, and the Galleria, opened in 1877 and famously known as the world's oldest shopping mall.

Bodie jumped out of the taxi facing the entrance to the cathedral, then realized he couldn't actually see the doors or anything at ground level due to the mass of people wandering through the square. The building itself rose magnificently toward cloudless blue skies, with the great arch leading to the resplendent Galleria on the left.

"This noise level is gonna affect the comms," Heidi said. "Could we have come at a busier time?"

Lucie joined her at the side of the road as the taxi eased away. "Somebody mentioned civilian security."

Bodie believed she was being honest, straight, and informative rather than sarcastic. He wondered if there was any way to get Lucie Boom to let her hair down. Heidi scanned the crowds.

"Stick together, people, and keep your wits about you."

Lucie nodded. "Alessandro is a well-known language guru. I hope you don't think your enemies will come too."

"He's not the *only* language guru capable of translating the text, though, right?" Jemma questioned. "I mean, if our competitors wanted to decipher the text, they could go elsewhere?"

"No. He's not the only one. But he is the best."

Carefully, they threaded through the crowds. The Italians and the local tourists certainly weren't shy, brushing past heavily and manhandling each other out of the way. Those who didn't move quickly enough were barged aside, and yet everyone who paused for a snapshot was mysteriously given their own space, the human traffic flowing around them.

Bodie gazed up at the cathedral and the surrounding architecture. An incredible vision, it made him feel humble. Who really needed the legend of Atlantis when they had wonders like this to admire?

They came to the steps at the foot of the cathedral. Bodie smelled coffee and sweet pastries on the wind and noticed the restaurants all around the square. His head whipped to the right as he heard Lucie's name being called.

"I am here!" A man he assumed to be Alessandro waved and held up a bottle of water. Bodie saw Lucie walk toward an older man, maybe sixty, with thin, smooth hands and salt-and-pepper hair. He was dressed in a suit, with the shirt undone down to the chest hair, and clearly kept himself fit. When the rest of the team approached, he ceased shaking Lucie's hand to address them.

"It is good to meet you."

After the introductions, Lucie explained more of what they required. The group sauntered to the edge of the square opposite the entrance to the Galleria. Cassidy, Cross, Jemma, and Gunn were tasked with watching the crowds and remained silent, taking it all in. Lucie and Alessandro spoke carefully.

"I will need to study the compass," the Italian said. "The text will likely be heavy. Dense. I will need to be sure of my translation."

Lucie nodded, but Heidi broke in. "We don't have time for that. What we need is a quick feel."

"A quick feel?" Alessandro studied her. "Is that not American locker-room talk?"

Heidi smiled, seeing the amusement in his sparkling eyes. "Yeah, I guess so. But we need your best theory, Professor, and quickly."

"If it ever existed, Atlantis has been there for ten thousand years," Alessandro said. "What is the rush?"

"We want to find it first."

"Oh, of course you do. Americans." Alessandro shook his head. "Will you save the world?"

"No, but we might change the world," Bodie said. "Imagine the right technology, ancient or not, getting into the wrong hands."

"That depends on your definition of the right hands," Alessandro said. "But you are the people who found the Zeus, yes?"

Bodie nodded, watching nearby windows and doorways.

"I respect that. It was done properly, and the artifacts allowed to benefit the Greeks. I do wonder what happened to the Illuminati, though. Did the American government make you release them?"

Bodie was surprised at the question and at the assumptions people generally made. "No," he said. "We took down everyone we could find."

But not the boss, he thought. *Who escaped.*

"Good, good. Like I said, I respect the way you handled it and I will try to help you." He glared at Heidi. "Posthaste."

"Thank you."

They found a table and ordered drinks, while the others continued to scan the crowds. Lucie fished her tablet out of her bag. Alessandro took it from her and studied the images of the runes. Bodie expected a lot of professional awe, perhaps even expressions of admiration or suspicion, but the professor didn't utter one word.

Bodie sipped his coffee, reflecting on how the team had evolved since agreeing to help the CIA—how their thief skills had developed and helped in so many other useful ways.

Alessandro leaned forward so that his nose almost brushed the screen. He flicked to the next image. Presently, he took out a ring-bound notebook and a pencil. With infinite care, he licked the carbon tip and began to write. Bodie leaned in but couldn't understand the Italian script.

Assuming it was Italian. He decided to keep quiet at the risk of embarrassing himself.

Lucie stared out across the square. Bodie looked for Cassidy, Cross, Jemma, or Gunn but couldn't see any of them. The respect he felt for both Jemma and Gunn had bloomed of late, with Gunn's vital support to the team in Rio, and Jemma helping out in the Alps, not to mention the superficial graze on her leg.

Hours later, Alessandro leaned back in the skinny, wrought-iron chair. "It is a mixture, as Lucie says," he said reflectively as if to himself. "And yes, it could only have been done on purpose. This man, Danel, specifically wanted a learned individual to uncover his secret."

Alessandro and Lucie peered at Heidi and Bodie with dissatisfaction.

"Spill, Professor," Heidi said. "I'm not getting any younger."

"Prettier, though." Alessandro crinkled a well-practiced smile at her.

Bodie winced inwardly for Heidi, and waded in to sort it out. "Suspicious movement in the square," he lied. "Can we move along?"

Alessandro didn't look convinced but tapped his notebook. "Essentially, most of the runes mean the same thing. They were added to cause confusion, to muddle the translation, which baffled poor Lucie here."

"And what do they mean?" Bodie asked.

"Poseidon." Alessandro nodded sagely. "The script includes seven different forms of the word 'Poseidon,' largely unknown, I might add, and just a single sentence."

"Please," Heidi urged. "Please tell us the sentence."

"'Go to the temple of Poseidon in the mountains of Atlantis.'"

Bodie waited for more, but Alessandro offered nothing. *Is that it?* crossed his mind, but then he realized he'd foolishly tempted fate.

"The friggin' Moroccan Bratva are here," Cassidy breathed over the comms. "I see four of them, including Cross's honey trap."

Bodie jumped up. "Time to leave. They made it pretty clear what they would do if they ever saw us again." He prepared his weapon without looking or drawing attention to it. In the shadow of the cathedral he peered into the square.

"How could they possibly find us?" Jemma asked. "It's not . . ."

"We'll deal with that later." Heidi grunted. "After we get these civilians to safety and get out of here."

"Cassidy said there were four soldiers, plus Yasmine," Bodie reminded her. "Wouldn't it be better to capture and question them?"

"Probably, Guy, and I do like your thinking, but we're walking on deadly thin ice. First, could you physically do that? And second, one wrong move could endanger hundreds of people. Something like this . . . you have to walk away from."

He didn't like it, but understood. Cassidy reported that the Bratva were searching the crowd without purpose, as if they weren't sure where to go. It was then that Cross came on the line.

"You say Yasmine's with them? Maybe I could draw her away and talk?"

"That's not a good idea, Eli," Bodie said.

"Why? The information we gain could be—"

"Listen," Heidi said. "There's no time. I've just been told the Chinese are here too. *Move!*"

CHAPTER TWENTY-FIVE

"But I need to explain about Poseidon and the kings of Atlantis," Alessandro said. "About men so influential they later became gods."

"Listen." Bodie helped him up. "During tenure were you ever shot, stabbed, or decapitated?"

"Umm, well, no, I don't think so."

"Let's keep it that way. This is what Heidi does, what we do. We'll keep you safe."

Alessandro went with him. Lucie came around the table and bumped into Heidi. Bodie saw Cassidy emerge from the crowd.

"Your ten o'clock, thirty meters," he said. "Heads down and walk straight across the square."

They complied, trying to maintain a pace that was brisk yet blended with the crowd. Jemma met them and joined in. Soon they were level with the side of the cathedral and moving past its arched windows, unable to ignore its imposing vertical walls. It lessened their escape options for now, but once they were past, it would increase them.

Cross's voice filled their heads. "Hey, Yasmine. Come with me."

Bodie cursed aloud. The man was jeopardizing everything. "You're putting lives at risk," he hissed. "Get the fuck away from her."

"How did you find us?" Cross asked.

Yasmine's voice was clear as crystal. "Run, Eli! *Run.* They will kill you."

Bodie skidded to a halt. He could see Cross through shifting figures to the left and Yasmine just a meter away from him. He couldn't leave his friend behind no matter what the odds were.

"Come with us," Cross begged. "Why are you with these monsters?"

"This is not the time. It's deep, Eli, my story is very deep. If I get the chance I will explain. But you must go now. They will kill you."

"Please join us."

"I can't. Not now. Look, they're coming. Just go!"

Bodie neared Cross, then met Yasmine's eyes and saw the faces of the men approaching her. One was the bald, spindly-armed man, flanked by three tough-looking henchmen. Bodie grabbed Cross and steered the older man out of there, arrowing clear of where he'd left the rest of the team.

"Stop it," Cross said, struggling.

"This is your one fucking pass," Bodie hissed at him. "Any more of this shit and you're done. You hear me?" Even here, even now, his chest hurt when he spoke that way to his friend.

Cross deflated. "Yeah, sure."

"I mean it. I know we're the original members of this team—we can tell each other and work through anything—but you're becoming a liability. You're drawing attention to the whole group, to Alessandro, chancing a firefight here, in this crowded square. Get it together, Cross, or go home."

"I hear you, I hear you. She's just . . . the love of my life, Bodie. I need answers. Isn't there anyone from your early years that you'd give anything just to talk to again? To find out . . . *why?*"

There was, but Bodie knew this wasn't the time for an in-depth conversation about it. He continued to force the pace, cutting through the crowd. At first he didn't look back, because looking back tended to get you spotted, but then Cassidy confirmed his worst fears through the comms. "They're coming after you."

"How many?"

"All five."

"Good. That means they didn't see you. Keep on going and we'll meet you back at the hotel."

"You sure you don't need backup?"

"I'm good. We're headed for the Galleria. There's a thousand ways out, I hope."

"Roger that. Speak soon."

Bodie sped up as they passed underneath the triumphal archway that led inside the shopping mall. Wide and airy and incredibly high, it was and always had been one of the most important Milanese meeting places. The glass and iron roof consisted of four barrel vaults crowned with a large dome, and effected an eerie atmosphere that held sway over the masses below.

Despite the crowd, Bodie felt that a respectful hush permeated the interior of the building. It was as if something sat coiled in the heights of the vault, devouring the clamor.

They pushed past glass displays and a restaurant, paused briefly at an intersection where the Louis Vuitton, Versace, and Prada establishments created a soft, golden glow of enticement, with the colorful glass dome high above. Bodie turned to see the bald man only steps away and didn't hesitate. A swift right was blocked but his hard left met kidneys and doubled the man over.

Bodie caught Cross's arm and ran.

They raced past Prada and fled up the arcade, looking for a large shop that might have multiple exits. Bodie didn't have to look back; he could see their pursuers' reflections in the windows. Four grim, intense-looking men and one woman. All around, curious patrons made way. A tall, thin woman in a tight-fitting dress pulled her young son by one hand and barely looked up. A tourist with two cameras whirled to take photos. Pigeons flew overhead and roosted on the architecture.

Bodie reached the end of the Galleria, emerging onto a street. Shockingly, the rest of the team was right in front of him, and they were in trouble.

The sudden scene of violence shocked him. Heidi was struggling in the grip of a Chinese man. He brought a knee into her groin, head-butted her, and then spun and flung her into a window all in the space of two seconds. Heidi hit hard, and Bodie saw the window crack from end to end behind her. She sank to the ground, dazed.

Cassidy fought two of them, holding both at bay, but the two-pronged attack was harsh. She tried to escape and help Jemma, but the men sidestepped and blocked her. She scowled, frustrated. Cassidy was bleeding and her pants were torn.

Jemma and Gunn tried to defend Lucie and Alessandro as best they could, standing tall and striking fists into the most vulnerable areas they could see. Twice Jemma connected with soft flesh, but then she struck bone. She cried out, backing away. She was no match for this man and he knew it.

Bodie saw Heidi's aggressor aim a kick at her head as she rocked from a heavy blow. He was too late to prevent the kick, and saw her skull slam against the wall. A line of blood appeared on the stonework. Bodie flew, adrenaline boiling, leaping and coming down with an elbow on the nape of the man's neck.

"She was already down, asshole."

The Chinese man staggered but used Heidi's head to steady himself before pushing off. He led with a spinning elbow, which Bodie blocked, then a left punch, which Bodie dodged. The ribs were vulnerable, so Bodie delivered hard knuckles to them. A fist connected with his skull, a knee slammed his stomach. He fell back, wondering how he could possibly beat these guys.

Chinese Special Forces. Isn't that what Heidi said?

We're in deep shit here.

Bodie kicked the bastard in the knee. Dirty tactics applied now, and he knew more than a few. When the man hit the ground, clutching his burning joint, Bodie sent a boot into his Adam's apple, further debilitating him.

Around them, civilians screamed.

It's all falling apart.

A brave young man ran up to Heidi and tried to inspect her bleeding head. The man Bodie had just felled struck out at him. Bodie waded in again, finally rendering the attacker unconscious, but didn't have time to check the groaning CIA agent.

Jemma screamed. Bodie whirled, expecting anything, but even then caught his breath. Mayhem ensued. Jemma knelt before a Chinese Special Forces man, blood running down her cheek. He had a hand tangled in her hair and was holding her close while fending off both Lucie and Alessandro. Gunn was on his knees, doubled over, wheezing in pain. Despite the admiration he felt for Lucie and Alessandro, his heart leapt for Jemma and Gunn. Ten steps away, he sprinted as if he was trying to outrun a bullet.

But then Cross ran past him, and the original five Bratva were just a meter away, piling out of the arcade and into the fight. Bodie couldn't avoid them. One man careened into him, knocking him off his feet and winding him. Bodie landed hard and rolled, shouting into his earpiece.

"Jemma. Fight him! Get up and fight!"

"You're kidding!" Her voice came across weak and muffled.

Bodie used the brick wall to gain his feet, looked over, and saw Jemma turn her head and sink her teeth into her opponent's thigh. Bodie cringed, because it wasn't the thigh at all.

Her opponent pulled away, letting go of Jemma's hair. It was one of the few times Bodie had seen her without her bun, and the difference was striking. She wiped her face. Bodie flat-armed a Moroccan in the nose and rushed past, leaving Cross to engage them.

Jemma forced Lucie and Alessandro back against the wall, shielding their bodies. Now Bodie saw Gunn, lying flat out and hopefully just unconscious. Cassidy continued to engage both opponents, her ripped pants now matched by a ripped shirt, and all covered in blood.

Heidi was barely moving.

And here they were, pitted against properly trained soldiers. They were no match. They were battered, not superhuman, having met more than their equals. Bodie hoped they could get out of it alive.

The Bratva's chaotic arrival had helped. In particular, the way they had poured out of the mall in disarray, just plowing into the brawl. The bald man engaged Cross hand-to-hand, while the others set about the two soldiers in combat with Cassidy. The redhead, allowed a moment of respite, collapsed onto her bottom, panting and wasted, arms hanging listlessly. Bodie stumbled under the bald man's assault, then spun and shrugged him off. The man fell into the street, striking the curb. The crowd watched, some crying out and others filming. A man in a wheelchair tried to ignore the entire fracas and force his way through, but was pulled aside a moment before Yasmine's stumble would have sent him flying.

An engine roared. Bodie whirled to see a black van flying up the road, knocking some pedestrians aside. With horror he saw it run over a man's legs and then saw two Chinese soldiers through the windshield.

No way out.

Fight, then.

The van roared past and stopped adjacent to Jemma. Sliding doors were flung open. Four men poured out like black lava, faces and bodies entirely covered. Bodie saw them reach for Jemma and felt a new level of fear.

"No!"

CHAPTER TWENTY-SIX

Jemma struck out as the Chinese came for her, but two men dragged her away from Alessandro. Two others grabbed the Italian and Lucie, and pulled them aggressively toward the van. Bodie was running so fast he was practically airborne. Striking Jemma's adversaries before they knew what was happening, he sent both of them sprawling to the ground.

Bodie landed well, rolled, then came face-to-face with one of the felled Chinese soldiers. The eyes under the mask were unreadable. Bodie made a wild swing, putting all his remaining strength into it.

Cassidy looked up, still wheezing hard, to see the Bratva being ground down by her two previous opponents. One man was already limping badly, another labored with one eye fully closed. The only way she'd stood a chance was to show them her ability to street-fight raw and dirty—a trait they became wary of very quickly. The Bratva might think they were street fighters, but they weren't even close to her league.

Still hanging her head, she looked to the left. It was the noise of the van's engine that had roused her. Now she saw Bodie struggling with the soldier he'd just taken a swing at and Jemma on the ground. Jemma looked out of it, exhausted. She saw Alessandro and Lucie being manhandled into the van. She remembered all too well what had happened to Carl Kirke.

Cross fell before her, groaning in agony, but she ignored it. Worse, she used his frame to push herself upright, then gingerly tested her limbs.

All there.

That was enough. She stumbled into the road, came up behind the van, and slipped around it. Sliding open the door, she took stock of what was inside.

A driver and a passenger, screaming at their comrades to hurry. Lucie lying prone, shocked by the sudden opening of the door, hands bound but legs still kicking. Cassidy gritted her teeth, just as shocked at the incongruous sight of Lucie's ripped signature woolly sweater as much as the blood and scrapes all over her exposed skin.

The Chinese soldier tying Lucie's feet together glared at Cassidy. She bared her teeth, grabbed Lucie under the arms, and hauled her out, dropping her unceremoniously onto the street. By the time Cassidy came back up, the soldier's feet were in her face. He was holding on to the roof of the van, swinging his legs, and the underside of his boots filled her vision. They connected solidly, made her see stars, and flung her backward over Lucie and onto the concrete path.

The van door slid shut with a deafening clang.

On the other side, Bodie saw Cassidy kicked away and then the doors slammed shut. *Alessandro was still inside.* The Chinese then ran for and piled into the front seat, doubling up. Bodie was on his feet, but the van was already moving.

Civilians and tourists jumped out of the way. Bodie saw that the Bratva soldiers had quit fighting and that Yasmine had hauled Cross up by the front of his shirt and was squeezing the man's throat.

Gotta be hallucinating.

But no. Her words came clearly through the comms as her lips brushed the older man's.

"I'm in charge now. He put me in charge of this and said if I fail he will throw me naked to the wolves. You caused this. You. It was fine before you came, before you spoiled my life yet again. Get in my way and I will kill you all."

As if to prove her point, she brought up a sharp knee between Cross's legs. When she let go, he slithered to the ground like a boneless snake, unable to move. She glared at Bodie once, tight faced, unhappy, and then ordered her men out of there.

What the hell just happened?

Bodie saw the van screaming away. Chasing it was out of the question. With limbs shrieking, joints pounding, and his equilibrium shot to shit, he set about rounding up the rest of the crew.

Barely conscious, they limped away from the scene.

CHAPTER TWENTY-SEVEN

Since they were all together and time was short, they stopped halfway up a dark back alley. Even before he recovered, Bodie spoke up regarding Alessandro. "We're not leaving him behind."

"We have very little time," Jemma said, leaning against a grimy wall. "They'll take him somewhere to interrogate him."

"Sorry, Jem," Cross said. "It's not like that in real life. They will interrogate him in the van and then . . ."

He broke off, unwilling to finish in front of Lucie.

"How can we find them?" the history expert asked.

"How did they find *us*?" Cassidy asked, scowling with pain.

Heidi tested her ribcage tenderly. "I already sent a local team after the van, so don't worry. They have full agency capabilities." She flinched as she moved. "Satellite. CCTV coverage. They'll find the van and grab Alessandro back."

"Tell 'em to be careful," Bodie cautioned. "Those guys redefined 'good.'"

"They *were* better than the norm," Cassidy said. "Beyond special ops? At least, that's what I'm hoping. If they're training them that well these days it's time to friggin' retire."

"Not a lot's known about the Chinese Special Forces and their training methods, but these men would have been trained to an incredibly high standard by the faction controlling them," Heidi said, still cringing. "Sorry I was taken out so quickly."

Bodie stared at her and then laughed. It was crazily funny to hear their CIA boss apologizing for being thrown against a window. "Don't worry about it," he said. "Happens to the best of us."

Gunn had slithered to the ground the moment they stopped. Jemma had already checked and found a large swelling on the top of his head. The team required medical attention and somewhere safe to lick their wounds. "Gunn and I," she said, "aren't cut out for this. Heidi, we're helping as you insist we do, but we're not friggin' warriors."

Heidi nodded in silence, accepting the rebuke.

"I hope you called an agency Uber too," Gunn said, "'cause I don't think I can walk another step."

Bodie listened to the noise that pervaded the city, chiefly sirens at that moment. It went without saying that Heidi would have called for an extraction. It was just a matter of waiting. He thought once more of the Chinese and the Moroccans.

"Quick patch-up," he said. "And then back at it."

Only deep groans met his words.

"C'mon," he cajoled them. "The doc's only gonna tell you to keep moving, don't let those aches stiffen up too much."

"Says our resident expert," Cross mumbled, still largely uncommunicative.

A black van came around the corner, stopped, and picked them up. Ten minutes later they were back inside their hotel rooms, taking turns being thoroughly checked over. The questions the doctor faced in each room were typical—Bodie asking how the rest of the team was, Gunn wanting a second opinion, Jemma clamming up completely, and Cassidy asking if he'd like to go dancing.

Later, they reconvened in Heidi's room.

"Alessandro?" Bodie asked first.

Heidi was seated at a table, sheets of paper scattered across its surface, folders in a large pile, a hot coffee mug steaming, and a bar of chocolate half eaten. "They never found the van, but they did find a badly beaten body. Must have left him for dead. He's in surgery right now."

Bodie closed his eyes as Lucie's face tightened, the neat exterior she presented to the world threatening to crack. Bodie saw her fists clench around the glass she held before she spoke softly.

"Will he be okay?"

"Too early to tell," Heidi admitted. "But they're hopeful."

"How did the Moroccans find us?" Gunn asked from over by the window. "I get the Chinese. Unlimited resources. Only a few people like Alessandro in the whole world. But how did they find *us*?"

Heidi cut in. "I can confirm that four other ancient-language experts were abducted and tortured today."

"And for what?" Jemma whispered. "'Go to the temple of Poseidon in the mountains of Atlantis.' Really?"

Cross cleared his throat. "We should also look at saving Yasmine. She can't be with the Bratva of her own free will, right? Not the Yasmine I knew. Those guys won't let her go easy."

Cassidy glared. "Are you kidding? She's running with them. Leading them now. She'd rather kill you than kiss you, Eli, and I gotta say, I'm feeling the same way right now."

"Me?" Cross looked over. "Why? What else can I do? I can't leave it at that. I need . . . closure."

Bodie held up a hand, saving that tussle for later. "Right now," he said, "we're on the clock. We know at least two other big players are trying to figure this out. Let's not be last."

"Figure what out?" Jemma asked, now trying to bind her hair back into its bun and wincing with every stretch of a muscle. "There's nothing to figure. Not forgetting the fact that both these players just kicked our collective ass. Do we really wanna face them again?"

"She's right," Gunn said. "Maybe you should call SEAL Team Delta or something."

Heidi regarded the room. "That's it? You're backing out? One rough thrashing and you're all quivering like babies? Where's your spine, people?"

"Hey," Cassidy growled. "We don't deserve that, and you can't motivate us with abuse. We don't play that way."

Heidi visibly caught hold of her emotions. "Yeah, yeah, I'm sorry. Been a rough day. Look, Danel's clues have brought us this far. I can't accept that it's a dead end."

Lucie used the desk to rise to her feet and steady herself as the bruises from her struggle to escape the van complained. All eyes turned to her.

"Alessandro wasn't done," she told them. "When we were inside the van, just for a few seconds, he whispered something to me. He said, 'Look at the ancient coordinates on the rose.' He knew what was going to happen to him and wanted to pass it on. Then Cassidy saved me and he . . . he was gone."

"You think he was about to push you out of the door?" Cassidy asked.

"Maybe, I don't know. But Alessandro was lying across from me and then you were there. He spoke the second you appeared."

"'Look at the ancient coordinates on the rose'?" Heidi mused. "I wonder what that means."

"Well, isn't it obvious?" Lucie regained a bit of fire in her voice. "Alessandro only saw one object and it was a direction finder, which essentially is the same as coordinates."

"The compass." Bodie nodded. "And the rose?"

"Every compass has a rose," Lucie said. "The diagram that shows north, east, south, and west. You align the rose to go in the direction you need. The compass has far more relevance than we first thought. As it should, I guess, being one of the Four Great Inventions. The others, according to the Chinese, were gunpowder, paper, and printing. Make of that what you will."

Heidi shuffled through the papers on the table. "So you're saying there may be a set of coordinates on the compass rose?" She squinted.

Lucie walked across the room to her side. "I certainly hope so."

Bodie pushed out of his chair, trying not to groan as bruised muscles protested. He found himself shuffling and then leaned over Heidi's shoulder. "Not the best photo ever taken."

"You try snapping a good picture," Jemma complained, "bent over in some billionaire's weird little trophy room."

"Good point," Cassidy said. "And well put."

Bodie squinted at the photo that Heidi must have printed out and blown up. The compass and the runes were easily recognizable, as were the directional figures and arrows around the compass rose. Whatever letters and symbols lay at the center, though, were blurred and seemed to blend with the arrow lines.

"Crap," Heidi said.

"Not a problem," Lucie said. "Jemma's original photo should still be on her phone. We can zoom in on that."

Every pair of eyes turned toward their chief organizer. Jemma laughed nervously. "Of course I still have it."

A few moments later they were studying the clearer symbols.

"Alessandro called them ancient coordinates," Lucie said. "But, essentially, they're simple compass coordinates." She shrugged. "Seafaring people, like the Atlanteans, used celestial bodies to navigate and combined that with dead reckoning. The ancient Greeks invented a coordinate system in a book called *Geography* that was lost at the Library of Alexandria in the third century BC. And, as we now know, the Greek gods were actually the kings of Atlantis, all our forefathers. The fact to bear in mind is that the Greeks never pretended to invent their gods or their mythology, rather saying that it passed from ancient peoples into the flutes of the Greeks. But, I digress. The greatest seafarers used a geocentric ecliptic system centered on the earth for their astronomy, and thus we can follow the paths they took."

She sat beside Heidi and asked for a laptop. "This will take a while," she said.

Dismissed, Bodie didn't complain but took the opportunity to pour coffee and wash down painkillers. Cassidy was already supplementing those with copious amounts of alcohol. He saw Cross with that faraway look on his face, and Jemma, battered and bruised. Gunn huddled alone with his comfort tablet clutched in one hand, a bandage wrapped around his head. Cassidy appeared shell-shocked, but still managed a smile.

"Been a while since I was taken down," she said.

"I have a special ops team preparing to join us," Heidi told them then, hoping to assuage their concerns. "Loaned to the CIA. All they need is a destination."

"Well, tell them to mount up," Lucie said with satisfaction, "because I know exactly where the Temple of Poseidon is."

CHAPTER TWENTY-EIGHT

Another plane journey, but more time to rest up. The team tried everything to dull the aches and pains. As relic hunters, they'd only needed their individual skills, but ever since Heidi and the CIA took control, they had found themselves being pushed more and more into mortal danger. So far, their injuries hadn't been serious, but it was only a matter of time before one of them received a harsh wound . . . or worse. Injury would lead to later complications, problems, or impediments that could hinder their effectiveness as relic hunters. A vicious circle. In the end, Bodie found the best plan to alleviate his pains was to stretch out along the leather seats, close his eyes, and listen to Lucie. He decided to table their issues with the CIA.

"The mountains of Atlantis," she said from her seat facing them at the front of the plane. "I should have guessed it. The most accepted theory is that the Azores—peaks that rise just above the Atlantic Ocean off the coast of Portugal and Morocco, and of course the Strait of Gibraltar—are the highest mountains of Atlantis and all that remains of the sunken continent. These coordinates"—she raised the printed photo of the compass—"point us to the correct Azores island and, hopefully, the very mountain where the temple will be."

"The Azores?" Heidi said. "Aren't they a semipopular tourist destination? I mean, if there was a temple out there, wouldn't a curious explorer have stumbled across it by now?"

Lucie nodded. "That is a worrying factor," she admitted.

The plane droned on. Heidi mentioned that they would be landing in Morocco first, before boarding a plane to the Azores islands. Bodie yawned and fell asleep. When he woke hours later, they were descending toward the Moroccan airfield. He stretched, disorientated, and immediately wished he hadn't. Cassidy wafted fresh, hot coffee under his nose and he rose gratefully, still wincing.

"We here?"

"Yeah. Thought you needed your beauty sleep."

"Amen to that." He grinned at her and it was in moments like this where he felt content that, after all this time, he'd finally found a new family. Oddly enough, he'd been thinking more and more about the old one recently. Not his parents, that was still too painful, but the Forever Gang, and how good it used to be.

If he stared into the middle distance he could still see their faces. They were long gone, but somehow still here too. He'd already realized he saw Brian in Cassidy's gregarious extrovert qualities. In Cross's slow, easygoing attitude he saw Scott. Was there a correlation between the past and the present? Between *his* past and present? Surely it couldn't be a coincidence that he'd gravitated toward similar personalities. He'd tried to hold on to them his entire life. Thinking even harder, was Jim similar to Gunn—the studious intelligence? And little Darcey—such a trier. Such a spirit. Did she remind him of Jemma? It couldn't possibly be so clear-cut—surely *he* was making it work to his own ends—but the reflections were there.

As if seen in a dream, misty memories continued to come back to him.

Maybe it was the rise and fall of the plane, the sudden turbulence, but something had resurfaced in his sleep and he contemplated it now.

Out of the five of them, only Brian and Scott had been scared of theme-park rides. Jim, Darcey, and he had loved them, thrill seekers since birth, always up and ready for the next daring thing. They had come to accept that Brian and Scott wouldn't ever come with them, and that was the one experience their tight-knit little gang would never enjoy together.

But one day they came upon a new water ride called the Grand Rapids. Three tried it first and pronounced it good. Bodie fancied maybe it was the joy on their faces when they left the rides. Maybe it was the excitement and laughter displayed by others, or perhaps just the bonds of friendship. But Brian and Scott, out of nowhere, articulated an interest and they shared the experience together, their incredible connection cemented forevermore—the laughs and shouts of glee, the soakings they braved; the sudden drops that made them squeal; the pure exhilaration and moments of utter happiness; every second a delightful capture of youthful glory, of immortality, of unforgettable bliss.

Except he *had* forgotten it. Bodie *made* himself forget once it all changed, and the worst part was that forgetting was the only way he made it through the rest of his life.

Until now.

Grand Rapids was long gone, a distant memory. He lamented forgetting it all, but maybe only because he could.

Go back there one day.

Remember the best times you ever had.

It was a promise to himself.

The plane jolted hard, bouncing up off its tires and then slamming back down. Bodie spilled coffee and Cassidy banged an elbow. Gunn dropped his tablet. They changed planes quickly and were then once more in the air, speeding toward the Azores. The second flight was a short one and soon they were landing again.

Heidi regarded them all.

"You poor ragtag bunch of beat-up, broken-down oddballs. C'mon, I dragged you all this far, I can get you a step farther."

"Excuse me," Cassidy piped up. "You dragged *us* here? I think you got that backward, girl."

Bodie braced as the door opened and they got their first look at the Azores. Oddly, it wasn't at all what he was expecting.

An exquisite deep blue sky oversaw a stunning green land primarily made up of lush, verdant mountains. Bodie viewed it from a wide stretch of tarmac where the plane had landed, but Heidi soon steered them away from the tiny terminal building.

Vehicles awaited, and also the promised special ops team, a poker-faced unit of Navy SEALs. Bodie saw them wedged into the lead car and immediately walked toward the second. Through the years of his clandestine travels he'd happened upon several elite American and British soldiers and didn't want anyone to recognize him. A glance at his friends told him they felt the same.

Heidi climbed in alongside Bodie and the rest of the team. "Don't worry. They won't bother you. Unlike some people, they follow orders."

Guiltily, because of the Pantera episode, Bodie and Cassidy looked at the SEAL team before realizing Heidi shouldn't have any cause for complaint. They were right here in the thick of it now, weren't they? Only Cross seemed remote, lost in his recollections of Yasmine.

The scenery grew more spectacular as they climbed out of the flatland and up among the peaks. They passed an impressive mountain with a circular crater, the center hollowed out and now full of sparkling blue water. Dusty trails meandered by the side of the road and off into the wilderness, hiked by tourists. At every turn there stood another splendid vista designed to take their breath away.

Heidi followed a GPS device preprogrammed with the coordinates Lucie had provided. Sometime after leaving the airfield, they stopped and exited the cars, leaving them parked in a fenced area. The SEALs ignored them and ranged out to the surrounding fields, leaving just two to walk with the team of relic hunters, who stuck together. After their skirmishes in the Alps and Milan, Bodie felt relieved to have a group of soldiers whose main mission was to protect them. A beaten trail marked by a fence led them along the side of a mountain, wind whipping their hair and the scent of the sea all around. Bodie took in the great span of the Mediterranean Sea ahead and to the left and reveled in the trek, feeling the aches and pains already washing out. To make matters better, Heidi took a call that confirmed Alessandro's recovery.

Lucie beamed for the first time. Bodie considered it a huge improvement.

The trail ascended for a while and then dipped, taking them around the edge of another mountain and allowing them to marvel at a lake below. Thick trees bordered every shore so that there was no beach and no easy way to enter the water. The entire area looked untouched, glittering, but then Bodie spied a couple of pale bodies frolicking in the water and smiled with a hint of sadness.

"I guess there's no place left where man's not been."

Cassidy raised a pair of field glasses to spy on the couple. "Skinny-dippers going at it. But you're wrong, Bodie. I know of at least one place where man's not been."

She looked sidelong at Jemma. The other woman colored and then squawked out a retort. "How the hell would you know? I've known you what, five years?"

"Four," Gunn said. "I know, it feels longer."

"Still getting to know each other," Bodie said and then saw Cross looking back at him. *Some more than others, I guess.*

The SEALs had been assessing what lay ahead and declared the all clear. They moved on. An hour passed with nobody in sight. The trail wound around another mountain and headed toward the east coast. At last they came to a place where Heidi's GPS let out a little beep.

She slowed. "We're close."

Bodie scanned the landscape hopefully. He didn't really expect to see anything and wasn't disappointed.

"A few trees over there," Gunn said dubiously.

"You think those trees mark a ten-thousand-year-old temple to the god of the seas?" Jemma asked sharply, still smarting from Cassidy's comment.

"Who knows? Maybe they used trees back then. Maybe it's rudimentary. Maybe—"

"Stop." Heidi walked across five meters of flat, green grass to the edge of what was the second crater they'd seen that day. Bodie saw straggly bushes and vegetation stretching down to a narrow sandy beach and a large expanse of water—yet another blue lake. Fingers of scrub dotted by a few unkempt trees extended toward each other on both sides of the lake. The SEAL commander signaled them to the ground immediately, radioing that his team needed to do a full reconnaissance before allowing them down.

Bodie understood. They might not be the first team to find this place.

Cassidy stared at the dirt. "So, we're on the ground again. Didn't take long."

Lucie crawled over to Heidi. "Does the GPS pin the location down?"

"Oh, yeah," the curly-haired American said. "It's in the middle of that friggin' lake."

"How deep is it?" Lucie asked.

"They're all volcanic lakes," Heidi said. "Not surprisingly, this was a largely volcanic area many thousands of years ago. So they now shape this tropical paradise, which is, thank God, still spared from mass tourism. We're lucky it isn't covered in clouds. The lakes around here range between three hundred to almost a thousand feet deep. I guess, judging by the color of the water, this is one of the deeper ones."

"You should send back for gear." Lucie's thought processes were spinning into overdrive. "Contact the main town and keep it quiet. They will surely have some top-notch diving gear here."

Bodie understood what she was saying. That those who could were about to take a trip underwater. Before he could inform the others, the SEAL commander crawled in beside them.

"Bad news," he said. "Your Chinese are already here. Good news? They're right across the lake and unaware of our presence."

"Can you take them out?" Gunn asked. "The last thing I want is another fight."

"That would be unwise. We can't be sure of the outcome, or how we would fare at this stage. Also, their resources could be as deep as ours. They could have more men here very soon. Best to let them think they're alone."

"That's the plan?" Jemma asked. "Wait and watch? That's not why we're here, why we put ourselves in harm's way. I'd say your plan's inadequate."

Bodie stepped in to stop another argument. "Don't worry," he said, waving them down. "I have a plan. It needs some work, and it's risky. It also means the soldiers will have to watch our backs."

The commander gave no indication of his thoughts. "I hear you. What did you have in mind?"

"First, Heidi rustles up the gear from a trusted local. Then we have to send somebody to collect it. Next . . . well, I'm sure you know our backgrounds. What do you think we would do?"

The commander pondered it, then nodded with a look of respect. "That just might work. Risky, though."

Bodie nodded and gestured at his team. "Just the way we like it."

CHAPTER TWENTY-NINE

That evening, the sky turned from blue to deep crimson and gold as the sun died over the horizon. The far waters swallowed it in a matter of minutes, and the black silhouettes of birds flying home at dusk disappeared completely.

Bodie watched the small waves, saw them lose all definition, and spoke into his comms. "Ready here."

An affirmative came back from Cassidy and Jemma. They had determined from the Azores Diving Academy that the absolute maximum depth of this lake was one hundred and seventy meters—about five hundred and fifty feet—which meant using a rebreather with open-circuit bailout cylinders. They would have to use hypoxic breathing gas to ward off the effects of nitrogen narcosis, and carry a large volume to compensate for decompression stops on the way back up. For somewhere like the Azores—where tourism is more likely than research—the equipment was a rarity and Heidi had managed to source only three pieces.

In the dark, Bodie waited, feeling slightly ridiculous. He was a good diver, reluctant at first, taught by one of Jack Pantera's marine instructor pals. Initially, he couldn't see the point, but when Pantera demonstrated the many ways diving would prove useful for egress and ingress to properties all over the world, he quickly saw the light.

Cross was also a good diver, but his head was still not on the mission. Instead, Bodie chose Cassidy to accompany him because he trusted her absolutely, along with Jemma because she was highly competent and clearly wanted to get into the field more. Suited up, they presented an unlikely trio.

Cross approached Heidi as they waited. "Any news on the Bratva yet? I mean, we're just a couple of hours flying time from their coast."

"And that's one of the reasons I'm guessing they're interested in the compass," Heidi said. "But no. Nothing yet."

Bodie studied the map they had made together. It broke the lake into zones, five in all, which they hoped to scour as quickly as possible. To do it right they would have to do it painstakingly slow, which increased risk, but that was why the SEALs were there.

From their hidey-hole ten meters from shore, Bodie, Cassidy, and Jemma crept toward the water. They carried their own gear, already secured. Bodie eased in first, adjusted his face mask, and slipped below the surface. They each carried industrial-strength through-water ultrasonic transceivers in their masks, enabling communication.

Of course, they could prepare all they wanted. The real test was finding clues in the deep waters of the lake.

Bodie felt frustration as they started their first meticulous sweep under the water. It took some time to systematically map out the zones they'd recorded. A live feed sent everything back to base, where Heidi, Gunn, and Cross watched for anything the divers might miss. Bodie sank through the murk, not especially claustrophobic but definitely feeling the black nothingness press all around. Everything was different underwater, and some of his muscles started to ache again, compressed by the increasing density underwater. They kept to the sloping shores at first, ranging left and then right and then moving farther down, but it was hard work, taxing work, and unfamiliar. Nobody expected to find a temple on the slopes of the lake, but they couldn't risk missing a clue either. Bodie stopped often and made the others pause too. He knew that unrelenting focus could make a mind turn to autopilot, so he relaxed them by chatting through the comms system. Underwater life came over to investigate, but the shadows were small and soon darted away. Other than that, their new world was darkly oppressive.

Hours passed. The divers found nothing. They emerged carefully, still under the cover of night, made their way up the bank and into a comparatively safe area. Cassidy immediately stripped off her suit, showing not an ounce of embarrassment in her tight-fitting underwear before slipping on loose canvas pants and a jacket. Bodie was slower and Jemma slower still, the pair stopping to rest even before they escaped their suits.

"No luck," Bodie said, disconsolate.

"Don't worry. We came up with a plan," Heidi told him, trying to avert her eyes from his broad chest. "The SEALs reported that the Chinese are out diving too. All of them. On the far side of the lake."

"Good thing we didn't bump into them down there," Jemma said, laughing.

"Hold on, Frizzbomb." Cassidy was watching the CIA agent closely. "You do realize the more you stare at his chest, the tighter those curls get?"

Bodie blinked and looked surprised. Heidi turned quickly to the stars, finding a particularly bright celestial body to study. Cassidy laughed.

Bodie changed the subject to save Heidi further embarrassment. "This chase to Atlantis is really coming down to the wire."

Heidi looked momentarily grateful for the intervention, but then her face clouded over. "Yeah, and that really worries me. If what we hear about Atlantis is true—that it was a highly developed, almost *futuristic* civilization—then those who find it could take a giant leap right through today's technological advances."

"You're saying they could rule the world," Bodie said.

"It's not as radical as it sounds, believe me."

Lucie took over. "The SEALs will lead you to the empty Chinese camp. Maybe you can find something useful."

"We can do that but I also have another idea. Where *exactly* is that waypoint? I know it's under the lake, but where? Can you find that?"

Lucie nodded. "Of course I can."

"Please have it ready for tomorrow night."

Bodie stood up and threw some clothes on. Within minutes they were following the SEALs to the deserted camp.

By the time they returned, the Bratva had arrived at the lake, slipping noisily down to a far shore. It would remain to be seen how they fared. Bodie imagined the Chinese would leave them alone in order to maintain their own secrecy and spirit any findings away undetected.

The next day passed uneventfully, leaving Bodie to relate what they had found in the Chinese camp and stay well fed and hydrated.

"Nothing telling," he said. "But they do have very high-tech gear. Whoever they are, they're well funded and well connected. I've never seen anything like it, and even one of the SEALs said the same. We took photos of what notes we could find, but obviously couldn't read them. Also, we couldn't move anything or go where we may leave footprints. They're too good not to notice."

"So you'd rather have been sleeping?" Gunn asked.

"Yeah. How's Eli?"

Heidi nodded at Cross, who was sitting with his back to a tree. "About the same."

Bodie slipped over and took a seat on the hard ground. "Hey, how are you?"

"What she said." Cross nodded at the CIA agent.

Bodie lowered his voice. "We've come a long way together, mate. I trust you more than anyone. Accept your judgment without question. Don't disappear on me now."

"I'm still here. I'm with you, Bodie. Trust that I will do the right thing."

Bodie did trust Cross, but it was becoming harder to do without question. He wanted to ask about Yasmine, but didn't want to delve into the complexities around why she worked with the Bratva. And why she'd threatened him. All that mattered was that they make it through this job and get the chance to break with Heidi Moneymaker and the CIA once and for all.

Night returned and the underwater search continued. The best tracker they had, a SEAL expert, departed to keep a closer watch on the Chinese. They didn't expect to hear from him, save checking in, unless something major occurred. The Moroccans were watched intermittently, seen as amateur but dangerous.

Bodie felt like they were floundering through the mire. It helped seeing the grid being checked off properly, but still one could only stare at, feel, and reposition a rock so many different ways. The darkness sometimes made it hard to know if they were going over a previously checked area. Lucie's isolating of the coordinates put the temple seventy meters down and ten meters out from the position they were at now, so the team had decided to continue where they left off. They should reach it tonight.

Time passed. The Chinese progressed on the other side. A SEAL crept over near the Bratva camp and reported seeing them wading into the water with their own diving gear. He didn't expect they'd make much progress. He also mentioned they'd completed a recon of their own, coming dangerously close to Heidi's well-camouflaged hideout but passing right on by.

By the time exhaustion set in, Bodie and the others were far from their goal.

CHAPTER THIRTY

Bodie was far too wired to sleep that night, brimming with disappointment and tiredness, nerves stretched taut at the chance of discovery. He sat back against a tree and stretched his legs out, inviting the others to sit and talk under the black canopy of sky. Heidi brought a liter bottle of bourbon, and if it wasn't for her odd reaction earlier, he'd have pretended to kiss her.

"Who's starting?" she said. "If you want to drink, let's hear it from the heart."

Bodie reached out. "I spent two hours at an eighth birthday party," he told them after taking a swig from the bottle. "It was six minutes from my home. My parents dropped me off and left me there because it was for my best friend, Darcey. It was interrupted by the police toward the end. They asked for me and sat me down, told me what happened. I didn't cry. It didn't hit home. I didn't believe them. Darcey's parents and others said they would look after me for a while and they did. It was a blur. I don't remember any of it. But what I do remember was the cold on that first night in the orphanage. The cold that was solely in my head and heart, because they kept that place at boiling point. It was the coldest night of my life."

Cassidy swigged from the bottle and went next. "All the horror stories you hear about kids are worse than mine. I had two parents who wanted me. But they never loved me. I was an ornament, a necessary object you take along to shows and parties. The thing is—and you should all hear this—a child knows. They know when love isn't reciprocal. They know when a parent or grandparent loves one child more than the other. They know at a very early age, and why would you, a grown-up, want to put an innocent child through that kind of trauma? The pain of realization. The pain of knowing. You will change them for life. I knew, and I cried myself to sleep every night. I fought it, denied it, finally accepted it. I tried to change them." She shook her head, the memory causing a tear to sparkle in her eye. "Imagine that . . . a child so starved of affection she tries to change her parents. But I wasn't strong enough. No child is. I ended up leaving them and never once looked back."

She passed the bottle on. A raft of stars painted the lightless vault with a pale, glittering patina above their heads. Jemma was up next.

"I can't match any of you guys. Honestly, I don't deserve to share the same bottle. My upbringing was fine, my choices all good. Maybe I was a loner; some kids thought I was different. Shunned at school by the prom queen and her pals," she said with a distinct eye roll. "I had normal kids' problems, I guess. Go figure."

Heidi wrenched the bottle from her. "You're right. That's not even trying. Spit that out right now!" She laughed and continued quickly. "Hard upbringing for me, but not dreadful. My father was tough, loud, and unfair. Taught me a lot, though, about life. He was a cop. Some gangbangers shot him in a convenience store. They didn't have to. He didn't pull on them. Didn't even move, just told them he had a daughter waiting at home. They gunned him down for sport, for a scalp. Later it made me want to become a cop of some sort. Maybe . . . maybe it shouldn't have. Because I'm sure not cut out to juggle work and family life. Not this kinda work, anyway."

"They catch those bastards?" Gunn asked.

"Yeah, caught 'em. Judge and jury'd 'em. Of course, they're back on the street while my dad rots in a grave."

Heidi took a second swig.

Bodie looked around the circle. Only Gunn and Lucie remained, since Cross hadn't joined them, and neither looked ready to accept the bottle. He sighed and took it again. "Best friends before the accident," he said, smiling now, although he didn't know it. "Scott, Brian, Jim, and Darcey. We formed this gang, a fun one. We did dares and had adventures and looked out for each other. We were the Famous Five, you know? We were untouchable, unbreakable, like all happy kids are. We were the Forever Gang." He raised the bottle.

"To you, my friends, wherever you are now."

"You never told us about them before," Cassidy said, interested.

"I know, and the more I think about them the more I understand why. You guys remind me of them, and the memory is . . . painful."

Heidi took the bottle back, draining another mouthful. "My daughter, the best thing that ever happened to me, the one who holds my heart in her hand, thinks I do this job *because* I don't love her." She stared at Cassidy. "I do. More than life. More than breath. But she's reading it wrong."

Cassidy held up a hand. "Then tell her. Face-to-face. There's no instant messenger or text between true family and friends. Between real partners. It has to be personal."

One of the SEALs came up to them. "Keep it down," he said. "Or go to bed."

"Yeeees, Dad," Lucie said to everyone's surprise, and gave him a salute.

She reached for the bottle.

Heidi kept it from her, staring, and lowered her voice. "You get it, right? You can only drink with us if you share something intensely personal."

"I understand perfectly." Lucie plucked the bottle away and swigged deeply. The circle sat forward, curiosity high.

She placed the bottle between her legs and stared at the ground. "My whole family are dead," she said. "My entire lineage. Every one of them has died from either natural causes or accidental death. Nothing sinister. But now, every day, every minute, I expect to go next."

Bodie swallowed hard, seeing the personal effort it took for Lucie to get those words out. He also saw what she felt: expectation, knowledge, and fear. How could you ever move on and forge a life, a career, friendships when you expected to die any moment.

"You can't let what happened to them ruin your life," he said. "No matter how bizarre."

"I know that," Lucie said. "And yet here I am."

"No." Heidi scooted over and shared the rest of the bottle with her. "Here *we* are. Broken souls. Tortured, even. Where do we go from here?"

Cassidy spoke for them all. "Fuck it," she said. "Let's go to bed."

"Yeah, who brought the fucking bottle out, anyway?" Heidi threw it aside.

Bodie rolled over to get comfortable under the tree and tried to get some sleep.

CHAPTER THIRTY-ONE

The third night of diving took them to the area around Lucie's waypoint. The entire team was antsy by now. The SEALs were itching for action against the Bratva. Bodie was entirely sure that if the Chinese hadn't been present, the SEALs would have taken them out that very night.

Still, his focus remained on the underwater quest, and although he wasn't scared of drowning, with every hour that passed beneath the surface he began to feel as if the black waters were eager to claim him. The grid was barely two-fifths explored. The Chinese were still hard at it, and left Bodie wondering if, sometime soon, they might actually run into each other. He crouched in the black depths and sifted dirt and rocks and sludge and tried to see through clouds of silt. He knelt, he sat down, he walked along rocks. Time passed without meaning down here, eternity lasting a lifetime. He was aware divers had been using the Azores for many years, but knew they were mostly part-time and recreational divers who wouldn't generally stray beyond thirty meters. The deeper they went, the less traveled the lakebed should be.

The dive's halfway point passed with no success. Bodie's air tank signaled that it was below half full. He checked another gauge to verify but dropped it, then reached along the hose to retrieve it and caught his hand inside a fissure.

He pulled gently, but his glove snagged on something. Slowly, he crouched, worked his fingers around, and managed to extricate it. *That was close, but I guess I could live without a glove if I had to.* He moved on, still searching, but then a thought occurred to him. Quickly, he moved back to the fissure, finding it after more than a minute of searching, and followed it down the sloping bedrock. The depth gauge read eighty meters, and he guessed he was fifteen out into the lake. The next drop-off was sharp and the fissure opened up. Bodie decided to follow it, relaying his movements back to Cassidy and Jemma.

Jemma tutted in his ear. "That's tomorrow's grid. Stay put. You'll hash it all up."

"Already there," he responded, still following the fissure, which, to be fair, was the only interesting feature he'd found in three nights.

"I have you on radar," Cassidy said. "But consider yourself reprimanded. Jemma's gonna slap you crimson when we get back up top."

Bodie measured the widening gap. "Promises, promises. You gonna use your hand, Jem, or your flippers?"

"Stop it."

"I think I'd prefer the flippers." Cassidy laughed.

Bodie grinned. Levity was one of the things that kept him sane, kept him moving forward with the knowledge that all of this was being done, essentially, against his will. And if that wasn't enough—he'd actually come to Heidi's aid earlier, saving her embarrassment. *Damn, that's confusing.*

His single light shone dead ahead from the front of his helmet, illuminating particles floating in the water. He unhooked a more powerful flashlight and waved it across the area. The fissure was stark white in the new light, jagged and partly hidden by sediment. It appeared to be narrowing again, and Bodie thought of moving on, but it wasn't narrowing. It was the deposit buildup. Bodie dug around, still following the tear, and then Cassidy and Jemma materialized out of the gloom, using the comms to let him know they were alongside.

"Thought we'd take a break and join you."

"Could be nothing."

Bodie showed them the fissure, then waved his flashlight ahead to see how far the opening extended. The underwater world revealed itself for just a moment, darkness pinpointed by hidden eyes and flitting silhouettes. The fissure ran farther down, out of sight. Bodie checked his depth and air gauges.

"Okay, for now."

The gap widened enough so that Bodie could put his head inside, then his shoulders. They dug furiously, causing an underwater cyclone that impaired vision. The farther Bodie slipped inside the fissure, the more excited he got, but he remained aware that they were descending meter by meter, farther and farther toward the bottom of the lake.

"Ten more minutes," Cassidy warned.

Bodie heard her, but he had to keep digging. Like a dog who'd lost his favorite bone, he dug and dug, moving on when his gloved hands came up against solid rock. The strange sensation when his fists punched through didn't register at first.

But the fissure broadened and Bodie slipped inside, purely by accident. His arms kept going, encountering no resistance. The angle of his body told him he was underneath the solid rock of the lake now, having crossed a thick lip. He forged on, swimming ahead, and heard Cassidy close behind.

"You pinpointed it?" he asked.

"Jemma's staying behind to make sure."

"No sign of the Chinese? From what I observed on the visit to their camp they appeared to know what they're doing, while the Bratva are clawing around in the dark."

"No, but dude, they could be a meter away and you wouldn't see them."

He knew that, just wanted to remind Cassidy of the threat. He was glad she was with him. Nothing like sharing a new experience with a friend. Time flowed by like the passing of water. Bodie swam with a strong breaststroke, pausing occasionally to cast the glow of his flashlight all around.

They touched the far end of the fissure.

"You're kidding!" Bodie had been sure they'd found something.

"Air low," Cassidy said, the comms starting to crackle. "We need to leave now."

Bodie ignored her, aiming downward, kicking his legs and searching for the farthest corner. The space closed again up ahead, narrowing down. Cassidy slapped his shoulder and pointed toward the roof.

"No time!"

He nodded irascibly, more frustrated than ever. With a last scissor thrust of his legs he found the spot where ceiling met floor.

Nothing. Just one more dead end.

He treaded water, still disbelieving. Jemma crackled across the comms, asking where they were. Cassidy swam in front now and pushed him away. Bodie's head went up and he saw something odd.

Another fissure, but in the wall above, higher than he might have expected. He started swimming up to investigate, but Cassidy got full in his face and manhandled him away. Bodie came to his senses, seeing the air gauge dangerously low. Together they swam strongly, collected Jemma, and made their way toward the surface.

"Something down there," Bodie panted.

"Yeah, and you'd have joined it forever with your bullishness."

"No time to waste." Bodie didn't acknowledge the reprimand. "We need to get back down there. *Fast.*" He broke the surface and started swimming determinedly toward the shore, suddenly brimming with excitement and purpose. It was all he could do to keep from cheering.

CHAPTER THIRTY-TWO

As dawn broke, Bodie paced the shore, desperate to be back in the water. The SEALs had stepped in, recommending a few hours rest for the trio, but as the time approached when they could reenter, Bodie couldn't stop speculating about the Chinese and how close they might be to locating the fissure. If these operatives were a splinter group loosely associated with the government, as Heidi conjectured, then he could only assume they wanted Atlantis for the same reason that the Americans did—to claim and *use* its riches, its potentially advanced technology. Whoever won the race to Atlantis might theoretically rule the world.

Then Bodie, Cassidy, and Jemma were back in the water, swimming quickly to the original fissure and squeezing inside. All the way they kept an eye open for the enemy, checked their radar for figures, but came up with nothing. Still, it didn't make Bodie feel any more comfortable.

Instead of angling down, Bodie swam in a horizontal direction, mindful of what he'd found the previous evening. At first, the gloom misled him, but then he felt his way up the wall and saw the same opening he'd seen earlier. It was undoubtedly a fissure.

This time, they quickly found the wider end, and all three fitted in easily. They swam into a narrow cavern.

"Underwater caves," Jemma said. "Nothing special for the Azores."

"Gotta be unexplored," Bodie said. "Judging by the amount of silt we pulled out of there."

"Maybe."

"Maybe?"

"What the hell do we know about debris buildup? Anyone?"

"It wasn't big on the curriculum at my high school," Cassidy said.

Bodie swept the cave with light, spotting an opening below. Swimming down, he called for the others to follow. It was barely a meter wide, and led to a tunnel.

"Follow me."

"Really?" Jemma breathed out heavily. "I'm not comfortable with that."

"Go before me," Cassidy offered. "I'll make sure you're safe."

Bodie performed a quick recon, ensuring all was well before venturing inside. Sure enough, the walls were close. Twice, his tank clanged on a sharp rock, making him reevaluate how strong it was. Twice, he forged on.

Three minutes felt like a lifetime, but they emerged from the tunnel into another chamber, this one with relatively clear water. Bodie spied some rubble buildup on the floor and dived down to investigate.

Piles of white rock, bare and smooth. He swore. All he wanted was a face, a carving, a bloody inscription.

A signpost would be even better.

Shrugging the frustration away with a small smile, he found another tunnel, this one angling downward and slightly wider. Their air supply was a quarter spent. Carefully, they levered their bodies inside. Another three minutes of careful jostling, shunting, and propelling and they felt a sharper tugging in the flow around them. Suddenly, they were caught in the current.

Unable to stop, unable to turn around, Bodie could only warn his friends with a screech as the current caught him and dragged him forward. The momentum increased as he saw the foaming flow draw nearer.

Oh, shit, we're in a waterfall.

In another moment he was tumbling, spinning, caught by a force far greater than he was.

Sent out over the edge, with no way of knowing what awaited him.

He tumbled straight down, the sensation terrifying, surrounded by froth and sheets of water. Any equilibrium he might have retained was lost. His head was filled with screams and rushing water.

Without warning, he hit a liquid surface, still caught in the waterfall's flow, and now his body was being pushed toward another extremity. Spinning, thrashing, Bodie managed to sprawl out of it rather than swim, and then kicked his legs in what he hoped was the direction of the surface.

His head and arms broke through with an enormous splash.

The first reaction was relief. *Sweet, I'm alive!* The second was worry for his friends. Cassidy appeared first in a plume of water, then Jemma. Both women fought for air against the surging flood for a moment before realizing they were alive.

Bodie got straight on the comms. "Relax, you're safe."

Then the realization hit him. *Were they safe*? Treading water, he surveyed the new cavern. First, he saw the waterfall twenty feet above. It poured powerfully, sending the torrent on its endless journey into the big cave below. Bodie assumed there had to be an equal-size exit point underneath them, since the cave didn't look to be filling up. He spun, anxious to sweep the entire chamber.

"Ah, girls," he said. "Is that what I think it is?"

Cassidy was already staring, dumbstruck. Jemma saw it next and almost stopped breathing. It wasn't perfect; it wasn't anything like intact, but it was stunning nonetheless.

At the very top, a pediment reached toward the roof of the chamber, almost brushing it at its apex. The triangular gable was supported by a horizontal plinth adorned with carvings, and then four columns that ended where the base of the temple began. The base consisted of four wide steps, which disappeared below the waterline, waves lapping at the discolored marble.

Bodie took it all in. The top arch appeared to have been a different color, possibly inlaid with gold, but time, and perhaps water, had dulled its original effect. Grime and mold clung to the pillars and the reliefs. Bodie guessed that, in relative terms, it was a small building, understated even, and wondered if it had been the effort of just a few men.

Still, without investigation they would never know.

Cassidy swam around him and then Jemma. Bodie took another few seconds to scan the area and the darkness behind the pillars. He saw nothing. Hopefully the weapons they had brought would not be needed.

Cassidy climbed out and removed her flippers, tank, and face mask. She splashed her bare feet in the water. Jemma followed suit.

"The air seems fresh," Jemma said. "Must be sucked down the shaft by that flow of water. It separates in the chamber and comes under pressure. The methane gauge is low. I imagine this cave was above sea level a long, long time ago, before the cataclysm. We must be careful, though. Most underwater caves are inhospitable, to say the least."

"Deadly," Cassidy affirmed. "Grab your camera."

Bodie rose in their wake, dripping wet. This close, he could see better where the building had been damaged. The pillars at first glance looked smooth, as if they had been evened out by time. But here and there Bodie spotted deep parallel lines. Pockmarks pitted their surface. Several piles of rubble lay farther inside the temple. Bodie paused and looked back as the women moved into the building's interior shadow.

All clear. The water fell and filled the chamber with noise. The far sheer wall of the cavern had rudimentary steps carved into it about halfway up, which led to another tunnel entrance.

The way out? Well, it's either that or forcing ourselves through the hole down below! Bodie knew which way he'd prefer.

With a practiced eye, he assessed the inside of the building. Nothing he could see shouted "Poseidon." The interior was about the same in width as it was in length, the rock face behind the temple just a meter distant from its rear steps. Bodie assumed the entire structure continued deep underwater and wondered if they would have to dive down.

Jemma used her flashlight to scan the columns; Cassidy used hers to illuminate the ceiling. Bodie shook off the quiet sense of foreboding that pervaded his mind with prickly, razor-edged fingers. He couldn't quite dismiss the thought that they had disturbed someone down here.

Why?

Jemma had scanned the front pillars and was moving to the back. Cassidy helped, her ceiling scan complete. Bodie wandered out front to take a look at the relief carvings high up on the plinth, reasoning that up there, at least, there was something to see.

Quickly, he removed the small telescope he'd packed in a waterproof bag. Lucie had indeed thought of everything. The telescope was fitted with a camera, and Bodie took several pictures, unable to comprehend the markings.

Cassidy came back. "Good boy," she said. "There are more on the other side. I'm going to shimmy up the building and take some photos."

"Be careful."

"Don't worry. I can only fall into water."

He sighed quietly. Cassidy knew the risks and happily shrugged them off, devil may care. It wasn't that he didn't trust her capabilities, it was more that he felt an obligation to keep his team alive.

More than a team. These people reminded Bodie of the best parts of his childhood. He regretted losing the Forever Gang, but he wouldn't lose touch with these new friends, who brought his old friends back to life without a crushing amount of angst.

Bodie was indebted to them a thousand times over and knew that they didn't fully grasp why. There had been a time when he felt he'd never find trust and real friendship again, but Cross and Cassidy, Jemma and Gunn had selflessly given it to him. He saw that now.

Finished taking his photos, he glanced over the roiling waters.

Saw the first face mask pop up and then three more.

Followed by waterproofed guns.

I saw figures in the water.

"Get down!" he cried. "They're here!"

CHAPTER THIRTY-THREE

Bodie ducked behind a pillar as two soldiers opened fire with automatic weapons, providing cover as their two colleagues swam powerfully for the steps.

Bodie looked back into the shadows under the building, and saw Cassidy and Jemma crouched to its side. He fired blindly at the water where the soldiers were. Bullets flashed back, smashing into the column, volley after volley. He slipped around the other side and managed to analyze the scene.

The lead pair were coming out of the water and onto the steps. Bodie saw weapons strapped across their backs and breathing masks hiding their faces. The two at the back bobbed in the water, firing every few seconds. Bodie readied his own weapon and waited for their enemies to come closer.

Cassidy fired first, the gunshot echoing around the small space. Her bullet skimmed the waves and embedded in the far wall of the cavern, but the attackers ignored it. They just fired back while their comrades continued to climb up the temple's steps.

Bodie leveled his gun at the closest climber and pulled the trigger, wounding him in the shoulder. His comrade instantly returned fire.

Bodie felt a tug against his right ear. Something trickled down his cheek. He fell back, breathing hard.

Too close.

He counted to three before peering out again. The man he'd wounded struggled up the steps and tore his face mask off, gulping down air as he fought the pain of the bullet wound. Bodie now saw that it was the Chinese who were attacking them. The man reached the top of the steps. The second soldier was now slightly ahead. He had ditched his pistol, and was readying an automatic rifle.

Cassidy and Jemma emerged from where they had taken cover, returning fire. But their shots went wild, missing the intended targets.

Bodie ducked back as shots came from the two swimmers at the rear of the cave. He saw them drifting nearer now, weapons aimed.

A figure came around the column. Bodie stepped back, firing, but the bullets went wide. The figure smacked him in the face, causing him to stagger, but he regained his balance by pushing off a column and dropping to a crouch. The attacker followed with a kick aimed at Bodie's face. Bodie twisted so that his shoulder took the impact. Pain flared. The gun came up and he wasted another shot as the Chinese soldier disappeared around the column, then appeared almost instantly on the other side.

A hand chopped at Bodie's throat. Agony exploded inside his lungs. The other hand came around with a knife thrust at his ribs. Bodie barely moved, but just enough for the knife to slice his suit and flesh and cause blood to pour. The other hand jabbed at his sternum, and this time he went down to his knees.

Damn, these guys are bloody good.

The Chinese soldier fell across him then, shot through the back by Cassidy. Bodie struggled to push him off. The second soldier was coming around a far column, held at bay by a flurry of wide shots from Jemma, who had taken cover behind another pillar. Bodie rasped, trying to catch his breath.

Cassidy was moving fast to intercept the second soldier. Hugging the outer wall, she padded quietly on bare feet until she reached the pillar that he was hiding behind, but didn't take anything for granted. Soundlessly, she dropped to the floor.

He reappeared around the pillar four seconds later, arms first, then head, standing about a meter above her, the gun pointed and already firing. Cassidy shot upward, twice, into his chest, sending him toppling back into the water.

Bodie watched as the two remaining swimmers came close to the steps. There was a lull. Jemma coughed. The waterfall roared. Bodie massaged his throat gingerly.

Cassidy waved. "You fuckers fallen asleep, or what?"

Nobody knew if they heard, but the swimmers' next actions terrified Bodie. They reared up, balancing on a sunken step, and aimed automatic gunfire at the building's entire façade. Hundreds of bullets tore chunks from the walls. Bodie shrank back, head down and filled with raucous noise. He was so close to the floor he couldn't focus, but knew he had to see what these madmen did next.

They fired ceaselessly, aiming at random. Only now they were pushing away, swimming on their backs with feet propelling them toward the far sheer wall with its steps. They passed close to the waterfall. Bodie tried to pick them off, braving the hail of bullets, but quickly ducked back down.

After a few seconds he looked out from behind his cover. Both swimming soldiers had ceased fire and were each about to pull the pin from a grenade.

You crazy fucking . . .

Bodie acted immediately on seeing the grenades, realizing they had ten seconds or less after the pins were pulled. Another major problem had occurred to him—they had left their tanks and face masks at the front of the temple, in full view of the Chinese. There was no living without those tanks and masks. He jumped into the open, grabbed masks for Jemma and Cassidy, and flung them behind him. The third mask was an easy kick across the floor. Then he bent down for the tanks as both grenades were hurled toward him. He was desperate to complete his task before they exploded. The first grenade landed and bounced, followed by its twin.

Bodie wrestled the first tank into his arms and threw it, then hurling the second tank to the rear of the building where, after a swift glance, he saw Cassidy and Jemma were already headed. His entire being was consumed now with one spinning grenade as it slipped off the building and plunged into the water.

And then the blast.

It detonated beneath the surface, sending a mighty deluge in every direction, an eruption that slammed Bodie off his feet. He felt the brief sensation of flight before striking the building's side and seeing the column that held it up start to crumble. The second grenade exploded on the floor of the temple, turning the cave into a hellish bedlam.

Bodie almost slipped between the building and the side of the cave. There was a meter gap down there, but the chances of being crushed were incredibly high. He scraped and scrapped and hung on. A deeper panic seized him when he saw the swimming soldiers hurling two more grenades. The column to his left shuddered, wavered, and then stopped moving, holding fast. One of the central pillars fell away, plummeting straight down in a jumble of marble, mortar, and dust. The boiling waters claimed it, dragged it back. Water poured from everywhere, and waves ran across the building's floor. Bodie lay prone, waiting for the next two explosions.

Meanwhile, Cassidy and Jemma had raced to where Bodie threw the masks, picked them up, and jammed them over their heads. They held on through the next explosion, huddled against the water blast, unable to stop themselves from sliding across the floor on the seats of their wetsuits, propelled by the detonation. As she slipped, Cassidy grabbed one tank and heaved the other in Jemma's direction. Jemma caught hold of it, snagged a strap with her hand, and looped it over her shoulders. The final explosion sent them farther back. Cassidy stopped herself by planting her feet on the rear wall of the cavern, suspended over the drop to the water below. She flung herself into the water as soon as she got the chance.

Jemma slid past, flailing.

Cassidy reached out, managed to grab her arm and hang on. She used her planted legs as a fulcrum, first arresting Jemma's glide, and then pulling her back to safety. The tank clanged off the marble floor between them. Through the viewing panel of their masks, they breathed out at each other in relief.

"Bodie?"

CHAPTER THIRTY-FOUR

Bodie's attention had been fixed on the Chinese as they escaped toward the rudimentary staircase. He'd lost his gun, maybe lost his life, but he watched them scale the wall and prayed that they missed a handhold and fell into the choppy waters below.

One important point did occur to him: *they found what they were looking for.*

Then the final explosions buffeted the chamber. Hell, he imagined, had never been so wet. Another column went down and the building began to droop. A wave big enough to surf dropped over him.

Cassidy's bare feet stopped just millimeters from his skull.

He looked up at her. She had clearly managed to escape the last two explosions. She grabbed him under the arms and hauled him to his feet. With unsteady legs he tried to keep his balance, but found he had to lean on her to stay upright. The world tilted. The floor cracked, a crazy, zigzag fault line passing right between his legs. When its edges parted, Cassidy dragged him through the crumbling pillars.

Above, the plinth shattered.

The pediment listed and then toppled outward, masses of carved marble coming straight down at him. Jemma ran and leapt into space; Cassidy ran, pulling him along.

Together they dived into the water. Bodie tried to see where his own air tank had gone but saw nothing. Desperate, he dived with Cassidy and Jemma straight for the bottom of the pool. As they skimmed through the water, the women strapped themselves into their air tanks and tried to attach the breathing tubes.

At their backs, the building started to topple and crash into the water. A displaced surge came straight at them. Debris smashed against Bodie's foot, propelled by the sudden rush. Cassidy allowed her body to straighten and drifted underwater for a moment to set her breathing apparatus properly. Jemma did the same.

Together, they pushed Bodie's mask over his face.

It was only now he realized he'd been holding his breath all this time.

Cassidy pushed her breathing valve into his mouth, a kiss from a good friend, and he took several lungfuls before giving it back. She sucked hard herself then, readying her body for the next big challenge.

She pointed. Bodie stared. *Oh, fuck me.* A million what-ifs barraged his brain. Below, the waters of the cave funneled into and through a narrow hole. The possibilities of what lay on the other side were endless.

Just remember what you've already passed through. It will be the same.

He gestured frantically to the far wall and the staircase. Cassidy made an explosive motion with her hands and Bodie realized what she meant. If they followed the soldiers they risked walking into bullets or bombs.

So down they went. They paused once more, this time Jemma pulling her breathing valve free and lending a lungful of air to Bodie. Cassidy went first, allowing her body to ride the spiral of water down through the hole wherever it led. Then Jemma and Bodie followed as he saw, to the left, an expanding wall of rubble coming toward them.

The master thief closed his eyes.

Cassidy fell through into another cave, splashing into the water from a height. This one was three-quarters full and had a staircase cut into two sides. There was no telling what ancient wonders were in here. She struck out for the side underneath the higher staircase. Behind her, Bodie and Jemma bobbed along, finally meeting the wall. Cassidy climbed a small part of the wall up to the stairs, seeing a narrow hole right above them. When she arrived at the stairs she peered up, wondering if the hole led into the cave they'd just vacated.

It didn't.

The shaft veered away from the underwater cave system. It occurred to her, finally, that these were air vents, and in fact the reason they hadn't been poisoned by the underground air. It made sense. In fact, it was perfect. She waited at the top and explained her thoughts to the others, while unselfconsciously hanging off the wall.

"Bollocks," Bodie said, now looking close to his old self. "And there I was just starting to enjoy swapping saliva from the breathing tube with the two of you."

Cassidy considered kicking him off the wall. Jemma screwed her face up in disgust. All three of them then climbed into the vent together and began to wind upward through the rock.

"Let's hope we don't meet anyone coming down." Bodie peered beyond Cassidy's haunches. "Since there're no wide spots."

The air was good, the going tough. The passage was narrow and hard on the hands and knees. Sharp pieces of grit and rubble assailed their flesh and suits. Small creatures scuttled around them and fell from the ceiling. When they stopped for a breather they had to lie flat, end to end, until they felt ready to continue.

"In one way I hope that wasn't the temple of Poseidon," Bodie said during one break. "But in another, I really hope it was, because it shows we're still on the right track."

"Yeah, those soldiers really cooked it. Do you remember what you saw?"

He recalled taking photos. "I was too busy clicking," he admitted. "Didn't register the images."

They forged on, the tunnel growing steeper until they had to claw their way forward. This continued until they could go on no more and collapsed in pain. Even after recovering and retrying, they found that the way ahead was nearly impossible. Cassidy groaned and slid backward. Bodie galvanized her with an ultimatum.

"Keep moving," he said, "or I'll crawl right over you and pull you with me—and, girl, I won't ever let you forget it."

A deeper groan and she was inching forward again. A grueling half hour later and the slope leveled off. The trio rested once more, took several gulps of air, and suddenly realized how much fresher it tasted.

A breeze wafted down the tunnel.

"We're close, be doubly careful," Bodie warned.

"I didn't come all this way to end up as soldier bait," Cassidy growled.

There was a surprise waiting for them at the tunnel's exit. An outcropping of rock and brush covered the opening, and when Cassidy angled her body into it, moving headfirst into waning sunlight and sliding slowly free, her eyes ended up looking down the side of a mountain to the rolling ocean below. Heart pounding, she grabbed hold before she fell out.

"Pull me back," she whispered furiously. "Just pull me back now!"

Bodie carefully dragged her to safety and let her readjust. "What's the problem?"

"Let me check." She let her eyes adapt to the light, gauged the vault of the crimson sky to determine the time, and saw the early sprinkling of stars above and a vertical space below her. "Shit, we've been in there a long time. It's dusk."

"Is that *it*?"

"No, that's not *it.* I'm staring down the side of a fucking cliff face. *That's* the problem."

"Ah, what's the distance?"

Glad to hear Bodie's thought processes matched her own. She estimated the drop. "Eighty feet?"

"Shit, that's a tricky jump. Not impossible, but tricky."

Cassidy shook her head. "Oh, great. So the mighty Pantera never taught you cliff diving?"

Bodie smiled. "Everything but."

Cassidy studied the area below. The truth was, there were no rocks, no rough surf, just rolling water. "Everything I can see down there looks safe."

"Cool. After you, then."

Cassidy smiled to hear the muffled voice from around her waist, where Bodie still held on. The bonds they had forged recently would only intensify. Her outlook on trust and friendship had been enriched, not least in the last few weeks. It even made her feel stronger inside, where it counted.

"Hold on," she called back. "I'm gonna see if we can climb up."

Wriggling, she shifted and angled her body until she hung out below the rocky outcrop. Then she grabbed hold of it and lifted herself up. *Damn, that was good exercise for the abs.* Bodie's grip was powerful, and she placed her life in his hands. She edged out a little farther and clung, staring toward the top of the cliff. The face wasn't vertical, but it was close. The sparse vegetation promised no handholds, and even the rock itself looked smooth.

"Pull me in. Climbing is not gonna work."

Quickly, she related her findings and then told them what they were going to do.

"Keep your chin up. Jump out, feet down, and do not look at the water. Use your arms to stabilize yourself, but put them down before you land. Land strong, feet together, knees slightly bent. And Bodie, cup your sack unless you want it to turn into a *really* bad day."

She counted eight seconds of silence and reflection before Jemma's scared voice filtered out of the tunnel. "You've done cliff diving before?"

"No, an old boyfriend of mine used to compete. Guess I listened more than I thought."

"We're jumping, then?"

Cassidy told Bodie to let go of her feet and then slowly shuffled into a sitting position. Using the outcrop as both a fulcrum and a safety anchor, she rose, shaking out the aches as she went. Dead ahead, the sun set spectacularly, casting a sheen of fire across the steadily rolling waves.

She launched her body right into them.

CHAPTER THIRTY-FIVE

With no functioning comms and no real clothes or shoes, the journey back to their camp took longer than it should have. They barely rested, conscious that an unknown but very real ticking time bomb now lay in Chinese hands, aware that with every passing minute the fate of the world hung in the balance. They were some way ahead now, and possessed everything they needed to find Atlantis first.

The night was dark, but an almost full moon and a million shimmering stars helped light their path.

They came over a rise, vegetation in their way, and stared down the slopes of the crater to the wide lake below. The whispering wind tussled and fought with the unyielding branches all around. Because of his relatively high vantage point, Bodie had eyes on the Chinese camp, and then the Moroccans', and then their own as the entire vista came into view.

They were fighting on the banks of the lake.

The Chinese had attacked, it appeared, from the water, their small dinghies lying forlornly there now, drifting close to the edge. Bodie could see chaos had overtaken the camp, with soldiers involved in fierce firefights, dodging equipment and using the natural cover of the undergrowth. The scene was illuminated by several small conflagrations, and most combatants exchanged bullets from behind whatever cover they could find. Bodie saw Cross and Gunn leaping in the firelight, but there was no sign of Heidi. Their camp was under siege, but maybe, just maybe, the three of them could turn the tide of battle.

The ground dropped off sharply below. Bodie hastened down with the women. They veered toward the camp, thankful when they passed below the lip of the crater and were no longer outlined against the sky.

As they arrived at the outskirts of the camp, the battle raged around them. Bodie counted five Chinese soldiers, most likely what remained of their force after they lost two in the underwater cavern. He saw two SEALs lying motionless, the rest holding the Chinese at bay. A figure was pinned down behind a twisting clump of brush close to the water. Bodie guessed this was Heidi or Lucie. He slowed as he hit the beach, coming in behind the Chinese positions. Ducking low, he crept along, one foot in the water, the other in the sand. He stopped and raised his hand.

"Slowly."

Cassidy placed the only gun they had retained after the cave firefight into his palm. They knew it was down to the last three bullets. Bodie saw this as a real chance of getting rid of the Chinese, who had been a heavy, life-threatening noose around the necks of the relic hunters. Taking care, he crept closer and closer, letting the noise of the battle mask any sounds he might make. Not once did a stray bullet come close; he was at a right angle to their position. When he reached optimum range, he settled and took stock.

Three Chinese were dug in between the curve of the bank and their camp, all hidden behind fallen logs and the trunk of a tree. A fourth hid cleverly in the shallows of the lake, using the slope for protection. Bodie slunk in closer, took a deep breath, and made sure he knew where the nearest cover was.

The area around Heidi suddenly began to blaze as flames cavorted and leapt between branches. The fifth enemy soldier kept her pinned down with gunfire. Bodie lined him up first and squeezed off a shot. The slug took him in the shoulder blade, sent him flying. Bodie switched aim smoothly, taking down the man behind the tree. The third and fourth were already changing positions. One moved too far and was immediately picked off by a SEAL, which left just two.

Bodie dived for cover. Bullets punished the undergrowth all around. Head down, he lay beside Cassidy and Jemma until more shouts went up.

"Look out!"

"Left, bud, on your left."

The three of them bobbed up. Bodie swore. The Bratva, it seemed, had taken the opportunity to attack, sensing easy prey. Maybe they were intent on just killing him, or maybe they had decided to join in the hunt for Atlantis. Bodie wouldn't put it past them. Criminals were opportunists, just like everyone else.

Bodie decided to hold on to the almost-empty gun in case he could find more rounds. He saw a Chinese soldier walking out of the water, but then another appeared out of the blackness behind the first, giving Bodie pause because he hadn't even sensed the man was there.

The Bratva waded in among them. Bodie counted six running through the crackling conflagration that was their campsite. Three SEALs were also present. Bodie ducked beneath a burning, collapsing branch to head-butt a large man, making him stagger backward. Fires raged all around, crackling and smoking high into the shadow-struck night. Bodie dodged another burning bush, turned, and shoved his adversary into the flames. The man's uniform caught fire, and he screamed and ran through a clearing. Up ahead, he saw Heidi crawling along the ground, keeping her head down.

Chaos crackled and spat and screamed all around. The SEALs engaged the Bratva, shifting from cover to cover, firing their weapons, and engaging in hand-to-hand combat, and the two remaining Chinese soon joined in. The camp was still in chaos. Cross elbowed a soldier before Gunn managed to push him down into a tangle of brush. Cassidy leapt atop him as he tried to sit back up. Gunn hadn't seen her coming and greeted her with incredulity, losing focus, and then had to jump free as a Bratva fighter tried to grab him beneath the arms. Jemma searched for a weapon. Bodie slid in beside Heidi and lifted her face.

"You okay? Injured?"

Her eyes cleared. "No, no, just the smoke."

She coughed. He dragged her away from the flames. The bald Bratva fighter with the spindly arms ran past him, followed by Yasmine, neither giving him a second glance. *How did they find this place?* Heidi grabbed his arm and pulled herself upright.

"Have you seen Lucie?" she asked.

Bodie frowned. "Shit, no. Where was the last—"

Bodie had ridden the odds too long. A Bratva body-slammed him, knocking him to the ground. The exertions of the last few hours had depleted his strength. As he tried to repel a second attack, he realized his capacity to fight was now dangerously reduced.

Raising an arm, he struggled to find the energy needed to fight effectively. His opponent kicked him in the ribs and then leapt, coming down hard with an elbow. Bodie managed to scramble clear and saw Heidi approach his attacker from behind, a boulder in hand. The rock crashed against his skull, made his legs fold. Heidi helped Bodie up and the two went in search of Lucie.

Cassidy was assisting Cross, peeling an opponent from the older man's back, forcing hands from around his throat, and sending his attacker spinning into a tree. He cracked his skull against the thick trunk, and collapsed to the ground. Burning debris from a spreading fire fell around him. Cassidy couldn't just leave him to burn alive, even if he was an enemy. She moved in to pull him clear, but he struggled against her as she tried to assist. She smothered the flames on his clothes, checked he was okay, and then punched him in the face.

"I think he would thank you," said a female voice at her side. "Maybe."

She fell into a defensive position. Yasmine and the bald man were there. Cross stumbled forward but tripped over a branch and went face first into the earth. The three regarded him for a moment, shaking their heads.

"Why can't you see what's right in front of your eyes?" Yasmine asked cryptically. "We don't want to kill you. We're trying to help you, even now. You are a damn fool, Eli Cross." She couldn't stop the small, genuine smile from creeping across her face.

"Couldn't agree more." Cassidy lunged first as she read the bald man's body language, a quick feint that told her he was about to strike. He leapt an instant later, catching a punch to the chin. Cassidy circled him as Yasmine stepped away from the encounter.

Bodie still saw the Chinese as the major threat. Their numbers may have been depleted but he knew from previous experience that they were formidable warriors. The SEALs had engaged them with knives, but one American was bleeding profusely and the other was attempting to beat a fire out on his friend's back while continuing to fight. Bodie left Heidi to continue her search for Lucie, and loped off. Jumping a fallen crackling branch, he hit one of the Chinese from the side, bearing him to the ground. All of a sudden Jemma was there too, real courage making up for lack of skills, her weapon a thick, gnarly bough. Bodie reared away from his opponent. The Chinese soldier raised himself up . . . right into the bough that Jemma swung. It contacted heavily with his forehead, making instant lights out, the body falling backward with a thud.

The remaining SEALs, looking grateful, took on the final Chinese fighter.

Bodie spun in the dirt and tiny fires, the wetsuit actually helping him move. "Still got your phone?"

Jemma patted her suit. "Tucked safely away."

"Really? Shit, I don't wanna know where." He surveyed the scene. Heidi dragged Lucie from underneath a flaming tree as parts of it sheared away and charred the ground all around. Lucie reeled when a spark landed in her hair and caught fire. Bodie was grabbing handfuls of water but Heidi managed to smother it, yanking Lucie upright and screaming into her face.

"Pull it together!"

She hauled Lucie away and into the clearing.

Bodie found his attention divided. So far he'd been too engaged with the Chinese to worry about the Bratva and had lost track of his own team. Cross had somehow fallen to his knees in front of Yasmine, and she was shouting into his ear. Cassidy was fighting the bald Bratva warrior. Gunn was lying prone as a heavily tattooed Bratva killer stood over him. Two Bratva soldiers were searching the remains of their camp, and Bodie wondered if they had been ordered to look for clues as to the whereabouts of Atlantis.

Bodie decided Gunn needed his help more than anyone. Cassidy could hold her own, although the bald Bratva's fighting style made him a dangerous opponent.

Bodie darted to where Gunn was being threatened by the Bratva soldier, hammering into the man from behind and knocking him away from the still-prone Gunn. The man spun to face Bodie, raising his knife. Bodie grabbed the man's wrist and twisted, trying to force him to drop the weapon. But the soldier was stronger than he looked and shrugged Bodie off with ease. He lunged with the knife and Bodie jumped back. He dropped and kicked out, striking the Bratva soldier's knees. A branch from a burning tree crashed to the ground nearby, distracting the tattooed soldier. Bodie took the chance and kicked the man hard in the chest, knocking him off balance. The knife fell to the ground. The man, though winded, still reached down to grab it. Bodie raised his boot and smashed it down on top of the man's head, laying him flat out on the ground and rendering him unconscious. Then he scooped up Gunn and checked on Cassidy.

The area all around her and the bald man, around Cross and Yasmine, burned with a hateful fury. Flames licked at their faces, their flesh, as they struggled and brawled and shifted positions. The blackest of skies outlined it all. Again, Cassidy threw a Bratva clear just as a burning branch would have landed on his squirming body, and the bald man stood down to give her a few seconds to quench her own blaze.

The Bratva were killers maybe, but respectful of a worthy opponent and with a deeply held honor code. It was what he was counting on when it came time to steal and return the statue that set them after him and Jack Pantera in the first place. He saw Yasmine had a hand around Cross's throat now, still yelling at him. Bodie's best guess was that she was desperate for information.

Which poor old Eli doesn't have.

Bodie ran up to the confrontation.

"Hey, Yas," he drawled slowly, using familiarity to gain her attention. "You two are not married yet."

He reached out and pulled her away, releasing Cross. Yasmine spun with an open hand, slapping him across the face. Bodie stood back, watching the interaction between the two.

"Why are you even here?" Bodie asked.

"Three reasons actually. You, Atlantis, and the Rif, which relies partly on us."

"The Rif?"

"Yes, the Rif is our home, but it has been a region of strife for many years now. We consider ourselves independent of the Moroccan government."

"I hear of it quite often. Mostly reports centering on the fact that it ignores narcotics and other criminal trades that are the mainstays of its economy."

"The government neglects the people. We help feed them."

"Is that what Viktor tells you?" Cross put in. "He's all about power, Yas. That's why he wants Atlantis and all the incredible secrets it may contain. Just one of those secrets could be powerful enough to put the Bratva in control for many years."

"Look, Viktor is not the boss. We work for the Frenchman called Lucien. And regarding the Rif—it *is* tyranny," Yasmine said. "There is no rehabilitation. No aid. The region is devastated. What do you expect them to do? They have to survive."

"Not in debt to criminals," Bodie said, trying to keep her talking. Again, they'd been told the name of the real Bratva boss of the region. It was uncalled for, and surely against any rule. What was she trying to tell them?

"The government always excludes the Rif from state development plans. It is devastated. A devastated population will not lie down and die, it will fight. It will resist until social and economic development arrives. Until then . . ."

"I'm guessing you are originally from the Rif," Bodie broke in, ducking as a branch exploded with the popping sound of gunfire. "But you can't confuse a state struggle with a criminal organization. How many like you does Viktor, or Lucien, have on the payroll?"

"He wants the clue. The clue you found down there." She nodded at the lake. "Give it to me and I can let you live." She looked back at Bodie. Her gaze was strong, but he sensed that behind the stare she was pleading with him to go along with her proposition.

Bodie glanced around. He could see the other confrontations had continued during their discussion. The SEAL team was forcing the remaining Chinese soldier to the ground, tying his hands behind his back. Cassidy and the bald Bratva soldier had reached an impasse, both still standing, both unable to continue. The fires raged in the treetops. The scene was chaos.

"We're evenly matched," Bodie said. "No, we're better than you. I recognize that you hit us without weapons and I respect that, but it was as much for you as for us. The Chinese were winning at that point."

"We helped save you."

Bodie made a face. "To kill us later? Not really, but you did cause confusion. Tell me, how did you know we were here? You didn't possess any of the information." He tried hard not to show how rattled he was, still surrounded by the Bratva. But he was grateful that Yasmine had been put in charge. At least she had reason to let them live.

For now.

Yasmine plucked at Cross's scalp until she came up with a tiny tracker. As she did so, the thief tried, ineffectually, to bat her away. "How did you . . ." He seemed lost for words then, staring at her.

"Remember the hug back at the Alps?" Yasmine shrugged. "I planted it then. Precaution. Always precaution."

Bodie scowled. "The CIA didn't detect that?"

"Signal can be turned on and off remotely," Yasmine said. "We just activated it a few hours after Moroccan airport CCTV scanned your faces."

"We didn't—"

"There's always CCTV, Guy, you should know that." Heidi shrugged.

The SEALs were around them now, two holding guns at a non-threatening level. Bodie backed away and signaled for the whole team to do the same. Yasmine stared at Cross, but the thief couldn't look at her, hanging his head as he trudged along. Having already noted their lack of firearms, Bodie didn't expect any protests from the Bratva and didn't get one.

"Stalemate," he said. "Everyone could die right now or we could all live to fight another day."

The bald man stepped in front of Yasmine. "You can count on it," he said.

CHAPTER THIRTY-SIX

Bone tired, the group trudged back to their SUV and drove into town. Reflecting on why they had been let go was deeply troubling. First, it had been a stalemate. Nobody had won, and no one had lost. Except the Chinese.

Second, Yasmine had offered mixed signals to both Cross and Bodie. But even the bald man had seemed reluctant to finish what he had started.

There was something else, something deeper going on here. But there was no time to stop. A large boat was waiting for them at a remote dock. Nothing fancy, just a rectangular vessel, pitted with rust, but bearing a powerful engine. Before they realized, it had motored them away from the Azores and out into the North Atlantic Ocean toward the Moroccan coastline from where they could view the jutting peaks.

From this distance, the Azores did indeed look like the tops of ancient mountains, all that remained of a deluged world. The boat dropped anchor a few miles from the coastline as the team gathered together in the small living quarters before separating to find their bunks and get some rest.

Bodie apprised them of the underwater find. They checked Cross for additional trackers, picking at his hair as if searching for lice. Cross looked dejected, lost, and was finding it difficult to cope. Everyone else nursed their wounds.

Bodie tried to lighten the mood. "I lost my camera," he said, shrugging. "I have no idea where, but there's still photographic evidence on Jem's phone. Everything we saw down there."

Expressions around the room cleared, especially Lucie's. "Really?" the historian asked. "Let's see them."

"Well, it's secreted carefully about her person."

Everyone stared at the tight wetsuit. Lucie frowned. Jemma grumbled, removed herself from the room, and then returned a few minutes later. She held the phone out to a suspicious Lucie.

"Don't worry, it's fine."

Heidi proposed a five-hour rest. The Chinese were dealt with for now and the Bratva had run out of clues to follow. The team could afford a small respite to replenish their reserves. Nobody questioned that the Chinese might send more men.

Whatever, Bodie thought. *I sure as hell can't function any longer without rest.*

He fell into a deep, dreamless sleep, and was still groggy when his alarm went off. Gunn, on the bunk below, complained loudly. Similar groans could be heard in the rooms next door through metal walls as thin as paper. He guessed it was now early afternoon.

Bodie was starving. He made his way to the galley, where steaming coffee and sausage sandwiches were available. Almost drooling, he polished off the first and started on a second. One by one, the others filtered in. Last in was Lucie, and Bodie saw immediately that she hadn't rested.

"You didn't sleep?"

"Later. We need information first." The historian's tone was entirely professional again and belied the bruises on her face and the bandages around both arms. Bodie remembered how she'd opened up when they drank from the bottle and wondered if she'd expected to die back there. After all, pitched battle wasn't exactly natural causes.

Heidi rested her chin on one hand. "So what does five hours get us, apart from zombie eyes and camel hair?" She flicked her eyes to Cassidy as she finished speaking.

"Oh, we can't all have perfectly tight, perfectly adorable curls, darlin'," the redhead protested, shaking her locks out.

Lucie poured coffee. "There were sixteen photographs in all. I sifted through them carefully. What we ended up with was an interesting frieze, which is the panel that runs along the top of the apex, yes?" She paused to drink, take a sandwich, and sit down at the table, affecting her schoolmistress air. "We have no way of determining the building's date, but we do have eight bas-reliefs. The first three, and the largest, depict the god Poseidon, so we can safely say what you found was indeed a temple devoted to him. These reliefs also contain other gods, whom the Greeks would refer to as Apollo and Artemis, but who the Atlanteans may have called kings. I saw traces that confirm the temple may once have been inlaid with ivory, silver, and orichalcum. Now, the white, black, and red stones you saw at the base of the frieze are typical of the volcanic rocks in the region, and would be the very stones the Atlanteans would have used, if Atlantis is indeed beneath the Atlantic. It appears that this particular temple was a personal project, rather than a public one. It is small, basically unadorned, and, in places, not even completed."

Jemma rubbed tired eyes. "You're essentially saying that it was probably situated in Danel's backyard? Like we might build a shed, or a barbecue?"

"Yes, why not? Danel was a lifestyle architect. A sculptor, a builder. He wanted to keep Atlantis alive for future generations. Is it not merely the equivalent of a man today burying a time capsule?"

"Putting your theory in context," Jemma said, frowning, "would mean Danel lived high up in the mountains. Near the very peaks, it seems."

Lucie shrugged. "Perhaps he knew the deluge was coming."

"All this is fascinating," Heidi said. "It really is. But can we get back to the temple?"

"Yes, of course. We're left with five bas-reliefs. One depicts a king, whom I assume was ruler at the time. Another depicts an area of land, which I believe Danel wanted to immortalize because it was his home, and, yes, it is among the peaks. Now, the three that remain are the interesting ones. The first is the Pillars of Hercules, the second an old mountain, whilst the third is composed of text, a translation of which I have messaged Alessandro for."

Bodie knew Lucie was enjoying stringing out her explanation, but then he was enjoying his second sandwich, and was prepared to let her waffle to her heart's content.

"And . . ." Heidi looked grumpy. "What does it all mean?"

"The Pillars of Hercules are the first marker, the old mountain the second, and the text the third. Simple. Each successive relief narrows the location down. The text, by the way, translates closely to 'In the mouth of the dead woman sleeping.'"

Bodie studied the others as Lucie explained. Despite all that had happened they were still engrossed.

"Since antiquity, the Pillars of Hercules was the name given to the promontories on either side of the Strait of Gibraltar. According to legend, Hercules performed twelve great labors. The tenth was to round up the cattle of Geryon. To get access to the far west, the furthest point reached by Hercules, he would have to cross the great mountain known as Atlas, a formidable task even for him. So Hercules smashed straight through it, connecting the Atlantic to the Mediterranean Sea and forming the Strait of Gibraltar. Never mind what Plato said about them, the Pillars have always held a startling significance in our world. They appear on Spain's coat of arms along with the Latin, *plus ultra*, meaning 'farther beyond' and implying a gateway. Dante's *Inferno* tells of a terrible voyage past the pillars and into the unknown. They appear in an unfinished novel by Sir Francis Bacon and bear the legend 'Pass through and knowledge will be the greater.' All of this implies that beyond the Pillars of Hercules a great, advanced land and civilization once lay."

"And the old mountain?" Gunn asked.

"Well, one Pillar of Hercules is the Rock of Gibraltar. The other is Jebel Musa in Morocco, also known as the Dead Woman because it resembles a reclining female figure." Lucie sat back. "And there you have it."

"Five hours well spent," Gunn said. "You can sleep now."

Bodie stared around the table. "Anyone else thinking what I'm thinking? Back to Morocco?"

Cross buried his head in his hands.

Cassidy shrugged. "Look on the bright side: we slip in, we slip out; the Bratva can't track us this time."

"Get some more rest," Heidi told them, tapping the table. "I have to report in, talk to the SEALs, and see what kind of provisions we need. Morocco is only a short boat ride away from here, but it's gonna be tomorrow before we're ready to leave."

Bodie stretched with a sense of luxury. "Doc," he said, "that's exactly what I wanted to hear."

CHAPTER THIRTY-SEVEN

A day and a half later, as dusk painted the waters in shadowy hues, the boat took them to Cueta, a city located in Morocco but belonging to Spain. From there they were due to travel to a tiny village nestled at the foot of Jebel Musa. At nine hundred meters, the mountain attracted tourists for its legendary view over the Strait of Gibraltar and even farther, to the Sierra Nevada. The team was well rested if still a little battered and bruised. Cuts and scrapes had been treated, as well as the odd burn.

The three remaining SEALs had been loaned to them in case of trouble, and now Bodie knew their names—Bass, Foster, and Hoff. The entire team was a silent bunch as they entered the harbor, Bass and Foster lost in their own imaginings, Hoff gazing intently at the approaching town. After docking, they didn't waste time, just hired vehicles to take them to a previously identified trail and then hiked until the sun sank fully below the horizon and darkness held sway across the land. Tents were erected and the team spent a restless night under the Moroccan stars. Morning found them cold and hungry and preparing a quick breakfast before setting out again, packs in hand, across a green field. Along the way they hopped over fences and pushed through a hedgerow, jumped a ditch and paused by a rushing stream. The sun climbed higher, but a swift breeze blew in from the Atlantic, chilling the air so that they turned their collars up and huddled inside their jackets.

Lucie explained a little more about Atlantis, and Heidi informed the team that they still hovered on the edge of legality because of some deep power play going on in Washington, DC. All "off-the-books" teams were affected, it seemed, but Heidi took the flak and told them not to worry. She explained that the power play involved a secret organization called Tempest, which appeared to be deeply embedded inside the Washington government, and was recruiting mercenaries and terrorists to further its own aspirations, while at the same time alienating and disavowing dozens of sensitively and internationally placed special ops teams. Her CIA bosses had complex, wide-ranging concerns on their hands and weren't prepared to throw any more resources at her.

The fields meandered on as uniform as military jackets. Hills rose to either side and masked most of the surrounding terrain, but the woman-shaped hump that was Jebel Musa stayed dead ahead.

"I see it now." Cassidy nodded at the mountain. "In fact, once you see it you can never really *unsee* it."

"Hair, nose, mouth . . . breasts," Bodie said. "The dead woman."

"I think those are her hands and arms," Cassidy said. "You know, in repose? Otherwise she'd have been called the *sleeping* woman."

"Well, the mouth is pretty clear," Bodie said. "That's all that matters."

Jemma was reading an international guidebook. "Says here that the mountain has over two hundred caves that attract cavers," she noted. "Which explains all those specialty stores back in Cueta."

The terrain rolled on, dusty brown dirt with patches of verdant bushes and grass. As they approached the slopes of the mountain, a patchwork of gray rocks dotted the landscape, markers of an unknown time, for an unknown reason. The team was forced to carefully thread a path between them so as not to break an ankle or graze a shin. They were coming up behind the head of the mountain, which sloped sharply but still allowed ascent by foot. The SEALs were ahead. Cassidy, wanting to stay sharp and at the height of fitness, ranged free as well, watching their right flank and looking back toward the village. Nobody had expected they would be followed, and they had traveled farther afield just to be sure, but Cassidy Coleman was never one to take chances.

By late morning there were still a few tourists around. Bodie spied two on the far side of the mountain, sitting upon what one might call the lady's "knees." Cassidy asked for a set of field glasses and everyone stopped.

"What's up?"

The redhead took the binoculars and stared back toward the village. "Probably nothing at all. There are five black Mercedes SUVs down there, parked in a row." She frowned. "I find things that are out of place, guys, and that's out of place."

Bodie borrowed the glasses for a minute. "You're right. Doesn't mean they're anything to do with us. Still . . ." He explained what they could see over the comms. "High alert."

"You think Frizzbomb has any intention of letting us slip away?" Cassidy asked as they stood alone for a while.

Bodie blinked. He hadn't considered their inevitable confrontation with Heidi and the CIA when they eventually pushed hard to break from them. The nonstop ride had all but consumed him. "I guess we'll know better after we find Atlantis," he said. "We have to make a stand, maybe throw down an ultimatum. I hate being at somebody else's beck and call. She certainly didn't like being denied when you and I decided to finish the Pantera op. But we also have the Bratva to worry about. Keep your claws sharpened."

"My claws are always sharpened, Bodie. It's a necessity of my life."

"I prefer to keep all of my parts well oiled," he said, laughing.

"Is that because you're old?"

"No, bitch, it's because I like to keep my assets lubricated."

"Disgusting. So, shall we call you WD-Bodie?"

He broke away as Heidi wandered over. "Five minutes to the head of the mountain. You guys ready?"

"All greased up and sharpened to a wicked point." Cassidy grinned. "You?"

As they moved out, Bodie allowed himself brief thoughts of Pantera and the man's family. The Bratva were not just here in Morocco; they were international, and incredibly resourceful. He just hoped that the safe house where Pantera was now established was proving safe enough.

The terrain rose, becoming rockier as it framed the head of the mountain. This close, the features were hard to discern so Lucie waved her GPS. The team came together and walked around the final feature toward the mouth. Nobody expected the find to be easy; indeed, nobody even knew what they were looking for. A cave was Lucie's best guess. The good news was that, to date, Danel's directions had been flawless.

It became a far steeper climb now, making each member of the team struggle a little. The mouth was a large delve in the rock, and they could climb both inside and above it. Bodie saw only hard, ungiving, jagged rock, but it looked like they were alone, so he resolved to take his time in the search. The SEALs moved up and on top of the mouth, checking the terrain on the far side. Jemma and Lucie walked straight into the mouth, hopping over the lip. Gunn waited close by, studying every nook and cranny. Cross crouched, still aloof, and stared at the surfaces all around as if searching for a vein of gold.

"There's nothing here," Lucie said in disappointment.

Heidi nodded toward the disappearing SEALs. "I'm gonna join them. See what's over there."

Bodie nodded. "Might as well join you."

"Ahh, thanks."

"Sorry, didn't mean that to sound derogatory. Cassidy just reminded me that we're not really friends."

"I don't see any cuffs, Bodie."

"You don't? Look harder, although they do tend to tighten just after an op."

"You think I'm a threat? I'm flattered."

"Don't be. We fear your resources. Therein lies your ability to hunt and locate us. But arguing aside, Heidi, there must be an end to all this and we must be able to see it. You want trust? Start by being transparent and state a contract termination date."

"Whoa, that sounds official."

"It does? Good."

"Give me some time, Bodie."

"You have until the end of the mission."

Heidi glared ahead, focusing on the brow of the elevation. She set off at speed for their destination. When she finally reached the brow, she was surprised to see the three SEALs on their knees with pistols to their heads. They had been taken prisoner by three elegantly suited older gentlemen. Heidi reached for her weapon, but then two more well-heeled individuals waved at her from the right, popping up from behind a boulder. Bodie took it all in, his face registering shock.

How did they do that?

Quickly, it was made clear to them. One of the men pointed to an iPad screen—a view of the woman's mouth that showed Lucie and Jemma searching undergrowth, oblivious to the scrutiny. The men then gestured at three red dots that overlaid the screen, and one of them showed Bodie a black detonator box.

"Bombs," he whispered. "Now, shout to your friends or watch them die. We do not need all of you."

Two of the suits remained watching the SEALs. A third broke away to join the two nearby, one of whom held the tablet. Each removed a long-barreled gun. Heidi stayed silent and so did Bodie. The speaker nodded at one of his fellows.

A shot rang out. Bodie gasped as Foster's skull jerked to the left and blood gushed out. The body toppled, unmoving.

"Shout for them."

Of course, now there was no need, but Heidi called anyway to preserve the remaining SEALs' lives. As Lucie, Jemma, Gunn, Cross, and Cassidy came over the brow of the rise, the suited men watched calmly, keeping their weapons trained on the captives.

"Submit, or die," the speaker and apparent leader said. "We do not need all of you."

The warning was made even starker by the newly dead body sprawled out on the rocks. The team put up their hands. Cassidy dropped her gun. They were made to line up, two bodywidths apart, as three of the five men patted them down. The other men stayed well apart, one above and one below, with their odd pistols trained.

Bodie submitted to a thorough pat down and feel, but it was worse for the women. There was nothing personally immoral on the part of the men but they were exhaustive and they were rough. After an array of guns and knives and other objects had been confiscated, the two SEALs and seven members of the team were told to kneel with their hands on their heads.

Two suits behind, three in front. They were proficient.

The leader addressed them, his gun never wavering. "You may call me Zeus. We are the Evzones. Do not look for anyone else. We are but five, and five is all we have ever been. Chosen through the centuries. The Evzones are happy to be the five."

CHAPTER THIRTY-EIGHT

Cassidy shrugged her shoulders. "I have no clue what you're talking about." She swiveled her head. "Hey, you guys have any idea what this old hobo's smoking?"

"Hobo?" the man repeated in a thick accent that Bodie guessed was Russian. "We are five of the richest men in the world. Oligarchs, I think the West calls us."

An oligarch was one with immense wealth and substantial political clout, enough to rule countries, Bodie knew. What, then, were five oligarchs doing in Morocco, at the very top of Jebel Musa, if indeed that was what they were?

"So this is, what, a Russian snobs' road trip?" Bodie asked.

"And hey, thanks for being so forthcoming with the answers," Cassidy said.

Zeus laughed. "We would prefer to kill you right now, but that is out of the question until we know all that you know. But you will die soon enough. That, I promise you."

"We have to repair the damage you have done in your search for Atlantis," another said. "You will tell us everything you learned, all the trails you followed, so that we may sweep away this disturbance. Only then will we allow you to die."

"You guys really make it sound appealing," Heidi said, shifting her weight.

Zeus looked left and right, as if remembering where he was. "We should go. It will become crowded up here all too soon."

Bodie had been wondering what would happen next. It wasn't what he expected. All seven of them were tied together with rope that looped around their hands and waists, and ordered to walk away from the head of the mountain and down the other side. As he walked, Bodie was reminded of the guidebook boasting of this area's several hundred caves. They passed two entrances before being herded into one. At first, it appeared small and unremarkable, but a rear overhang led to a wider chamber and then a third.

At last, Zeus turned. "This will do."

"Not much of a secret base," Bodie said with a sniff as he looked around.

"It is a public cave, idiot, but it will do for now. Apollo, please make sure we're not disturbed."

"I understand you now," Bodie said. "You're billionaires who can't bring your resources to bear on Atlantis because it's your little secret. No goons. No HQ. No paper trails and definitely nothing digital, 'cause everything worth hacking's already been hacked. Even now, you're winging it. What's it all about? Does it bring purpose to your boring, pampered lives?" The Evzones reminded him of the Illuminati leaders they had encountered in their previous quest: single-minded, wealthy men with no care for society outside their own small circle. Men who influenced world events in all ways to accomplish personal aims.

"Purpose, you say?" Zeus looked genuinely surprised. "Since we were born, our single purpose was known to us. There *is* nothing else. Do you see?"

"My bad." Bodie shrugged. "I envisaged you with a shred of sanity."

Lucie spoke up, voice cracking. "Please, please don't antagonize them. Have you forgotten they killed Foster? Just give them what they want and let's get out of here."

Bodie didn't have the heart to answer, because answering Lucie meant he would have to tell the truth. They weren't getting out of here unless one of the SEALs made a goddamn move. He'd been distracting Zeus long enough.

It happened then. Hoff and Bass slipped their bonds and lunged. The rope around their waists pulled taut, but they'd been expecting that. Two Evzones drew their guns and fired, and two stepped back. The shots rang out in the narrow confines. Hoff dropped like a stone, shot through the head, and Bass collapsed to one knee, bleeding from the right cheek. Another shot finished him and then Zeus was shaking his head.

"You think we're stupid? You talk while the special forces men make ready? I anticipated moves like that before you were born. I haven't put a foot wrong since I was five. Do not insult me again."

Bodie closed his eyes, trying to shut away the image of the dead, bleeding men, the spatter on Cassidy and Gunn. Their best chance of escape had just been gunned down, and it seemed the leader of the Evzones was not just dangerous but crazy as well.

"Ares, Artemis, grab the first. Chain them up. I want to get started right away."

Bodie saw them lunging for Jemma.

"Now," Zeus said. "Where are my tools?"

CHAPTER THIRTY-NINE

Jemma lay prone on the hard slab of rock, staring up at the ceiling. Artemis pulled her boots and socks off, then sat her upright. Bodie saw what they were going to do—torture each one in front of the rest and not even pretend that the right information would get them released.

Quite the opposite. The SEALs lay where they had fallen. Bodie watched as Jemma was positioned so that her bare feet were over a shallow bowl of water.

Zeus reappeared, a yellow box in one hand, some coiled wire attached to metal plates in the other. "Right," he said without emotion. "The drill is very simple. Tell me everything you know about Atlântis. The research, the findings, the people you came across. Leave nothing out and this will soon be over."

Bodie tried to save Jemma and the situation. "Why can't you just walk away? You're billionaires, right? Are you so privileged that you can't see when you are wrong?"

Zeus regarded him. "Protecting Atlantis is our life's calling. Our resources allow us to monitor every snippet of information, and to know if anything threatens the secrets we keep. My father did it, and my grandfather before him. We revel in our mission. It *nourishes* us, provides purpose in a world that has grown cold and indifferent. I have seen many changes in my life, but nothing I see tells me that the world deserves to find Atlantis and its secrets."

"But should that be up to you?" Bodie asked.

"As I said, I am part of the Evzones. It is up to the five of us. This world, the state it is in right now, would take Atlantis's technology, its advancements, and then destroy itself. Our mission is to prevent that from happening."

Bodie disagreed. "Five men? Five oligarchs deciding the world's future. How do you know we wouldn't benefit from new innovations?"

"Because of terrorism, and why it happens. Because of oil. Because of nuclear weapons and the greed of politicians. Because of global warming. Because of the world water crisis. And because of a small group of fighters called ISIS who, from a standing start, overran the sovereignty of nation-states."

"You're saying we could self-destruct at any moment." Bodie understood the man.

"Yes, and if the secrets of Atlantis added fuel to that already raging fire . . ." Zeus let it hang because he didn't need to go on.

Artemis lit a torch and placed it firmly inside a hole in the wall. Then he crossed to the other sides of the cave and repeated the act, illuminating their surroundings and their faces in an eerie, flickering orange light. Bodie half expected him to pull on a mask, but then remembered this was no Illuminati ritual. This wasn't a cult. Just a privileged few, selected by an odd birthright to join the world's most secret private club.

Zeus rattled the yellow box in Jemma's face. "Defib," he said. "We can tune it up to five hundred volts, but we'll start lower just to give you a taste. We don't want your heart giving out too soon."

Jemma's eyes went wide, a tear forced out of one. Zeus saw it and smiled. "Good, good. We have an understanding. And yes, I'm aware the cave doesn't have electricity, but my toy is fully charged and will last through three of you, maybe four. After that we'll have to improvise."

Jemma opened her mouth, but no words came out. Bodie spoke for her. "You don't have to hurt her. We'll talk."

"Of course you will. But how can I be sure it's the truth. Pain will reveal the truth. Pain is the great leveler. Now, put your feet here. Hermes, shoot her if she does not comply."

Jemma complied, placing her feet in the bowl. Zeus turned on the defib, placed it carefully on the ground, and unwound the paddles.

"Start talking." He held the paddles apart threateningly.

Bodie couldn't help himself, and rose to her aid. A gunshot rang out, the bullet skidding off the rock floor to his side, making him pause. There was a chance, then; these men wanted answers first, not to kill them outright. If they rushed in, some of them might live. But several would die.

Better some than all.

The same dilemma he'd faced during the hunt for the Statue of Zeus.

Jemma spoke rapidly, telling everything she knew. By the time she was finished, she was breathing heavily, mostly from stress, but it was then that Zeus hit her with the first electrical charge. Jemma screamed, stiffened, and whipped her head to the side. Zeus held the paddles to her chest for a few seconds and then pulled them away. Jemma went limp. Bodie felt pain in his own heart.

She looked up, her face twisted. Zeus smiled as he hit her again, this time for longer. Jemma thrashed and grunted in agony. Zeus signaled Artemis to ready the next person.

"Her." He pointed at Heidi.

"She told you everything," Bodie said. "Please."

Zeus didn't let Jemma rest, just jammed the paddle over her chest for a third time. Once that was done, he leaned in close to her right ear.

"Anything else you want to tell me?"

Jemma could barely move, let alone talk. Spittle flew from her mouth. Artemis hooked his arms under her shoulders and dragged her off the rocky perch, throwing her untidily in a corner of the cave. Zeus gave her a cursory glance.

"Weak."

Something occurred to Bodie right then. They were so far out of their depth here that he couldn't even see the surface anymore. They were thieves, used to clandestine planning and furtive operations. Human contact was generally considered bad form, and remained at a minimum. Even so, he knew what he *should* be doing to salvage their situation: Gauging the distance to the corner where Artemis had stashed their weapons. Slowing this whole session down. Attempting to galvanize the others into a concerted effort. And much more.

"So, *what* do you do exactly?" he tried.

Zeus loved to talk. He switched off the defib to save the battery and watched Artemis pluck Heidi out of the lineup. "The Evzones," he said, "are tasked with using any and all methods to keep outsiders at bay. We will totally eradicate any line of enquiry that may lead to the truth about Atlantis." He shrugged. "In *any* way. The options are endless."

Bodie saw the glee on his face and knew these men were more than guardians. They enjoyed every second of what they did to safeguard Atlantis. He saw Heidi struggling against Artemis and tried in vain to quell a sudden upwelling of fear for her safety. He didn't like to think where it was coming from.

Heidi fought, hampered by the ropes that bound her. The suited man dragged her to the center of the room and removed a cattle prod from Zeus's bag. Heidi focused on the tip and moved away. Artemis waved the prod in the direction of the stone plinth.

"And what is the truth?" Bodie prolonged it.

"Atlantis," Zeus said simply. "And all its varied wonders. That is the only truth that matters."

Heidi sat heavily. Artemis knelt to take her boots off and received a full-on kick to the face. The man reeled, holding his nose. Zeus darted in, picking up the cattle prod before Heidi could lever herself off the perch. The remaining two men didn't move, never once letting their aim waver. Bodie cursed inwardly, knowing their lives depended on distracting them.

Zeus jammed the prod into Heidi's stomach. The CIA agent folded, wailed. He kept it there until Artemis returned and wrenched off her boots as she tried to recover.

"Tell us what you know," Zeus said.

"What she said." Heidi nodded at the still face-down Jemma. "We've been together the whole time."

"Who at the CIA knows what you know?"

Heidi grimaced. *So,* Bodie thought, *they know exactly who the team is, not just faces.* He watched as Heidi bit her lip before he looked over at the rest of the crew.

"Just my boss, I guess," she said. "But I haven't spoken to him since the Swiss Alps. Not properly."

"The compass came from the Swiss Alps," Zeus confirmed. "He knows about the compass?"

Without warning, he pushed the paddles against Heidi and watched her suffer. Three times more he did it, and then dragged her away. They picked Cross next, and the older thief hung his head, dejected, preferring to remain in a world that was all his own.

Bodie silently implored Cross to get it together. He could be such a huge asset, and had been Bodie's rock for so long. The loss of Cross's input since Yasmine appeared on the scene had become a physical pain for Bodie.

The torches flickered in response to a slight breeze. Long shadows were thrown over the scene, and Bodie saw denizens of hell standing over his team, death in their hands. The ropes weren't too tight and he loosened his wrists as best he could. Through simple deduction he'd narrowed his attack to one man—the member of the Evzones he could reach most easily, the one standing three meters in front of him. That long-barreled pistol surely weighed a little more by now, that tensed arm surely ready to drop. Cassidy, beside him in the line, had already whispered she would cover his attack and distract the man watching their backs.

Distract?

She meant get shot, for that was what they both knew would happen. If there was any other way out of this, Bodie couldn't see it.

Cross ignored Zeus, looking instead to the exit of the cave and toward Jemma and Heidi, huddled together. The defibrillator buzzed and the charge went through his body. Cross writhed as much as the women had, pain etched into every contour of his face, but he spoke not once, didn't even favor Zeus with a single glance. He couldn't stop himself from hyperventilating, though, and then clutching his chest as he went rigid with agony. Bodie clenched his fists and teeth, terrified his friend was having a heart attack, brow suddenly wet with anxious sweat, a stark desperation filling his brain.

Cross relaxed a moment later, falling back onto the slab and breathing easily. His limbs moved weakly and he managed to open his eyes. "Just a twinge," he said in a defiant voice.

"Good." Zeus nodded, indicating that Artemis should throw him away. "The little bag of tricks will open him up a bit more later."

Gunn was next, and the young nerd looked so scared that even Cassidy spoke up for him.

"There's nothing else," she said. "Take a goddamn break, asshole."

The defib whirred to life but died, battery depleted. Zeus looked disappointed and then smiled with a deep malevolence.

"It appears we're on to the manual tools."

CHAPTER FORTY

"The history of Atlantis," Zeus said. "What do you know?"

Gunn stammered a reply, but nothing intelligible came out. Bodie guessed Zeus was asking the question of the team nerd because he might have carried out internet research, which would have as much fantasy wound through it as fact. That left Lucie next, of course, who would know the investigated background to everything. Bodie determined that he could not let them get to Lucie. It would be worse for her.

Zeus started with a box cutter, waving the tiny blade before Gunn's terrified eyes. "What do you know?"

"Destroyed by . . . by an earthquake or tsunami. Maybe by . . . by the Great Flood. Huge, a continent that joined Europe to the Americas. An active volcanic area still runs between the Canaries and Ireland, which would intersect Atlantis perfectly. Deep soundings were made by the US, the UK, and Germany separately, which mapped the bottom of the Atlantic and showed a large elevation reaching from Britain to South America and then to Africa. It rises nine thousand feet above the immense sea depths around it and reaches the surface around the Azores. And, taking the recent proof found in the Nebraska badlands that the horse originated in America, how . . . how did this wild animal cross to Europe and Asia in this predomesticated state? Answer: he walked." Gunn gulped. "Or trotted, or something."

The computer expert had gotten carried away, rambling because he was nervous. But then he saw Zeus's blade and clammed up in fear.

"Go on." Zeus nodded with approval. "Everything you say is a matter of record, free on the web, but I need to hear the conclusions a man like you would draw."

Bodie had hoped Gunn would drag it out, and, purposely or not, he did. "The animal thing is not reserved just for horses. Camel fossils were found as far apart as Kansas and Africa. Norway elks are identical to the American moose. And so forth. The same species of plants exist in America and Asia. And, of course, there is the banana. A seedless plant. It can't survive a voyage through a temperate zone, and yet traveled from tropical Asia and Africa to America . . ." He paused as Heidi shifted in the corner, turning and resting on her knees. For now, Bodie saw her head did not come up, but he guessed she was ready.

Zeus was pleased with Gunn. "Go on, lad."

"There's the question of the Aryan race, which we haven't come to yet. I examined the information in advance. According to Genesis, all the races that escaped the flood with Noah, the Thracians, the Cyprians, the Ionians, and more, are all now recognized as Aryans. The center of the Aryan migrations is Armenia, in which lies Mount Ararat where the Ark rested. The Mediterranean Aryans are known to have been a sea people some four thousand years ago. Their faces are painted on Egyptian monuments. The Greeks trace their descendants back to the Aryans, and everyone—Persians, Celts, Germans, and Romans—shares the same traditions. Of course, all this is relevant because the Aryans are long thought to have been a *superior* race—more intelligent, stronger, better. The Atlanteans who survived would be identified as *better.* It was Hitler and Himmler who searched for a decade for any remnants of the Aryan race, using an SS unit by the name of Ahnenerbe, which only came to light in 1945 when soldiers discovered many thousands of documents in a cave in Germany."

"But no real trace of the Aryans?" Zeus asked.

"They found nothing, but Hitler was beyond crazy. He thought measuring the circumference of a man's skull would determine his race."

"Fascinating. Now . . . how high can you scream?"

Zeus buried the tiny blade into Gunn's thigh. Screaming, Gunn threw his head back. Zeus withdrew and buried it again. Two small but vicious cuts welled with blood.

Gunn squealed, kicking furiously. Zeus avoided the reflexive strikes and gave an evil leer. Blood leaked through Gunn's jeans in small beads. Bodie could wait no more. He eyed the man in front, then nodded at Cassidy.

"See you on the other side."

"Yeah, wherever that is."

Together, they both knew that they had no choice but to risk their lives for their friends.

CHAPTER FORTY-ONE

Bodie had been stretching his legs in anticipation, feigning a cramp a few minutes earlier, so when he lunged, his limbs responded instantly. The guard in front of him—Hermes—was watching Gunn striking out at their revered leader; his gun was dipping, and Bodie covered half the distance without being noticed. When Hermes saw the resolute blur streaking toward him and started to react, Bodie flung the grit and gravel and dust he'd scooped up right into the other man's eyes. It wasn't much but it did the trick.

Hermes flinched away from the cloud, stumbling backward. Bodie tackled him at the waist, bearing him to the ground. Both men struck with a crunch of flesh and bone, winded.

Cassidy used both Gunn's and Bodie's actions to cover her leap at Ares. She jumped and then dropped and kicked out, leading leg striking Ares's shins. The tall man cried out in pain, dropping to his knees, but it wasn't that simple for Cassidy.

Falling, he leveled the gun at her head and fired.

Lucie pushed her aside, seeing what was about to happen. The bullet passed millimeters above them, but there was no coming back from the tangled mass they ended up in on the floor. Ares staggered up, with the gun still aimed.

On the floor, Bodie gasped for air. To his left, Gunn kicked out at Zeus from his position on the slab of stone. Heidi, close to Bodie, was trying to gain her feet, her equilibrium at odds. Jemma still sat in the corner, out of it, while Cross crawled toward Zeus, a look of grim determination on his face. Despite what he had been through, he was not about to give up.

Bodie rolled toward Hermes, who battered him with the butt of his gun. Bodie took a blow on the bridge of the nose and saw stars. When his sight cleared, the first thing that came into focus was the metal barrel, the evil face behind it.

"I do believe I'll enjoy this."

"Wait, wait, you haven't tortured me yet."

"By your smart mouth I'm guessing you were dragged up rather than properly educated. We'll see how the class system works in the next few seconds."

"So this is all about class system? You believe you're better than everyone else on the planet because you were chosen to protect a myth?"

Hermes frowned as if listening to the inconceivable. "Of *course* we're better."

The moment was over. Bodie knew that their attempted coup had been doomed from the start. He looked around the room. Cassidy was on her knees, hands on her head, as one of the Evzones trained his weapon on her. Gunn was on his back, having been taken out by another. And Cross could barely stand. The Evzones remained confident. Bodie wondered if this was it: the end for him and his relic hunters.

There was movement, a scuffle at the mouth of the cave. Bodie saw several bodies entering, which ruled out it being Apollo. From his position crouched on the floor he suddenly felt shock and awe, and fear, as the bald Bratva man, Yasmine, and several other figures dashed inside. Their guns were drawn.

"Get down!"

It was Yasmine's voice. Bodie echoed her words for the benefit of the rest of the team. Then he flattened himself as fast as he could.

Gunfire resounded from wall to wall, deafening reports that scrambled their thoughts. Bodie saw muzzle flashes, figures falling, leaking blood. He scrambled over the fallen Hermes, making sure the suited man had taken his last breath. As he did so, Bodie shook his head at the idea that he and the Bratva were now working toward a common goal. Two of the Bratva were down. Bodie twisted Hermes's gun free of the dead man's grip, and checked on Zeus, Ares, and Artemis.

Artemis was dead, blood flowing from a head wound. Heidi sheltered behind his body with Jemma and Cross, but they were dangerously exposed. Zeus had ducked behind the stone plinth, pulling Gunn down too. Ares had initially stood his ground—the superior entity—but a bullet to the shoulder had convinced him to take the low road. When he ducked he didn't reckon on Cassidy's boot in his face, or his nose exploding all over her sole.

His shout filled the cave. Cassidy descended like an avenging angel, battering him into unconsciousness and taking his weapon.

Which left just one of the Evzones standing—Zeus.

Bodie saw Yasmine and the bald Bratva soldier converging on the plinth from both sides. He saw Cassidy creeping up too and lent his own weight to the endeavor. Gunn was the major concern; they could see his legs sticking out from behind the plinth. They couldn't see Zeus.

"Give it up," Bodie shouted. "Your cronies are all dead, pal."

In a flurry of movement, Zeus shot to his feet, dragging a protesting Gunn with him. The weapon was leveled at the young man's head, and Zeus was dripping blood from a shallow arm wound. His expression was feral, at the very edge of sanity. Fingers paused on a hair trigger all around the cave.

"I go free. He lives," Zeus growled. "That is the deal. And I'll never let you near Atlantis. You'll die first."

Bodie didn't ask anyone's approval. "Run then, piggy. We'll catch you later."

But Zeus dragged Gunn to the back of the cave. Gunn grimaced in pain, right leg limp, the wounds already clotted, but still clearly painful. For the first time since her ordeal, Jemma regained her composure and tried to stand.

Zeus pointed the gun at them and then back at his captive. He fired quickly, three shots, threw Gunn's body at them, and spun toward what Bodie had thought was a solid wall. In a split second, he saw Heidi lining a gun up on Zeus, and Gunn collapsing to the floor. Cursing the choices, he let Gunn fall and bellowed at Heidi.

"No! Let him go."

Confusion swept her face, but she paused with her finger on the trigger.

"Thief's choice," he said. "Always think 'sneaky.'"

"I'm okay," Gunn gasped, leaning on his leg to test the pain levels. "He missed me on purpose, I think."

The shots were a distraction, then. Cassidy ran past and carefully surveyed the back of the cave. "Another way out." She peered inside. "Hidden behind this outcropping. Do we go after him?"

"Leave him for now," Bodie said, keeping the plan he had started to form to himself. It wouldn't do to explain it all now, but he'd noticed Zeus's blood on the floor of the cave. A potential trail to find the madman. "Too many of us need medical attention."

And the Bratva want something too.

"We don't have time," Jemma said. Lucie nodded, taking up the thread.

"That man will destroy the evidence. It is all he has left. We never found the cave on Jebel Musa which will take us to the next clue, but it has to be there. If we tarry . . . we lose."

"I'm not dragging badly injured friends into another confrontation," Bodie said. "No discussion. But we're not done yet."

Yasmine approached him, and he became aware of the size of the Bratva crew now—six strong—standing with their weapons lowered and faces expectant. "We have a medic," she said. "Right here." She indicated a young man with an earnest face. "Field trained. He's an army deserter, but that's another story. He can patch your people."

Bodie stared between them, torn. Why the hell did Yasmine keep on saving them? Even now, why offer her help? And Viktor, her boss. Had he promoted her for a specific reason? But there was no time to ponder the mysteries of their new Bratva friends. Zeus was escaping and Lucie was right—he would rather destroy Atlantis than let it be discovered.

"Okay," he said. "You saved our lives, so I'll take it on merit that your man's not a quack. I don't like it, but Lucie and Jemma are right." He stared at Heidi. "If you still want Atlantis, we have to stay in the middle of this."

"After all we've gone through?" Heidi groaned. "Yeah, I still want it."

"I want that bastard's balls too," Cassidy said. "For what he tried to do to my team."

"Get in line." Jemma limped gingerly across the floor. "Finding Atlantis will be a poor second compared to finding Zeus."

"Didn't we already do that?" Gunn tried to inject a measure of humor as the young medic looked at his wounds.

"Very droll," Bodie said. "Look, I'm fine, but everyone else get checked out." He turned to Yasmine and the bald man. "We need to talk."

CHAPTER FORTY-TWO

Can I trust the Bratva? No, but I do trust Yasmine. Maybe she helped them because of Cross, a way she could make up for the mistakes of her past. He had to believe she wouldn't betray Cross and that the trust he placed in her was well founded. Bodie was speculating, but couldn't think of any other reason.

Bodie listened to them speak and assumed they were wondering the same thing about him. The situation they found themselves in was based on mutual faith and hope, and a whole lot of supposition.

"I took one tracker off Eli, and Hakim planted another on your Cassidy." Yasmine shrugged. "Distraction. Smoke and mirrors. It is Spy Craft 101."

Bodie winced at that. "Not entirely our fault, love."

"Maybe. But professionalism is everything in our business."

She was right, he knew. Cross should have stayed in the game rather than wallow in lifetimes lost. God knows, Bodie himself had a plethora of great memories that would allow him to do just that. Right now, though, those old memories were solidifying his love for this team.

"I'm not sure we can trust you," Bodie said.

Yasmine smoothed down her midnight-black hair. "Of course. But we have goals that, for now, outweigh HQ's orders, at least in the minds of Viktor and Lucien, and we have similar numbers."

"Speaking of goals—what is your ultimate goal?"

"You mean, will we try to steal the discovery from underneath you? I would obviously ask you the same."

Bodie knew this was going nowhere. "You need us," he said, "to solve the clues. You lost men saving us. I'm not so sure we need you."

Yasmine shrugged. "Viktor is the head of an incredible worldwide criminal organization that can call on thousands of members. The best thing you could do is kill him."

Bodie agreed, and was surprised at the candidness, especially in the light of recent developments concerning Pantera, himself, and the Bratva.

"We should share," Yasmine said, "in the glory of finding Atlantis."

"How is that even possible?"

She pushed him hard then, right in the chest. Bodie staggered in shock. It was the last thing he had been expecting. The bald man held him up and laughed raucously. As this was going on Yasmine leaned in and whispered rapidly into Bodie's ear.

"Because . . . this beautiful bald man and I are Interpol agents, and with Lucien's help we intend to bring Viktor to justice, to destroy his businesses and incarcerate his crew. We're on your side. We've been *inside* for years and are close," she breathed. "So close."

It was good the bald man was holding him, for Bodie suddenly felt limp. Shock coursed through his system. *Yasmine was . . . what?* Shit, Cross would have a seizure.

Was that why she abandoned him all those years ago? Because she was an Interpol agent? It drew a few parallels to Heidi's issues with her own family.

He spun away before the others reacted. Just in time, as Cassidy was headed over. "We all good here? Playing nice?"

Bodie nodded. "Yasmine and . . . umm . . ."

"Hakim," the bald man said.

"*Hakim* . . . were just convincing me of their sincerity. And wow, they're pretty good at it."

Bodie stared at them. Yasmine betrayed the most emotion, no doubt scared he would reveal their secret, but Hakim stayed impassive, watching everything, including his own comrades. Bodie wondered what kind of enduring state of mind it would take for somebody to remain in the lion's den for so long. Of course, all he had so far was their word, but perhaps Heidi could make some covert inquiries.

He nodded. "We'll do this together."

Yasmine looked relieved.

Gunn stood up and tested the weight on his damaged leg. All seemed well. Bodie would never say it aloud, but if Gunn wasn't complaining about a wound, then it sure as hell couldn't hurt worse than a scratch.

Only twenty minutes had passed since Zeus had escaped. The Bratva started to file out of the cave, no doubt to secure the perimeter. Yasmine had already told Bodie that they took care of Apollo earlier.

"Jebel Musa," Jemma said. "Luckily, it's not far."

Bodie laughed, buoyed by her quick recovery from Zeus's shock treatment, but didn't kid himself. It would be superficial in the short run and she might need a ton of help. He'd keep her busy for a while. Outside, they found a windy, overcast afternoon belied by a lowering sun that glittered across the ocean. Jebel Musa was a short hike, but the large group took their time, some still sore and hurt, others just gauging their new companions. It was an odd group that came once again to the mountain top and stood staring down into the Dead Woman's mouth.

Bodie shrugged off the sick feeling he harbored for all the men they had lost. Grieving would come later, and the same for the Moroccan Bratva. Drawing in a long breath, he studied the terrain below.

"For an area full of caves," he said, "I don't see many, but we have to rule this out first, I guess."

"Right, well." Lucie sat down among the rocks and made sure her laptop was connected with a good signal. "I've already done all the hard work. As you know, this place is a honeycomb of caves, which means there are always new ones waiting to be found. New passages. Ask any caver. Where there's no real published literature that helps, there is a little information on caving blogs. Experienced men and women and old-timers have weighed in on a local thread and, if you compare topographical and geographical maps, we can identify a couple of likely areas for unexplored caves. Right there"—she pointed—"is a sinkhole, and over there another, but it is easy to pass a cave entrance—a small pit or brush hole for instance—and not see it. We need as many people as possible to search, but . . ." She paused. "I don't think this is it."

Bodie blinked. "Why?"

"Too easy. Surely somebody would have stumbled across it by now. If you want my opinion, we should locate the cave closest to the GPS coordinates and search for a new passage."

Bodie agreed, but the consensus was to search the area. They toiled for half an hour, coming up with nothing, knowing with every passing moment that Zeus was a little closer to implementing his plan. In the end, though, the answer was easy. Jemma pointed it out.

"We follow the damn clue," she said, "that Danel left for us. Instead of second-guessing and backtracking."

Bodie nodded. "It's as I thought."

They found the closest cave network and immediately felt dumb. It left them back at the cave they'd vacated a half hour ago, and when they searched harder, painstakingly probing the tunnel that Zeus had taken, they found one more dark offshoot toward the end. But they weren't superheroes. They were fallible and therefore needed to cover every eventuality. Bodie found, if he was being honest, that the path they traveled was standard enough. Nothing out of the ordinary. They had no way of knowing if they'd found the right tributary, but the direction followed Danel's celestial coordinates more closely than any other route appeared to.

And they found spots of blood on the floor. This was the sneakier way of finding Zeus that Bodie had imagined, and was now their last hope of catching the madman. Zeus was intent on derailing all their efforts. Where would he flee to?

They spurred themselves on, ramping up the speed. Tunnel after tunnel and chamber after chamber passed until Jemma voiced the concern that they should be looking at finding some serious caving equipment. A few spots of blood here and there gave them hope that they were following the right track. Bodie smiled when Heidi congratulated him on letting Zeus go.

"It's how my mind works," he said. "Slyly."

"I knew there was a reason we tamed a thief."

Hours later they stopped, weary to the bone, hungry and thirsty. Bodie perched on an outcropping of rock, simply longing for a soft bed, any bed. Just somewhere to lay his head. Everyone shared his exhausted look, and Jemma mentioned again that they needed equipment and supplies.

The thought of retracing their steps—twice—to get back to this very point spurred them on once more. They did have a small amount of water and shared three chocolate bars among them. Bodie nodded at Zeus's latest blood trail.

"It's getting fresher."

"We aren't far behind that bastard now." Gunn alternated between limping and striding, but still gamely hung in alongside Cross. The older man looked like he wanted to speak to Yasmine, but she didn't look his way.

Eventually Cross forced the confrontation by moving to her side, despite Hakim's glare. "You're going to have to talk to me sometime, Yasmine."

"Not yet, Eli. Danger is . . . everywhere."

Cross was no stranger to hidden signals. He waited until he could pull her to the front of the group, away from the rest of the Bratva and close to Bodie. "I thought my world was made up of two people," he said, "before you left."

"Truly, I saved your damn hide. The cops knew all about you. They were ready to descend, until I fed them better, more significant prey and diverted their attentions. *That's why I left, Eli.* To protect you."

Cross was speechless for several seconds, then said quietly, "And you couldn't come back?"

"That was impossible. I'm a cop. I work for Interpol now." Her voice was so low Cross had to strain to hear it. Bodie moved behind them to make some noise, to help.

"The love of my life . . ." Cross sounded bereft. "My enemy. Did you pretend to love me . . . to catch me?" His throat sounded like a mixture of gravel and knives were caught up in it.

"I never stopped loving you, Eli. Not once. My feelings ran so deep, conflicting with everything I did, everything I stood for. If you had found me . . ."

Cross glanced over at her. "What?"

"I'd have changed everything for you."

Tears formed at the corner of Cross's eyes. The thief looked away, but Bodie saw it. He felt deeply for the man, even more so because Cross was his immovable rock, the mainstay he relied on. Now, though, he saw an imperfect, human side to him.

After another twenty minutes of walking, following a gentle descent, they turned a sharp corner, astounded at the size of the chamber that suddenly lay before them.

A wide stream ran through the middle of it, flowing so quickly it lapped up and over the edges and onto the cave floor. The ceiling arched high above, lost in darkness. The far side was over ten meters away and lit only because a madman stood there, holding a flaming torch in each hand.

"Gunpowder," Zeus shouted. "Who do you think invented it? The Chinese? No, it was invented far, far earlier than that."

Bodie pulled up short, wondering what the hell was going on. "Thanks are in order," he called back. "We'd never have found this place without you. Well, not this week, anyway."

"Is that what you think?" Zeus all but cackled. "That I led you here like a witless oaf?"

The team walked closer, approaching the stream and the chamber's halfway point. Some of the detail behind Zeus came into sharper focus. The incredible wall was covered in some kind of extensive bas-relief or mural, the depictions of kings or gods—possibly Zeus himself, among the other names that the Evzones had taken for themselves from this very chamber. Five in all.

"I let you come all this way to show you how close you came . . . but still lost. We are sworn by our birthright to protect this secret at all costs."

Constellations filled the upraised hands depicted in the mural. A map of the stars. Bodie saw a trail within a trail . . .

Zeus brandished the flaming torches, sending the representation into blackness and flitting shadow. Heidi nudged Bodie on his right hip. "Umm, look at his feet."

What the . . .

A trail of black powder surrounded Zeus and then led in a sweeping curve to the edge of the stream. Bodie realized he'd been distracted by the leader and hadn't properly assessed his surroundings.

"Is that . . . a barrel?"

"Yeah," Heidi said. "Four, actually. Four barrels of real gunpowder."

"Fuck."

The team shone their meager lights on the barrels, gauging size and distance. Zeus read their minds.

"Don't worry," he cried out. "There's enough fire to cleanse the entire chamber and everyone in it."

"My friend." Yasmine stepped forward, speaking gently. "You do not have to do this."

Zeus glowered at her. "Of course not, but I *want* to. I was born to make this decision *for* you. My station in life demands it."

Bodie gritted his teeth, holding back the retort, which was a decidedly *lower-class* curse. In the end, though, he could see only one real option. Before Zeus blew it all to hell, they had to get a look at that frieze.

"You won," he said, feeding the man's ego. "Fair and square. You beat all of us."

Zeus's chest expanded and the smug smile flourished as he reveled in his apparent victory.

"But I wonder, since we're all now at your mercy . . . what is so mind-blowing that you would give your life to protect it?"

Zeus raised the torches without pause, illuminating the frieze. "The five great kings of Atlantis later became the gods of lower beings like yourselves. The Greeks. The Phoenicians. Their gods were based on real men. Remnants like this—cave paintings, petroglyphs—helped to cement that belief, fashion the faith. The ignorant Greeks thought those who came before worshipped these figures, not that they were familiar to them. Do you see? Atlantis and its secrets were so extraordinary that their lords became our gods. They were years ahead of where we are now, and we can't allow anyone to gain access to that."

Jemma, Gunn, and one of the Bratva had taken advantage of Zeus's distraction with his own prideful revelations to take a few photos of the mural. Bodie thought it was sound and quick thinking, given what may happen. The whole group drifted closer to the fast-flowing stream, though Bodie harbored intense reservations.

Zeus suddenly seemed to realize that something was wrong, turning his attention away from the cave wall and back to them. The fire surely had to be blinding to his eyes, and Bodie assumed the man's vision was limited. A gunshot would send Zeus flying and ignite the powder. Waiting would only lead to the same outcome, as would an attempted retreat.

"Shall we get on with this?" Cassidy hissed. "I'm super tired of listening to this asshole."

And there it was—the spark to the touch paper that controlled their situation. Zeus yelled something unintelligible and threw the torches to the ground. Bodie saw a sacrificial inferno leap up around the man as two sparking trails of fire streamed toward the waiting barrels.

Everyone leapt into the stream, immersing their bodies in the rushing waters. Sometimes, privileged men and women were just too arrogant and blind to realize their well-laid plans and opinions might be slightly askew. Bodie turned over in the stream, eyes narrowed against the water, and saw a blazing conflagration pass right over him. In his bones, the depths of his body, and the bedrock all around, he felt the percussive *whump* as the barrels exploded. Fire rolled across his vision, surging, undulating, taking everything that lay before it. Debris fell on and alongside him, shards of timber and rock. The furnace lasted many seconds. Bodie felt a lifetime pass before his eyes, from those glory days of youth to the friends that surrounded him now—and in those moments he experienced a startling revelation.

Here, now, immersed in this stream, surrounded by fire—*I'm where I should be. It feels right.*

The flames died away; the debris stopped falling, at least for now. Bodie rose from the stream, expecting anything. The sight that met his eyes was a sobering one.

Zeus's burning body, dead and sitting on its knees, now deceased to protect a birthright, having remained loyal to the colleagues who had perished before him. The corpse's muscles had contracted in the fire, and now the limbs appeared to be clawing at Bodie in a defensive posture.

Bodie then stared beyond the nightmarish image of Zeus to the wall they had traveled so far to see. He couldn't help but step forward, feet dragging through sodden timbers and still flickering remnants. The barrels Zeus had positioned beside the frieze had done most of their work, destroying a good portion of the detail on the outer rock face, but not all. Bodie could see three upraised arms, constellations scattering from them like celestial spray. A faint line joined several constellations, the path to Atlantis. Ares's head was still intact, as well as portions of the gods' bodies. Even as he watched, Bodie saw a part of the ancient depiction crumble away.

"Madman," Hakim growled.

"The world is full of them," Bodie agreed. "Is everyone okay?"

The only grumbling came from Gunn, whose leg now throbbed despite the medic's earlier attentions, and Cassidy, who claimed she'd swallowed half the stream. They took a few moments to photograph what remained and check the cave for more petroglyphs or hidden passageways. The Bratva verified that their exit tunnel was intact, and then they were heading back up to the surface, evidence in hand, aware that they now possessed a potential map to the lost city of Atlantis and all the ancient knowledge and wonders it might yet contain.

CHAPTER FORTY-THREE

Two Sikorsky helicopters thundered through the dawn, rotors black against the rising blush of daylight. Beneath, the enormous breadth of the Atlantic Ocean rolled and swelled, dangerous waters as far as the eye could see.

The only speck on the horizon grew larger as they came nearer—a battered research vessel called the RV *Philias* out of Greece, which had been retasked and directed to a particular set of coordinates.

Lucie had followed the celestial map that outlined the Dolphin Ridge, which the US ship *Challenger* had mapped out many years before. Using deep-sea sounding, the *Challenger* found an Atlantic plateau rising nine thousand feet above the incredible depths around it. When this plateau proved to be one thousand miles in width and three thousand miles long, the community still did not recognize this Atlantis-shaped, immersed land right where Plato said it would be. Within this elevated ridge lay several trenches, some deep, some narrow. The celestial map pointed them toward something called the Atlantean Trench.

Follow the coordinates, Bodie thought. That was all they had to do. Lucie had put to bed any further skepticism by finding an assertion in *Scientific American* that the mountains and valleys of the plateau's surface could not have been formed underwater but had to have been fashioned by elements scouring the land *above water.* And to explain the travel of plants, animals, and races between continents, connecting ridges were found, whereupon great journeys between continents could be made.

All of this was moot to Bodie, and to most of the rest of the team. And in particular, the Bratva. Zeus and his cronies had already persuaded them that *something* existed. All they had to do now was find it.

Bodie surveyed the seas and the skies. *As clear as a mirrored surface.* Such tranquility did not lull him into dropping his guard, and he noticed Cassidy scanning the terrain too. Despite the fact that the Bratva were with them, it was perfectly possible for another enemy to appear—more Chinese, or perhaps some new foe whose curiosity had been piqued by the discovery of the statues.

Bodie didn't trust the Bratva's intentions. Yasmine and Hakim had their own agenda, and Atlantis was understandably not their priority. A reckoning was definitely coming, especially as Bodie didn't remember Viktor Davydov being agreeable in any way. Then there was the mysterious Lucien, the big boss, who apparently knew about Yasmine's infiltration and was helping her.

The research ship's impressive size became more apparent as the choppers glided toward it. The landing was hard, skids bouncing multiple times off the metal deck. After disembarking, Bodie found the ship's captain and some of the crew gathered at the side, staring suspiciously at them. The wind bit strongly, sharp and cold and unwarmed by the blossoming sun.

"The vessel is ready," someone said with a heavy accent. "You follow me."

The "vessel" turned out to be a submersible, an odd hunk of metal that looked even older and more battered than the ship. The team eyed it suspiciously.

"You're kidding me, right?" Cassidy grumbled.

"*How* far down are we going in this thing?" Gunn asked.

A man came up to them, short, stocky, and with a face seemingly carved by the wildest winds. "My name is Alec, and I am the pilot," he said in practiced English. "We have been told to assist you. But this is *my* vessel, my baby. Yes, it is old. Yes, it is fragile. So you treat her with respect because, believe me, you really do not want to break her."

"Understood." Heidi came forward and reached out to shake the man's hand. "How many can she hold?"

Alec didn't even acknowledge the hand. "Listen to me. There are no parachutes. No flight attendants. Just one captain. We put a foot wrong down there and we die. You may have your mission," he said, shaking his head, "but that does not mean you are in charge."

"We get it," Heidi shot back. "You don't like us being here. You don't like us commandeering your boat. Tough. Get over it. And don't worry, I have no intention of overriding an expert in his own field."

Alec, looking somewhat mollified, gestured for them to follow along the ship's top rail. Bodie fell in line, ignoring the crew and heading toward the submersible, a dirty, great oblong bulk of metal and tubes. Alec paused, staring over their heads at the ship's captain.

"Anything?"

Bodie heard a negative answer. Maybe they were appealing to call it off. He wondered if they should at least explain their mission to the pilot. The boat rolled and creaked; the submersible reverberated even standing still. Heidi ignored the wind as it whipped ineffectually at her curls.

"Problem?"

Alec glared at her. "No. No problem. But I need to know which three are coming, and what you are looking for."

Heidi shook her head. "Not a chance, man. But I *do* know who will accompany you."

Bodie couldn't help feeling an icy thrill as she spoke his name along with Cassidy's and Jemma's. He waited a beat, then reached out a hand to Heidi's shoulder.

"You're staying behind?"

Heidi grinned. "Are you kidding? Of course I'm staying behind. The Devil himself wouldn't get me inside that deathtrap."

"Ah, thanks." Bodie nodded. "We're expendable, you're not. Good pep talk."

"It is one of my fortes."

"This arrangement between us," he said. "It ends very soon."

Bodie followed instructions all the way. They climbed a ladder and lowered themselves through a circular hatch, then descended into the bowels of the submersible. Inside it was nothing but clinical, all metal shelves and computer screens, large buttons and ribbons of wire. Bodie was extremely cautious, aware that he couldn't break anything. The pilot's own pep talk had served its purpose.

The interior was cramped. Bodie, Jemma, and Cassidy sat on the floor. Alec picked his way between them to the front of the small craft. Even Cassidy looked a little nervous as the round hatch was closed and the interior wheel turned to seal them inside. Luckily, the pilot soon diverted any anxieties they might have.

"Leave the weights for now, we're not overloaded," he said through an intercom. "Minimal prep time." He tapped at a laptop that rested on his knees. Bodie was pleased to hear and see the professional tone and manner.

"Send me the coordinates now. Checking outside lights and temperature . . ." A few more presses and then an adjustment of a small wheel that, to Bodie, looked like a radiator control. "Yes, we're good. Master arm is functional and we have . . . eight hours of power on the main cells." Alec looked around at Bodie.

"No more than a six-hour dive. You understand?"

Bodie nodded. Six hours sounded like a lifetime. Cassidy mentioned the restroom and received a scathing glare. Jemma asked about the science of the submersible and received a grudging reply. There was no placating their pilot.

"We ready?" he said into the handheld comms.

A crackle came back that, to Bodie, sounded rather ominous. If the connection was crackling up here, right next to the antennae, what would it be like a thousand meters below the surface?

"Video feed live," Alec said.

"Live," the black box sizzled.

"Then we're a go. Sit back, relax, and let's get this journey over as soon as possible."

Bodie nodded in agreement. "Pal, do I ever agree!"

Bodie reined in his imagination as they sank through murky depths. Who knew what they would find, or what they might encounter on the way? The ocean depths were the most unexplored regions on the earth, and home to incalculable secrets. The actual descent wouldn't take as long as they'd thought—probably forty-five minutes—but the sense of water pressing all around was something he was increasingly forced to ignore.

He concentrated on what might be happening aboard ship as the submersible sank toward unfathomable depths.

Heidi, he was certain, had kept herself and Cross up top to make sure Yasmine and Hakim were handled. Together, they would be able to keep watch on the other Moroccans. Bodie knew Heidi's initial communications to Interpol had made them aware of the situation.

The ship's captain would be privy to this knowledge too. Hopefully, his men were prepped.

So . . . *smooth sailing?* Bodie laughed at the image, and the chances of anything on this mission going smoothly. The only thing he knew for certain was that Alec was prepping the outside lights and master arm. Visibility remained good, the main screen showing a blur of greenish water illuminated by a single bright light, shapes of small fish darting away. The pilot guided them lower and lower, saying nothing, just following the readings and calculations on his monitors that showed a colorful map of the approaching seabed and the distances from rocks and trenches to channels, sea mounts, and valleys.

"How close to the exact coordinates will we get?" Jemma asked.

Alec grunted. "Close. We can't risk striking a rock or coming too near a ledge, but the seabed looks flat enough at that point. We're ten minutes away."

Bodie took a breath, now feeling anxious about what they may find down there. Each small TV monitor showed a different view of the sea around them.

On the one hand, he knew there had been prior expeditions to locate Atlantis that had come up empty-handed; but on the other, not a single one of them had known the exact coordinates of where to look.

Knowledge was everything. He'd discussed something similar with members of his own team: why, every time a plane went down, wreckage from the lost aircraft was sometimes never found, even though a portion of it might still float. The sea was far vaster than most could imagine, and looking for a seat or a life raft in the wide waters would be like searching for the tip of a spire or a dilapidated wall across the bulk of the murky ocean floor.

Impossible.

With the seabed coming closer, the team edged nearer the screens. Alec waved them back impatiently, but didn't ask again what they searched for. As they descended, he took a sonar reading that more clearly showed the upcoming floor.

"Slow, slow," Jemma said. "We're looking for a mass. A large mass. A building, almost."

Bodie understood. "You're thinking the temple?"

"Why not? So far, Danel's used it as the focal point for every clue, even building a representation of the original."

He waited and watched, reminded that Jemma had recently suffered electrocution and proud of how calm she acted now. The entire team had taken their new CIA status in a remarkably unruffled manner, at least outwardly.

Bodie guessed some part of it was down to legitimacy—it was good to be hunting and not *hunted* for a short while. But the lack of freedom, of free will, *that* needed addressing.

Alec drifted lower still. The coordinates clicked closer and closer until a low-key siren sounded among the submersible's instruments. Jemma leaned in to the small screen that focused on the sea floor.

"Can you enlarge?"

"On the laptop, yes." Alec clicked some buttons.

Bodie peered harder at the expanded picture that appeared, crowding close to Alec's shoulder. "What is that?"

Alec fired off another sonar reading, which told them the looming object was not silt, though silt covered almost all of it. The sediment mounds rose and fell, swirled by the current and built up through countless years.

"Could be a ship," Alec said. "Although the bulge there"—he tapped the screen—"is actually all silt, so the shape is distorted."

"Can we get rid of the silt?" Jemma asked.

"Yes, we have a vacuum, but wait . . ."

Alec reported their findings to the ship and slowed their descent. He spent a moment firing off a series of sonar scans and then cleaned up the image. "If we remove the silt like so, then we are left with a shape." He shrugged. "Is this what you are searching for?"

Bodie watched, electrified, as the picture suddenly became clear.

CHAPTER FORTY-FOUR

A roof shaped like a pediment. A frieze potentially across the length of its front plinth. A series of columns, some collapsed. The building was an exact match to the one in the Azores but on a far larger scale. It lay at an angle, much of the structure broken but so well made by the Atlanteans that it hadn't crumbled and scattered across the seabed on impact. The team took screen shots and Alec spent a little time vacuuming the silt away, but soon realized the task was far beyond the capacity of their vessel.

"Whatever that is," he said, "you will need special surveying, safety, and lifting equipment to continue this journey."

Bodie understood and wholeheartedly agreed, but secrecy was still paramount. Enough people already knew about their search—including several at Interpol now—and they didn't want it broadcast further without a cautious plan in place. Jemma asked Alec to inform Heidi that their operation had been successful and to take the next step.

Bodie sat back, eyes closed, feeling a deep sense of achievement, but most of all, relief. Mission accomplished. Perhaps this was one time that they could actually rest on their laurels. Nobody was crazy enough to assume Atlantis would be properly discovered in the next few days or months, perhaps even years, depending on budget, but their own job was done, and they had done it well.

Alec guided the craft upward without comment, clearly glad to be done with them. As they approached the bottom of the ship and the water's rolling surface, the Greek pilot turned to them with a frown.

"I am getting no reply from the ship."

Bodie stared. "How do you mean?"

"The frequency. It has been turned off. We are now on our own."

"I don't understand."

"The communication channel has been—"

A blast cut him off, a booming explosion, and the vessel tumbled sideways. Bodie hung on, grabbed Jemma by the arm. Cassidy fell to her knees before clutching a metal strut. A spark ignited a flame in the console, making the lights flicker. Bodie saw a leak spring forth as the submersible slowed and Alec reached frantically for a fire extinguisher.

"Plug the hole!" he cried. "Now!"

Struggling to remain upright, he sprayed with abandon and put out the flames. Another spark flashed in front of his eyes, but didn't catch fire. Bodie saw a tiny hole along one seam and crawled over as fast as he could. The water was just trickling, but still an incredibly scary sight inside the metal chamber. The pilot threw Bodie some special clay and he molded it to the hole.

Gradually, they righted.

"What was that?" Jemma breathed.

The pilot brought them up beneath the ship. "A bomb," he said carefully. "Somebody dropped something over the ship's side. I heard other explosions too. Possibly grenades."

"The Bratva?" Cassidy asked.

"Unlikely," Bodie said. "Surely they would make their move after we returned, but I guess it's possible."

"Maybe Zeus wasn't alone after all," Jemma said.

Alec eyed them doubtfully. "Zeus?"

"It's a long story, dude," Cassidy said. "Now, can you get us quietly onto that ship?"

"Won't we still be registering on radar?" Jemma asked.

"Sure." Cassidy nodded. "But they won't know we're alive, right?"

"Communications are down," Alec said, nodding. "All transmissions lost. They might think we are floundering, bobbing around, and I can simulate that. As for letting you out of here . . . we would have to surface."

"You can't . . . flood it?"

Alec looked scared. "The sub would sink faster than it filled."

"Understood," Bodie said. "Then we surface. Fast."

He was aware the comms system had been fine not so long ago. Whatever had happened up there had happened recently, *and might still be happening.* There was no better time to act and no better cover for their vessel.

Alec brought the submersible higher and higher, and Cassidy moved into place, ready to twist the wheel and open the hatch the moment the vessel surfaced. Another minute and Alec nodded at her. Cassidy opened the hatch carefully, pushing it upward until daylight streamed into the metal chamber.

"It's not dry land," she said. "But it's better than the bottom of the sea."

Bodie watched as her muscles bulged, the cords under her skin standing out as she climbed into open air and the shadows cast by the ship. He was right behind her, the two crouching on the sub's unsound curved metal surface. The first thing he heard was yelling, then laughing. A gunshot rang out. More laughing. Jemma joined them and the three crept vigilantly toward the rear of the vessel and the stern of the boat, where it floated low, probably due to the weighty cranes bolted to its rear deck. Due to the height of the submersible, they were able to leap to the side of the ship, where they hung for a moment before pulling themselves aboard.

More gunfire rattled overhead—automatic this time. A man fell over the top rail, tumbling from the highest deck. Bodie turned away as he landed a few meters to their left.

Without pause, Cassidy ran over and checked the body. Bodie recognized one of the Bratva soldiers. Cassidy shook her head and looked for any weapons. Her expression said it all.

Nothing.

They ducked for cover, running parallel to the side of the ship and forward. Bodie found an open door and checked inside. It was clear, but revealed nothing except a rickety, rusted ladder leading to the second deck. Bodie took his time while Cassidy watched their rear. He emerged behind a wide, white-painted stanchion that supported a small gantry crane. All the commotion now seemed to be coming from the front deck. Bodie waited, not liking it, the thief's instinct taking over. Spotting the way forward, he quickly signaled the other two to join him.

"See there? Steps leading up to the control room? If we can sneak inside we can see what's going on."

The coast was clear, all the noise emanating from beyond the bridge. Bodie led the way, pausing after each step, and soon they were easing open the rear door and ducking inside.

A thin man with a ponytail whipped his head around. Bodie saw the firearm dangling off his shoulder and darted in. The man registered surprise and reached for the gun, but Bodie slammed him off his feet, staggering as he did so. Both went down. The man retained the gun, scrabbling to bring it to bear. Bodie fell awkwardly and couldn't react in time.

Cassidy picked up a metal chair and slammed the legs hard into the man's face. Immediately, all struggle stopped. She reached out to help Bodie up.

"That's how you do it, Flash."

Bodie gave her a grin, and then crept over to the broad window that looked out from the control room across the front deck and over the ship's prow.

"It's worse than I thought."

"A terrible understatement." Cassidy groaned.

Jemma's sharp intake of breath was enough. They saw a large group gathered on the triangular deck. The bulk of it was younger men wearing T-shirts and jeans and carrying semiautos, currently being held next to their thighs as they stood watching. Others were older, more important-looking, and standing closer to the man who appeared to be in charge.

Viktor Davydov.

Bodie gently cracked a window so they could hear what was passing among the rough crowd.

At the center of the loose circle were Heidi and Cross, Lucie and Gunn, kneeling alongside the ship's captain and other members of the crew. The Bratva fighters who'd accompanied them were there too.

All but Yasmine and Hakim.

The small crane at the ship's prow had some adornments—Yasmine and Hakim, chained to the uprights with cuffs and rope, both with arms stretched up high and faces bloodied. They were struggling to remain on tiptoes, their bodies swaying a little.

"You think I didn't know?" Viktor's voice came across as such a shriek Bodie imagined him spraying spittle. "You two? Fucking in private and then fucking me over? You think you're clever?"

He aimed a handgun at them and fired. Bodie assumed the bullet passed between them because nobody screamed in pain.

"I *knew* you were Interpol! I *knew.* It pleased me to corrupt you, to taint you, to watch you suffer in all those little ways. Turning the screw!" As he cried out the last word he fired again. Both Yasmine and Hakim flinched, their bodies swinging. Behind Viktor, several men stood guard, guns trained on the captives, but even from here Bodie could see Cross and Heidi tensing as if preparing to attack.

"This is gonna go so bad," he whispered. "Cross knows and Heidi is experienced enough to know that they're not walking out of this. Whatever happens, they'll all be shot."

"And I know where Eli's head is," Cassidy breathed.

"Right there on his shoulders," Jemma said. "Where we want it to stay."

Bodie searched for a plan. They had one semiautomatic and a couple of grenades that Ponytail had been carrying. It would have to be enough. He studied his companions and knew he'd have to make a hard decision.

"I need Cassidy with me," he said, and then explained his plan.

"I'll do it," Jemma said, nodding. "For family, right?"

For our family.

Bodie and Cassidy exited, taking a circular staircase down. The clock was ticking. Thirty seconds—that was game time, which he hoped wouldn't be too long and too late for Yasmine and Hakim.

"A week ago, I was going to kill you." Viktor leaned forward, leering at his captives and spitting. "Slowly. Painfully. And then grind your flesh and bones into my garden. But this . . ." He gestured all around. "This came up, and I thank you. I am pleased to have waited, for now . . . now I can kill you knowing that you led us to Atlantis."

This time he aimed his gun, sighting down the barrel, and started to pull the trigger.

"Who?" Hakim shouted. "Please, Viktor, who betrayed us?"

Maybe he was playing for time, maybe he was just desperate, but Bodie thanked the bald man for the question. The countdown was almost up.

"Who betrayed you? Nobody here on their knees. They are all too dumb to see, and that's why they will die here too. Who betrayed you? It was the Frenchman. Lucien, of course."

"Our boss?" Hakim sounded incredulous. "I don't believe you."

Viktor shrugged. "It does not matter, but why would I lie? Lucien has been whoring in every pocket for a decade. He's my boss, your boss, and a double agent whenever it suits. His power . . . his global reach, gives him immunity."

Yasmine had stayed quiet until now. Bodie saw the pain on her face, the hurt in her eyes. "Eli!" she shouted. *"Eli! I never stopped—"*

Then Jemma did her job in the control room, changing what everyone thought was about to happen.

CHAPTER FORTY-FIVE

The control room exploded. Gouts of fire surged through broken windows as glass shattered onto the deck in a lethal, glittering rain. A moment later, a hail of gunfire rang out, bullets hammering into the deck's machinery and railings. This was followed by a second explosion on the other side of the ship, behind the control room, that again sent up an eruption of flame and smashed mechanical parts.

Bodie had hoped the new Bratva arrivals would react instinctively rather than with forethought, which is exactly what happened. Viktor spun and screamed an order. Men peeled away, heading to the sources of the fresh trouble. Bodie waited for a clear deck in front and then made his move.

He ran straight for the captives with Cassidy at his side. At first, their appearance was lost in the general upheaval. Bodie caught Heidi's eye. The CIA agent reacted instantly, berating the guards and drawing their attention. Bodie ran into one, elbow first, sending him tumbling, and grabbed his weapon. Cassidy felled another, and then Heidi was up and grappling with a third. Bodie turned the gun on more guards and then went down to one knee as the captured Bratva fighters surged to life. Cross, he saw, had started moving toward Yasmine, probably intent on her safety over all else.

Viktor stared in pure anger, seemingly unable to believe his speech and executions had been interrupted. Bodie saw his lips move but couldn't read the words. The half-dozen men guarding him raised their weapons as the freed Moroccans attacked.

Bodie fired, felling one of the guards. Viktor ignored it all, turning his back with disdain and concentrating once again on Yasmine. Viktor's five remaining guards took on the Moroccans, bullets flying and then bodies crunching as the dead littered the deck.

Cassidy rolled with her opponent, smashing him on the side of the head until he went limp. She saw Cross relentlessly beat down one of Davydov's men, then immediately look toward Yasmine.

"I won't let you die!"

A blow landed on the older man's right side, one he hadn't seen coming. Cross was going to die unless he focused on things besides Yasmine. Cassidy saved him, then gave him a punch of her own.

"Get with it, granddad!"

She rose, evaluating her surroundings. She'd counted eight men rushing off to deal with the distractions Jemma had set, and figured they had maybe a minute before at least some of those would return. The surviving rebel Bratva were fighting a losing battle against Viktor's guards, but now the ship's crew were running to aid them.

Bodie grabbed the captain. "Arm your men." He threw the man a weapon. "Watch our backs when the others return. We're going after Viktor!"

The remaining crew hesitantly grabbed weapons, but the captain fought to rally them, pointing out that fighting and winning was the only way they'd ever see their families again. Some scrambled for cover. Others knelt, aimed, and waited. Bodie felt sure Jemma would be okay since they'd told her to find somewhere safe to hide.

Viktor raged at Yasmine and Hakim. His cracked, frenzied voice brought Cross's head up quickly, snatching his attention.

"Eat my food, drink my wine, *try my drugs*!" The gun came up, leveled at Hakim. "This is my answer to you!"

"No!" Cross yelled, his face twisted with pain.

Viktor squeezed the trigger, and the bullet tore through Hakim's chest. Yasmine screamed in distress. Cross, still too far away, scrambled across two dead bodies to stop what was happening. Bodie saw Hakim spinning away from Viktor, blood gushing from his wound. Viktor fired once more, the second bullet ending the bald man's life. He raised his gun.

"And one more traitor must die."

Too slow. They were all too slow.

Viktor realigned the pistol, leveled it at Yasmine's throat, and pulled the trigger.

Cross threw himself at Viktor. Bodie fired but Viktor was no longer there. It took him a moment to realize that the Bratva boss had been distracted by Cross's attack, sent staggering sideways but managing to shrug the thief away. Yasmine still lived, swinging slightly, screaming, spattered with Hakim's blood, and losing some of her own where Viktor's askew bullet had torn a ragged wound in her left arm.

Viktor bludgeoned Cross with the empty weapon, striking him around the temple and ear. Cross slumped and Viktor wriggled away, leaving the thief to crawl desperately after him. Viktor ran right up to Yasmine, drawing a wicked blade as he came close.

Cassidy went down to one knee, sighted Yasmine herself, and then elevated the barrel one meter higher. Two shots severed the chains and sent her figure crashing to the ground. In his haste, Viktor stumbled over her torso, sprawling headfirst.

Bodie nodded his satisfaction as he dashed in, but Viktor was faster than he could have imagined. Still holding the knife, he slashed at Yasmine's unprotected throat.

She couldn't move, muscles spent from hanging upright for so long. Bodie heard an outburst of gunfire behind as he moved in. The first wave of guards had returned.

It was Cross who saved Yasmine, coming just close enough to drag Viktor away by the leg and deflect the Bratva boss's swing. Even so, the knife nicked Yasmine, causing her eyes to open wide and a burst of adrenaline to fire her veins. She folded in on herself, bleeding from two wounds. Viktor leapt in again, landing on her and furiously gripping her arms as he tried to avenge her betrayal.

In a chaotic second, he raised the knife. It flashed down at her throat, but Cross was there, intervening in the only way possible, striking Viktor from the side and grabbing the descending wrist to wrench it upward. Viktor rolled off Yasmine and pulled Cross over her, their two bodies together again at last, their eyes meeting briefly and poignantly.

Then Viktor thrust the knife back toward Yasmine, turning at the last instant and plunging the blade up to the hilt into the side of Cross's neck.

Yasmine screamed, a torn, desperate sound that resounded through the chaos of the battle.

Bodie arrived and kicked Viktor in the ribs so hard that the cracks were audible. He saw Yasmine and then Cross and couldn't comprehend it, not at first. Staying upright, though, was a risky move at best.

Bullets riddled the air.

Cassidy, Heidi, and Gunn knelt together, sheltered behind a lifeboat davit that kept getting speckled with gunfire. Lucie lay behind them, having somehow wedged her body beneath the huge piece of steel until she could no longer move. To their credit, the ship's crew had surprised Viktor's returning fighters and all but wiped them out in the first minute. Only two lone snipers remained. Cassidy worried for Jemma, but knew in her heart the girl would have found some good cover. It was just a matter now of waiting for the well-armed crew to flush the last of Viktor's goons out.

Bodie knelt over Viktor and dealt him a hard blow to the head, making sure the mafia boss was at least bordering on comatose before checking on Cross and Yasmine.

Pure shock made mush of every bone in his body. He could barely stand. The deck rose up to strike his knees before he realized that he'd dropped down as if he'd been shot dead. Cross lay in front of him, bleeding out, eyes flitting to and fro and mouth moving, but no words coming out.

"Help!" Bodie screamed. "Oh God, help me!"

The knife moved as Cross tried to speak, but pain registered so badly in his eyes that Bodie almost turned away. In that moment he saw it, saw there was no help for his greatest friend, and simply reached out to take hold of the man's hand.

"I'm here. I'm here for you."

Yasmine laid a hand on Cross's heaving chest. "Oh, Eli."

Bodie leaned forward to whisper into Cross's ear. "You know what we say—family is a sense of belonging. And nobody ever belonged more to my family . . . than you."

Bodie registered the two grenades before he actually saw them. Two tumbling black objects that signaled mortal danger inside the deep, intuitive recesses of his mind. There wasn't time to pick both objects up and throw them into the sea, but there was just enough time to roll Viktor's broken body over them.

He grabbed the Bratva boss and threw him across the grenades.

Yasmine sensed the danger too, but with her eyes locked with Cross's, she did not move a muscle, choosing to spend his and perhaps her last moments in the place where they should always have been.

"Please don't leave me. I loved you so much," she said, and then the bombs went off, two loud explosions. Bodie flung himself aside, traumatized to the core. Yasmine then laid her head over Cross's chest and, teary-eyed, met Bodie's gaze.

She wept. Bodie punched the ship's deck in anger before crawling over and taking just a moment to watch as Viktor's guards gave up their fight and came out with hands high and heads down. The crew surrounded them and bound them. Cassidy, Heidi, and Gunn were loping across the deck.

"Cross?" Cassidy asked first.

Bodie opened his mouth but the answer choked in his throat. He reached Cross's inert body and saw the lifeless eyes.

"Oh my friend, what have you done?"

Yasmine reached for him and he held her hand. Cassidy was at his back, making strangled noises of misery. Heidi was on her knees and Gunn was trying to catch a breath. They stayed like that for some time, scoured by the sea breeze and rocked by the steady waves.

In time, Heidi answered a question Bodie could not bring himself to ask.

"Don't worry, Jemma is safe, inside that small deck on top of the control room. Lucie is stuck beneath a lifeboat. I'll help her out . . . eventually."

Bodie slowly became aware of the cold breeze, the waning skies, and the uncontrollable thumping of his heart. "Did we win?"

"No." Cassidy surveyed the dead. "But we are still alive."

Bodie sensed a change in Yasmine's ragged breathing and let go of her hand so that she could sit up. When he did, he stared in sorrow at Cross's body and wondered aloud if they deserved his sacrifice.

"We can only try to live up to it," he said. "Those who die are never truly gone unless we let their memories fade from our head and our hearts. I won't let that happen, Eli. I'm sure none of us will. You were the best of friends, mate."

"He sacrificed himself for you." Cassidy was staring at Yasmine, a hard edge to her gaze.

"But I . . . I'm so, so sorry."

A chopper approached from the rolling horizon. Bodie sighed as he saw it. "Now what?"

"Don't worry." Heidi held up her hands and shouted that everyone should stand down. "Don't worry, it's the CIA."

CHAPTER FORTY-SIX

A few days later, the team was on a plane, en route back to the United States with Yasmine on board, a protective detail around them, and a Lockheed Martin F-35 shadowing them through the skies.

"You really think we're this vulnerable?" Bodie asked tiredly.

"No, buddy." Heidi smiled briefly at him. "I think your story about the Bratva, their subsequent attack on Jack Pantera, and their latest threat is . . . what would you say . . . a load of bollocks?"

"And bollocks it is," Bodie said. "They would never try something in the air."

Heidi opened her mouth and then clamped it shut. In the end, she settled for a whisper. "And there I was thinking the news often reports mysterious plane crashes and disappearances."

Bodie tuned it out. They were flying back to America at the end of their operation. Atlantis was discovered and being diplomatically revealed to hand-picked nations, although Bodie guessed the term "international waters" was about to become one of the most frequently used on the planet. Cross was with them, but his carefully wrapped body was a suppressing factor for the team, overpowering any thoughts they may have had of victory or satisfaction. It even overrode their need for escape, for now.

As they prepared to leave Morocco and return home, Heidi had gotten word that the Bratva had issued a worldwide kill-or-capture order not just for Bodie or Pantera but for the entire team. Including her. No doubt this was in reaction to the outcome of the battle for Atlantis, and because Bodie's team had, again, bested them.

Which meant the Bratva just declared war on the CIA.

Not for the first time. Heidi had increased their fears by explaining that the Bratva were composed of over six thousand different groups, with over two hundred of those enjoying the resources of international reach.

Bodie accepted the glass of dark rum that she held out to him. "Thank you."

Heidi eased herself into the empty leather seat to his right. "Don't get used to it."

"I won't. I prefer it with cola."

"And why do I need to know that?"

"For next time," he said quickly, and then kicked himself. Instead of continuing the banter, he let her see his true feelings. "For Eli," he said, holding the glass up. "The best friend and colleague a team could ever have."

Heidi saluted the toast, as did everyone else. Long minutes of brooding, soul-searching silence followed.

"So, what's next?" Bodie asked Heidi. The team had a right to know where they stood, especially in light of their most recent success and loss.

"What's next? Slow down, dude, you'll run out of relics to hunt."

"I don't mean that and you know it, Heidi. Are we free? Are we still owned by the CIA? I think you'll find that's two wins out of two."

"Either way," Yasmine said darkly from the rear of the plane, "we root out Lucien and cut short the rest of his days."

Bodie nodded, but wasn't sure they would get to the Frenchman who had betrayed Yasmine and Hakim. Not personally, at least.

"We're thieves, not assassins," Jemma said. "Or at least we were prior to joining the CIA."

Heidi drained her glass before she spoke. "The CIA is not known for releasing its grip lightly. I have no agenda, Bodie, not of my own. Remember, I am only a minion."

"Clean records," Bodie said. "Worldwide. We don't want to run anymore. You come up with that and we'll consider a third run out, but only after we sort the Bratva and the guy who has their statue, and Lucien."

Heidi remained silent as she took the demand in. "You trust me?"

"Of course we trust you." He didn't have the energy to argue right now and knew it was what she wanted to hear.

"And does that mean no more repeats of the Pantera sideshow?"

Bodie was caught off guard. "The . . . what?"

"You thought I'd forgotten the insubordination you showed? Bodie, I ordered you back to DC and you ignored me."

Bodie recovered enough to affect a glare. "And I saved Jack, his wife, and his son."

Cassidy coughed loudly. "He means *we*."

Heidi sighed with a touch of exasperation. "If you run it through your head, my friend, you will find it was *I* who saved Pantera and his family. By placing them in a safe house after you tore through Winter Park. But that's not the issue here—the issue is your mutiny."

Bodie gave her his best gleaming smile, spread his arms, and said, "Hey, welcome to the world of a thief." It was too soon, and thoughts of what Bodie was brought back thoughts of Eli Cross and the remarkable man he had been. Bodie blinked tears from his eyes.

Heidi shook her head and relented. "To answer your earlier question, I'll look into the pardons, but don't expect an answer soon. And people, please don't fracture our relationship *too* often. I have enough of that in my life without the relic hunters adding their own crap."

"Fine by me." Cassidy stretched out. "I'll wait for my pardon. I need me some downtime anyway."

"Downtime?"

"Yeah." The redhead glared at Heidi. "This Bratva thing is gonna run and run. I'm thinking a safe house somewhere around Daytona Beach. Somewhere we can party, then chill. Somewhere to forget for a while. Party again, then—"

"Surprisingly," Heidi broke in drily, "Daytona Beach isn't high on the safe house list."

"There's a safe house list?"

"Not officially, but . . ."

"Can we choose?"

"This isn't an open house, darlin', and besides . . . don't you have a plan for the Bratva?"

Bodie assumed she'd been reading between the lines because, realistically, there was only one way out of it. "I guess we have the beginnings of one."

"And I have a choice of *new* relics to hunt."

"Not a chance!" Jemma snapped. "My friggin' bones are still aching from this jaunt. And . . . and . . . it will never be the same."

"You'll heal," Heidi said. "Time heals all."

"Bollocks," Bodie said. "Time dulls the pain, but only until you let yourself remember."

"And me?" Lucie asked quietly. "What will I do?"

Heidi assessed her with an inquisitive glance. "The Bratva are unaware of you," she admitted. "I'll give you a choice."

"What choice?"

"Leave or stay." Heidi shrugged, curls bobbing up and down. "The pay's not good here but you sure do see some sights."

Lucie sat back, clearly thinking it over. Bodie hoped partly that she would join them—the historian's help had been utterly invaluable—and partly that she would break away from the grip of the CIA. He wasn't surprised by her next question; in fact, he'd been expecting it from her inquisitive mind for some time.

"I have to know what you plan to do about Atlantis," she said to Heidi, speaking in calm, even tones.

"Teams are on their way to secure the site," the CIA agent replied, "and the larger area. We're moving fast, before other interested parties can get close. It's going to take some time, Lucie, but we will explore the ruins and potential treasures that are down there; we will study them and, perhaps, share them with the world. But for now, it will be behind closed doors. Do you want to help?"

"I think I'd love to."

"And the Chinese?" Cassidy asked. "I doubt they've simply slunk home with their tails between their legs."

Heidi nodded her agreement. "The government faction in question has denied all knowledge, as you'd expect, but our field offices in Morocco are seeing the arrival of a much larger group of men. They're gonna be trouble, for sure." She shrugged. "But not for us. Not anymore. We won!"

Bodie smiled at her dismissal of their enemy and enthusiasm for the hard-won victory. He looked at the future of his small family then, and saw nothing but pure turmoil—a barely controlled, barely survivable madness.

His past was little else. All the way back as far as he could remember . . . all the way back to . . .

The friends of his youth. The Forever Gang. Solid companions before any of this new life existed. Solid companions who reminded him of his current crew. They represented the real path his life should have taken. *How can turning a different corner change the course of a person's entire life?*

But there it was. Fate. Destiny. Whatever it was—a man or woman could change it if they chose. Grab it, twist it, mold it to the shape you wanted. If the friends of his youth had taught him anything, it had been how to *belong* to something bigger than a single person.

He looked around now, took in the whole plane and every person with him. It didn't really matter what the CIA did next. Or the Bratva.

Family is a sense of belonging.

Seated there, among friends, he felt almost content again.

AUTHOR'S NOTE

While *The Atlantis Cipher* is the second part of a new series, it shares the same theme of escapist adventure, camaraderie, and cinema-style action as my Matt Drake series, starting with *The Bones of Odin*, which is also available for the Amazon Kindle.

My next novel, Matt Drake #19, will release in November 2018.

If you enjoyed *The Relic Hunters* or *The Atlantis Cipher*, please consider leaving a review.

And keep up with all the latest news and giveaways by following me on Facebook—davidleadbeaternovels—or at my website: www.davidleadbeater.com.

ABOUT THE AUTHOR

David Leadbeater has published twenty-three Kindle international bestsellers. He is the author of the Matt Drake series, the Alicia Myles series, the Chosen trilogy, and the Disavowed series. *The Atlantis Cipher* is the second in his Relic Hunters series of action-packed archaeological thrillers. David has sold over three-quarters of a million e-books on the Amazon Kindle.

For a list of his books and more information, please visit his website, www.davidleadbeater.com. You can also join him on Facebook for news and paperback giveaways: www.facebook.com/davidleadbeaternovels.